W9-BBM-562

24.
06.
08

WITHDRAWN FROM
TORBAY LIBRARY SERVICES

# The Tell-Tale Tattoo
# and Other Stories

# The Tell-Tale Tattoo
# and Other Stories

*K. K. Beck*

**Five Star • Waterville, Maine**

Copyright © 2002 by Kathrine Beck

All rights reserved.

Additional copyright information on page 285.

This collection is a work of fiction. Names, characters, places, and incidents are either the product of the author's imagination, or, if real, used fictitiously.

First Edition, Second Printing

Published in 2002 in conjunction with Tekno-Books and Ed Gorman.

Set in 11 pt. Plantin.

Printed in the United States on permanent paper.

**Library of Congress Cataloging-in-Publication Data**

Beck, K. K.
    The tell-tale tattoo and other stories / K.K. Beck.
    p. cm.—(Five Star first edition mystery series)
    Contents: The tell-tale tattoo—Hollywood homicide—Rule of law—A romance in the Rockies—Peril under the palms.
    ISBN 0-7862-4570-0 (hc : alk. paper)
    1. Detective and mystery stories, American.  I. Title.
II. Series.
PS3552.E248 T45 2002
813′.54—dc21                                2002023178

# The Tell-Tale Tattoo
## and Other Stories

# Table of Contents

# Introduction:
# Mystery Master Means Murder

*by Elizabeth Foxwell*

"If [K. K.] Beck wrote the phone book," I declared in *Publishers Weekly* in 1998, "I would read it."

It's still true. One of the most versatile and talented of today's mystery authors, Beck has delivered ably plotted historical mysteries (*Mrs. Cavendish and the Kaiser's Men*), modern whodunits (*We Interrupt This Broadcast, The Body in the Volvo, The Body in the Cornflakes*, the Jane daSilva series), chilling suspense novels (*Unwanted Attentions*), and thrillers (*Bad Neighbors*). Many of her works are darn funny, such as *The Revenge of Kali-Ra*, an affectionate send-up of the over-the-top style of Sax Rohmer, H. Rider Haggard, and E. Phillips Oppenheim. Who can resist this dramatic opening: "The Queen of Doom Awakens from Her Slumber." Other Beckian tales are gripping, such as this collection's Agatha-nominated "Rule of Law" in which a Dutch attorney contemplates a dark fate for the Nazi collaborator who destroyed his family.

What deserves special mention, however, is Beck's lively series with Iris Cooper, that 1920s "comely coed" admired for her brains and sense and unafraid to dig beneath the glamor of the Jazz Age to the darker doings of her social set.

9

Inspired by the heroine in Ethel Lina White's *The Lady Vanishes*, the redheaded flapper is abetted by her kind Aunt Hermione and ace reporter Jack Clancy who speaks in tabloid headlines. Iris appears in *Death in a Deck Chair*, *Murder in a Mummy Case*, and in this book in the Agatha nominee "A Romance in the Rockies" (Iris hot on the trail of missing pearls and a feckless suitor), "Hollywood Homicide" (Iris investigates the mysterious death of a movie starlet), and "The Tell-Tale Tattoo" (Iris searches for the heir to a set of Italian paintings). Also included is *Peril Under the Palms*, the Hawaiian adventure featuring family secrets and a dead spinster, where our heroine bests a big "palooka" with the assistance of a smart blue T-strap shoe.

"Say, Iris, were you swell in there," says Clancy. Enjoy the swell gems in these pages, and dial M for Marvelous.

# The Tell-Tale Tattoo

**Portland, Oregon,** seems like an odd choice for someone looking for a place to die, but that is what I believe Miss Spencer chose to do. I first heard about her in a letter from my Aunt Hermione.

*April 1928*
*Portland, Oregon*
*Dear Iris,*

*Our neighbor Professor Poindexter has finally gone off to the Amazon on that expedition in search of giant spiders he has been planning for so long. I pray he does not bring any live specimens back with him! Mrs. Poindexter will accompany him. She is such a devoted wife. What a shame that her husband's specialty shouldn't be something more pleasant. Butterflies, for instance. In any case, they have rented their house, furnished, to a lady from back East.*

*Mrs. Poindexter introduced her to me before she left. Miss Spencer is living alone with a maid she brought with her and has hired a woman to do the cooking. She told me she had come here to be near her only living relative, a nephew who I take it is trying to set up some sort of business here about which she seemed rather vague.*

*She appears to have spent a great deal of time in Europe, where a lot of her relatives tragically died all at once in an avalanche. They were from Boston and had something to do with railroads. Miss Spencer has brought with her only the things she loves most: a magnificent collection of Italian pictures, and a few books and things. Iris, I do believe she is not well. She is very thin and tires easily. Still, there is a strange serenity about her, rather like one of the sadder but resigned Madonnas among her wonderful paintings. She is about thirty-five or so, and handsome in a haggard sort of way, with pale skin and a cloud of soft, light brown hair.*

*There is, I feel, some sad story in her life—apart from the fact that she may be suffering from some serious illness. I have been perhaps friendlier than I usually would be with a new neighbor because she seems lonely. I will be very interested in your impression of her.*

I smiled when I read the letter. Aunt Hermione had managed, with her usual efficiency, to find out a great deal about Miss Spencer. When I came home for my summer vacation from Stanford, my aunt and I paid a call on her. While there was indeed a brave sort of languor about Miss Spencer, she became very animated when I asked about her pictures. I particularly admired a small, square portrait of a young Venetian woman of the Renaissance period with wavy pale gold hair and a pearl necklace.

"It is one of my favorites," she said, touching the ornate gilt frame. "Not a Titian, but almost certainly from his *scuola.*" She looked at me thoughtfully and said, "She has that Titian red hair, just like you, Miss Cooper, and she is probably about your age." I blushed and said I hoped I hadn't admired the picture just because of that, and she laughed quite merrily. It was a nice throaty laugh, and suddenly she seemed much younger and more vigorous, and I realized that she must have once been quite lively. How sad that her poor health had robbed her of her true nature.

As we were sitting down to tea, the maid, a trim French woman, came in and said that Mr. Spencer had arrived.

"My nephew," she said to us. "Always dropping in unexpectedly. My late brother's boy, Sidney. I'm really just getting to know him. He ran away from his prep school and ended up out West somehow." She smiled indulgently. "He's rather high-spirited, as I was when young." One of her brows arched, giving her a suddenly jaunty air. "My family didn't want me to run off to France during the Great War to become a Red Cross nurse either."

I was glad that she had something of the same temperament of her only living relative. So many people have a slew of relatives and nothing in common with any of them.

A young man with brilliantined hair came into the room. He was dressed for the links in plus fours and a scarlet and yellow argyle sweater with matching socks. "Hiya, Aunt Edna!" he said heartily. After brief introductions, he refused to join us for tea. "No, I'm in a hurry. I just stopped by to see how you are and to let you know I'm having a fella come over and appraise these paintings. For the insurance, you know. I know how crazy you are about 'em, and if anything happened to 'em I know you'd be heartbroken." He grinned happily at the walls and gave her a wink. I had the impression he had been drinking.

Miss Spencer sat up a little straighter. "These pictures mean a great deal to me," she said, "but I don't see what having them appraised for their monetary value has to do with my feelings about them."

"Of course not, of course not," said Sidney hastily. "I just wanted to make sure your affairs were all in good order." There was a little silence, and he added nervously, "I'm only thinking of you. Well, never mind, then. Is there anything else I can do for you?"

"I don't think so, Sidney," said Miss Spencer with a narrow-eyed, thin-lipped look.

"Say, listen," he went on breezily, "you wouldn't happen to have a little moolah on you, would you? I seem to have left my wallet at home, and I'll need something to tip the caddy with. I'll square it away with you next time I see you."

"How careless of you, Sidney," she said with a forced little laugh. "Please excuse me, ladies." As she left the room with Sidney in tow, presumably in search of her handbag, Aunt Hermione and I exchanged glances. How sad that Miss Spencer's only relative should be such an oaf. And, as her only relative and presumably sole heir, it was pretty tactless of him to take such an obvious interest in the cash value of what might someday be his while the present owner was still alive.

About a week later, Mrs. Jones, the lady who does our ironing, told us that her sister Muriel, who is a friend of Miss Spencer's cook, reported that Sidney and Miss Spencer had had an unpleasant conversation, in which Miss Spencer had been heard to say loudly: "I'm afraid you have been a great disappointment to me, Sidney."

A few days later Miss Spencer asked Aunt Hermione to recommend a lawyer. "She specifically said she wanted someone who could do a will," reported Aunt Hermione with relish. "I gave her Mr. Musselwhite's name."

In the coming months we saw a good deal of Miss Spencer. She seemed quite happy to see us, but in a quiet, distracted way. She spent a lot of time in her rose garden, which was particularly lovely that June. By late July, however, she was frail and weak, and although nothing was ever said, it was clear she was very ill indeed. The doctor came often, but of Sidney, there was no sign. Near the end, I read to her—Browning, Keats, and Shelley was what she wanted to hear.

She died in August while we were away at Lake Oswego,

and when we returned, I was astonished to learn from Mr. Musselwhite, the lawyer Aunt Hermione had recommended and an old family friend, that she had left me the picture of the young Venetian woman. As a legatee, I also received a copy of the will, and its contents were fascinating. I read it in Mr. Musselwhite's office downtown.

The will was handwritten, and Mr. Musselwhite told me he had not drafted it, but that it was properly witnessed and perfectly legal. Miss Spencer had simply given it to him for safekeeping and asked him to probate it for her.

The will didn't mention Sidney at all. A large bequest went to her maid. The rest of her estate, including the paintings, went to someone named "Captain Reginald Montague of the Royal 21st Barsetshire Fusiliers, who shared my love of Art and of Life, as it can be, but so seldom is, lived." She had underlined "lived" three times. She had also elaborated. "Though Reggie and I had just that one glorious month together in the spring of 1915 before his wounds healed and he rejoined his regiment, it was a month that lasted a lifetime: I cannot believe that any two people could ever have experienced such intense love in every meaning of the word as we did during those few short weeks. Only he and I will ever know what there was between us."

At least until now, I thought. I was absolutely thrilled with Miss Spencer's indiscreet will. Knowing that she had had a past and had really lived made her short life seem so much less tragic. I saw a younger Miss Spencer in her crisp uniform, giving her arm to a tall, clean-limbed Englishman in a maroon silk dressing gown and walking him around the leafy grounds of the hospital. In his cool gray eyes lay the sadness of knowing he would soon be back at the front, perhaps to die. And if he was to die, she must have reasoned, surely there was no reason to hold back.

15

Mr. Musselwhite must have seen my eyes glowing as I read this, for he clicked his tongue and said, "I am sorry I have to show one of your tender years such a document. I would never have advised Miss Spencer to reveal her most intimate feelings. Nor would I have encouraged her to reward some foreign cad, who, it appears, took advantage of an innocent American girl. But I was not consulted."

I wondered what had kept them apart after the war. It must have been something awfully big to thwart such a deep love. Were they promised to others? Maybe he had died in battle. This thought caused me to ask Mr. Musselwhite sharply, "What happens if Reggie isn't alive?"

"Then her nephew Sidney gets everything," he replied. "Except for your picture and the bequest to the maid." He shook his head sadly. "Had I drafted the will, I would have suggested she name a residual legatee. I am not sure she intended her nephew to inherit." Mr. Musselwhite sighed. "But perhaps it is for the best. I don't believe in cutting out relatives on a mere whim or caprice. Especially when there is a family fortune of many generations standing. The ties of blood are surely more important than a brief, sordid, youthful attachment, however intense." He glanced up at me, looking embarrassed, and coughed, no doubt thinking he had been too frank with a young girl.

"I hope Reggie's alive," I said defiantly. Reggie wouldn't, I felt sure, care about mere money, although as a sensitive man who loved art I'm sure he would love the pictures as she had. The thrilling part, however, was that now he would know how much she had loved him. Perhaps that knowledge could sustain him throughout the rest of his life.

"I'll try to find him," said Mr. Musselwhite dubiously. "His old regiment seems to have lost track of him. Some mis-understanding about mess funds. Apparently, he left England. He could be anywhere. I've advertised in the English papers to see if anyone knows where he is."

"We've got to find him!" I said.

Mr. Musselwhite sighed. "I'll do my best. Meanwhile, I wonder if you and your aunt could do me a kindness."

"What is it?"

"Well, Miss Spencer's maid seems pretty overwhelmed, and her English is poor. We need to get the effects in order. The lease will be up on the house soon, and everything must be packed away. I will see about proper storage of the paintings, but there are clothes to be gone through, that sort of thing. It needs a woman's touch.

"It wouldn't be right to have Sidney Spencer go through the effects, as he's not mentioned in the will, but as the likely heir, he has expressed concern that if these matters aren't taken care of, the estate will be liable for rent beyond the terms of the lease."

Sidney seemed pretty smug about getting his hands on everything. Mr. Musselwhite had probably encouraged him. He'd practically come right out and said he should have inherited. Reggie had to be found!

As I left Mr. Musselwhite's office, I figured out just how he could be found sooner rather than later. I went directly to the Western Union office and wired my friend Jack Clancy, a reporter for the *San Francisco Globe*. Back home, an hour later, a long distance operator announced there was a call from San Francisco. I grabbed the telephone and told Jack all about the missing heir.

"Pretty hot stuff," he said appreciatively. " 'On her deathbed, lonely heiress reveals her one moment of happiness. Their forbidden love blossomed as the world went mad. Where is Reginald Montague now? Did he spill his blood on the fields of Flanders, his last thoughts of the pert little American nurse who had brought him back to health and life? Or is he alive, a lonely man whose youthful spirits were crushed by the horrors he saw around him in the trenches?' "

"That's the ticket!" I said enthusiastically. "But I don't think Miss Spencer was ever pert, exactly. She was more pale and interesting."

Jack continued his story in a sad but indignant voice. " 'Where is Reginald Montague now? Will he have learned too late how much she cared for him? Is he alone and friendless, lamenting his lost youth and lost love?' "

"I hope we can find him," I said. "The poor man."

Jack switched offhandedly to his regular speaking voice. "Reginald Montague probably has a wife and five little Montagues by now."

"How can you be so cynical?" I asked indignantly.

Jack laughed. "We'll find out soon enough if enough papers pick this one up. Think we can get a picture of either of them?"

"I'll find out," I said, delighted that Mr. Musselwhite had asked me to go through Miss Spencer's things.

I didn't find any photographs next door, but I found something else that proved to be quite useful. While Aunt Hermione and Miss Spencer's weeping maid, Yvonne, went through her closets and laid her clothes out on the bed to give to charity, I went through the small shelf of books. When I had read to her, I saw a small, blue cloth-bound book on the shelf, and it had aroused my curiosity. Examining it now, I saw that it was a diary covering the war years. Flipping through the entries for 1915, I found this:

*Captain Montague—I call him Reggie now when we are alone —is so much better. Really, he is incredibly frisky and energetic, fairly bursting with vigor I can scarcely keep up with him. His recovery has been astonishing. What cruel irony! I have nursed him back to health, and given him all the cheer and comfort I could, only so that he can be sent out again to the trenches. But we never speak of it. We live only for those sweet, stolen moments behind the sheet cupboard or in the shed at the back of the garden. It came up just once when I ran my fingers lightly over the tattoo on his right arm—his regimental crest with its moving motto—Valor and Fidelity—beneath it. The very qualities which he embodies! "It wasn't my idea," he said, glancing down at his arm. "The CO suggested we all get one. Makes it easier to sort out the bodies on the battlefield." "Oh Reggie!" I said. "Please don't even speak of it," and fell weeping on his manly chest. "Buck up, old thing," he said. "No need to be gloomy. Let's enjoy ourselves while we can."*

It was a few days later when Mr. Musselwhite called. "Are you responsible for the story that ran in the *Oregonian* this morning?" he asked.

"Well, I guess I am," I said. He sounded annoyed. I had only been trying to help.

"I wish you'd told me. Sidney Spencer is hopping mad. He says this kind of publicity will bring out all kinds of charlatans and impostors and we'll have a devil of a time sorting them out. He may be right."

"It won't be too difficult," I replied with a certain feeling of triumph. "I happen to know that the real Reginald Montague has a tattoo of his regimental crest and motto on his right arm." I explained about the diary, and described the tattoo in detail. Mr. Musselwhite seemed to be taking notes.

A week later Mr. Musselwhite called and asked me to come to his office immediately with the diary. "Two Reginald Montagues have made an appointment to see me this afternoon," he explained. "One of them wired me last week and

arrived by train from Vancouver, British Columbia, this
morning. The other telephoned me this morning. I'd like to
have a copy of the description of that tattoo. That should stop
any charlatan in his tracks."

When I arrived at his office, slightly out of breath and very
excited, I saw two men in the waiting room eyeing each other
warily. They both looked to be in their mid-thirties. One was
tall and bald with a fresh pink complexion. He wore a well-
tailored suit with a white camellia in his buttonhole and a red
and white striped tie. There was a monocle on a black silk
cord around his neck. The other was shorter and stouter. He
had a small reddish mustache and a slightly rakish air due to
the fact that he had a light overcoat draped over his shoulders
like a cape. He too wore a red and white striped tie. I tried not
to stare at them.

Mr. Musselwhite's secretary, a severe-looking woman in a
black dress, with steel-gray hair in neat waves, rose and said,
"Mr. Musselwhite will see all of you now." We followed her
into the office, where Mr. Musselwhite was sitting behind his
desk. To my surprise, Miss Spencer's nephew Sidney lolled
in a nearby chair, a worried expression on his face.

"Captain Montague?" said Mr. Musselwhite.

"Yes?" they both said.

Mr. Musselwhite sighed. "Gentlemen—and I use the term
advisedly, as at least one of you must be an impostor—would
you be good enough to roll up your right sleeves and show us
your right forearm."

"Certainly," said the bald man in a plummy English accent.
He removed his jacket and began fiddling with a cuff link.

"This man is an impostor!" said the man with the mustache. "This is an outrage." He turned to the bald man.
"Who *are* you, sir!"

"Why I am Captain Reginald Montague," said the bald

man. He was rolling up his shirtsleeve calmly as he spoke. "I imagine you're looking for the old regimental tattoo," he said to Mr. Musselwhite. "Stag couchant on a field of red, with crossed white bars."

"Iris, would you please find the passage you told me about in the diary," said Mr. Musselwhite. He turned to the other man. "This is all very unpleasant but I believe we can save a lot of time if you would please show me your right arm."

"I can't do that," said the man with the mustache, shedding his coat with a flourish. "I left my right arm at the Somme!" Indeed, the sleeve of his tweed coat lay flat and was neatly tucked into the pocket.

The bald man held up his arm triumphantly. "There it is," he said, looking down at a tattoo. "And our old motto. 'Words to live by'." I looked down at his arm. There it was, all right, in capital letters: VALOR. FIDELITY.

"The motto was in Latin," said the man with the gingery mustache irritably. "Virtus, Fidelitas. That's what my tattoo said. I believe you are an impostor, and furthermore that you were never even in the Royal 21$^{st}$ Barsetshire Fusiliers at all! You have no right to wear that tattoo, or that necktie!"

"But the diary said Valor and Fidelity," said Sidney. "Surely we have to pay attention to what it says in Aunt Edna's diary."

"Oh," said the bald man with a look of great sadness. "Was Edna your aunt? Let me offer you my deepest sympathy. She was a wonderful woman." His eyes glazed a little. "A remarkable woman. So full of life and vitality."

"How dare you speak of Edna in that familiar way?" said the other Captain Montague.

"I think she translated the motto when she wrote it down in her diary," I said. "But even if it *had* been in English, it would not have been spelled without a U. That's the Amer-

21

ican way. In England it's spelled V-A-L-O-U-R. I imagine you got this tattoo this week, right here in Portland. Soon after Sidney Spencer heard from Mr. Musselwhite that a Reginald Montague was arriving from Canada. It will be easy enough to find out, I imagine. Just a matter of the police asking a few questions at tattoo parlors."

The bald man stared in horror at his forearm. I turned to Mr. Musselwhite. "The tattoo wasn't mentioned in the newspaper stories. I found out about it after I talked to my reporter friend. And I know you told Mr. Spencer here about it, because he just acknowledged as much by saying the motto was in English. Did you tell anyone else?"

Mr. Musselwhite glared at Sidney. So did the bald man, who said in a different accent entirely, without a trace of Englishness, "You stupid idiot. Now I've got to wear this stupid tattoo for the rest of my life!"

"At least you will have your right arm, which is more than the brave Captain Montague has," said Musselwhite angrily. "Get out of my office, both of you! In fact, why don't you both get out of town? We don't need riffraff like you around here. If you don't, I will call the police."

"Here is my passport," said Captain Montague briskly after they had departed hastily. "I also have some of her letters and a photograph of her." He handed them over to Mr. Musselwhite. "Poor Edna," he said sadly. "Had she no other relatives?"

"A lot of them died in an avalanche," I explained.

"And she never married? I always assumed that she was a wife. There was some boy in Boston her family expected her to marry. If I had only known she was here, and alone," he said sadly.

"Did you ever see her after the war?" I asked. I had to know.

"I wasn't myself after the war," he replied. "I was feeling pretty low. Lost my bearings. Didn't want her to see me maimed like this. And there was her immense wealth! Why would she have wanted half a man—and a poor one?" He sighed.

"I got to know her in her last days," I said. "I believe that she faced her death bravely. She didn't seem to be alone. She had her pictures, which she adored. And poetry. And some very happy memories." I handed him the diary.

# Hollywood Homicide

**Come on,** Iris, you're a swell typist. And I've got it all arranged. The landlady, Bessie LeBeau, has a place for you to stay. I've even got your train tickets."

"But Jack," I said, "I only have a week before classes start again. I can't just go gallivanting off to Hollywood." Jack was calling from Los Angeles, which lent a sense of urgency to the proceedings. I had rushed to the parlor of the women's residence hall in a panic, wondering who could be calling long distance and if all was well at home in Portland.

Jack is not a college man, and doesn't seem to understand that there are rules. "Stanford University is acting *in loco parentis,*" I explained. "Coeds aren't allowed to smoke. Or run off on mad adventures." I looked nervously over at our housemother to see if she was listening, but she seemed preoccupied with sewing on a button for one of the more helpless girls.

"Get your aunt to wire them, say she needs you at home. I'll do it, if you want."

It was very difficult to say no to Jack Clancy, the newspaperman who had played such an important part in my adventures. While it was perhaps not quite proper to act as a spy for his newspaper, The *San Francisco Globe,* the chance to have anything to do with another mystery interested me strangely.

But was it a mystery?

I had read all about the death of Blanche Talbot, the promising young movie actress. Her body had been found at the

24

bottom of a swimming pool in the Moorish Court Apartments in Hollywood, where she lived. She had apparently taken a night swim alone, dived into the pool at the shallow end, knocked herself out, and drowned. The papers had said her death appeared to be accidental.

I pointed this out to Jack.

"You can't always believe what you read in the papers," he said, an interesting admission from a newspaperman, "or what the DA's office says either. I have good reason to believe Blanche Talbot was the victim of a brutal crime. This wholesome farm girl, whose matchless beauty proved to be her undoing, thrusting her as it did into the hotbed of sin that is Hollywood today, was a human sacrifice on the altar of youth and beauty and her killing must not go unavenged."

"You always have too many clauses in those leads of yours," I said.

"That's what Rewrite is for."

"Come on, Jack. Of course it would be more interesting if she'd been murdered, but what makes you think she was?"

"First of all, I got it from a source in the coroner's office that the head wound seems a little too spectacular for the kind of bump she would have got. The skin was broken in a way that seems more as if she was struck with a sharp object."

"Was there water in her lungs?"

"Yes, a little. It's my belief she was knocked out, then thrown into the pool where she drowned. But that's not all. I just made a little trip up to Castroville and talked to some of her childhood pals. Get this. Little Blanche was terrified of the water. Ever since she fell into an irrigation ditch when she was a tot of three. Wouldn't go near the stuff."

"But she was wearing a bathing suit," I protested. "I read all about it. The newspapers said it was scarlet wool with white stripes across the bodice."

"Of course she was wearing a bathing suit," said Jack impatiently. "She was a professional bathing beauty. I've been down snooping around at the Moorish Court Apartments, where the tragic beauty lived and died. She spent a lot of time lounging around the pool half dressed, drinking cocktails. It's that kind of place."

"Well then, I won't I have to pack much, will I?" I said.

"I'm not suggesting you join the revels with too much enthusiasm," said Jack. "In fact, you'll probably do a better job if you act quiet and mousy."

"I would much prefer to act abandoned and wild," I said, hoping to annoy Jack.

"Don't be silly," he said patronizingly. "You're supposed to be a respectable young lady there to type a manuscript for this writer who lives there. I fixed the whole thing up for you. This Baxter Carlson fellow didn't have much to say about Blanche's last days, but he did mention he needed a typist, so I said I had just the girl for the job."

"You mean *the* Baxter Carlson? The Baxter Carlson who wrote *Young, Wild and Doomed?*" Like a lot of people my age, I had read this novel of college life which had been banned in Boston but praised for its ruthlessly honest picture of modern youth casting off conventional morality while suffering intellectual despair.

"That's right. Now that there's this craze for talking pictures, he's making some dough writing photoplays, but he's also working on another novel and he needs someone to type it while he's at the studio. Kind of a tortured soul, I gather."

I was terribly excited at the idea of meeting Baxter Carlson. I'd seen his photograph in a magazine, and he looked awfully sensitive, with a high forehead, a soulful expression, and sad, pale eyes.

I was intrigued by poor Blanche Talbot, too. I had seen her last picture, *Dancing Debutantes*, about a society girl who wins a Charleston contest at a disreputable roadhouse and falls in love with a handsome rum runner, and she was sensational. I had also read how the studios predicted a great future for her, how she had been discovered in Castroville, California, when she won the Miss Artichoke crown, and how Elinor Glyn had proclaimed that she had "it" in spades. On campus, the boys had voted her "the girl we'd most like to be stranded on a desert isle with."

"Well," I said to Jack, "I suppose I could go down there for a little while. At least until the semester starts. But I can't think I can learn anything. Just because the poor thing fell in that ditch doesn't mean she didn't go in the water later. I almost drowned in Lake Oswego when I was five, but I still learned how to swim."

"There's more," said Jack darkly. "I got a tip that her studio is trying to hush something up. It's possible they put the fix in somehow. The word is, some goons from Corinthian Pictures were at the scene before the cops were. I can't be three places at once, so while I cover that angle and follow another big story I've got down there, I want you to make friends with all those Moorish Court people and find out what they think happened."

The next day, I took a train down to Los Angeles and arrived in the afternoon at the Moorish Court Apartments on Santa Monica Boulevard near Fairfax Street. Jack said he'd pick me up for dinner at seven, by which time he was sure I'd have plenty of copy for him. I wasn't so confident.

I wore a plain navy blue dress with a white collar and cuffs and a simple black straw hat, from which I had removed a bunch of bright yellow silk poppies too gay to adorn the millinery of a quiet office girl. Carrying my portable Underwood and my suitcase, I wandered into the central courtyard under palm trees and past beds of bright flowers.

The apartments were a collection of Spanish-style bungalows arranged around a swimming pool. Also arranged around the pool was a trio of laughing people sprawling on garden furniture. They turned to look at me. A young man in a one-piece bathing suit with hair slicked from a perfect center parting wielded a cocktail shaker. A dark woman of about thirty-five, in scarlet silk pajamas, heavily rouged, her eyes outlined with smudges of kohl, her hair in a smooth Colleen Moore bob, eyed me over a cigarette holder. I recognized Baxter Carlson in a white linen lounge suit looking blasé and smoking a pipe.

I immediately felt dowdy and thought I might have overdone the simplicity of my ensemble, so it didn't take much acting to mumble shyly, "Mr. Baxter? I'm Iris Cooper."

"Oh, the typist," he said, giving me a searching look from top to toe which seemed rather insolent. Although perhaps novelists, who made their living as observers, did get into the habit of staring. "Have a drink."

"Well, all right," I said, although it was barely past lunchtime. I set down my typewriter and suitcase and sat gingerly on a lawn chair.

The young male with the cocktail shaker poured me something from it and handed it to me. "I'm Adrian Fleming," he said pleasantly. "And this is Alice Chester. You've probably read her stuff in *Movie Mirages*."

I accepted the drink and thanked him. Feeling overdressed, I removed my hat and pushed the waves of my hair back into place.

"Oh, my dear," said Adrian, "you mustn't sit in the sun without your hat. Redheads should stay out of the sun

28

entirely. It's devastating for the complexion."

"That's what my aunt Hermione tells me," I replied, taking a sip of what seemed to be a lethal potion.

"Adrian's a studio makeup artist," said Alice Chester. "You should listen to him if you want to be a movie actress, as I'm sure you do."

"It had never occurred to me," I said, annoyed.

"How very original. You must be the only pretty girl in Hollywood who doesn't."

"Miss Cooper will probably succumb to the lure of fame," sighed Baxter. "The producers will whisper sweet promises into her shell-like ears. We all become corrupted here. I just hope she finishes my manuscript first."

"I'm sure you will find that I do a very good, professional job," I replied, setting down my half-finished drink. Frankly, the cocktail was so strong I feared that if I drank the whole thing and rose too quickly, I would fall into the pool. "I will start immediately, if you wish."

"Oh, please do!" said Alice Chester. "The world has waited so long for Baxter's next novel it's almost forgotten him."

"Pay no attention to her," said Baxter. "Alice is the poor man's Dorothy Parker. All of the malice but none of the wit."

"And Baxter is the poor man's Scott Fitzgerald," said Alice in return. "The aristocratic good looks, but none of the talent."

"Come on, kids, knock it off," said Adrian. To me he said, "Come with me, Miss Cooper. I'll take you to Bessie. She's expecting you."

"Goodness," I said to Adrian as soon as we were out of earshot, "they sure seem to have it in for each other."

"They have a past," said Adrian, arching a well-shaped

eyebrow. "She followed him out here and gave up a good job in New York to write for that gossip sheet just to be near him. It's officially over, and he chases young girls, while she still carries the torch and pretends to despise him. I don't know why he puts up with it."

"Perhaps he finds it flattering that she still cares," I said. Or perhaps he enjoys being despised, I thought to myself.

Adrian took me up to a big house overlooking the Moorish Court Apartments, and walked inside without knocking. The room was decorated in an opulent, gloomy style, with plenty of polished tiles, brass ornaments and potted palms. "Bessie, darling, she's here," he trilled out. A stout, middle-aged woman in a plumed turban and what looked like an Oriental potentate's robes appeared. There was a large tropical bird on her shoulder, which nibbled in turn at the turban's feathers and its own.

"Hello, my dear," she said. "I am so glad you are here. Mr. Baxter needs your help. That book of his was to have been sent back East months and months ago. I can't let my boys and girls allow their careers to go bust. They must learn to think of the future."

"You remember Bessie, don't you?" said Adrian. "She was in *The Terrors of Tatania*. I spent my entire childhood worried about her."

I nodded, but my attempt to feign familiarity with *The Terrors of Tatania* were apparently unsuccessful, because Miss LeBeau waved her hand, bracelets jangling, and said, "Aw, she's too young to remember. It was almost twenty years ago. They had me tied to railroad tracks and going over Niagara Falls in a barrel every week. I was younger then, but not as young as I said I was. Thinner too." She shook her finger at me in a schoolmarmish way. "But I wasn't ever stupid. I saved my money and bought this place.

These dopey kids I've got staying here aren't planning for their future. They'll get old too."

"Except for poor Blanche," said Adrian solemnly.

Miss LeBeau's eyes brimmed up with tears. "Ain't it awful?" she said. "We still can't get over it."

"I read about the tragedy in the newspapers," I said, then added in a kind of naive way, "Gosh, she sure was pretty. What was she really like, in real life?"

"That kid was going straight to the top, and she was doing it on the square. She told me, 'Bessie, I don't care if it means I can't be a star. I'm going to respect myself, and someday, when I meet the man who'll be the father of my children, I'll be glad I did.' " Bessie leaned over conspiratorially. "There's not many girls at Corinthian Pictures who've had the nerve to slap Fred Green across the kisser."

"Who's Fred Green?" I asked.

Adrian clicked his tongue. "Number two man at Corinthian Pictures. He was *crazy* about Blanche."

"I hope you don't mind my putting you up in her old bungalow," said Miss LeBeau. "You aren't superstitious or anything, are you?"

"Anyway, she died in the pool," added Adrian. I thought I detected a little ghoulish pleasure in his tone. "Not the actual bungalow."

"Oh, I don't mind at all," I said.

Draperies swirling, Bessie led me back down the paths to the courtyard once again, while the helpful Adrian went back to his cocktail shaker. Baxter Carlson and Alice Chester had now been joined by a quartet of very odd people, three of whom were sitting by the pool in formal evening dress at two o'clock in the afternoon! They were a stout couple in their fifties and a rather washed-out girl of my own age.

The gentleman wore a swallow-tailed coal and white tie,

31

and there was a silk opera hat on the wicker table beside him. The lady wore a lavender blue evening gown that matched her marcelled hair, which was topped by a precarious-looking rhinestone tiara. The girl was dressed in a flouncy bright pink dress with a white satin sash around the hips and inserts of lace in the skirt. It was much too fussy and babyish for her. I couldn't help but think that she would have looked much better in something simple in a pale, clear shade that would have set off her delicate coloring better.

What was even more extraordinary, however, was that this overdressed trio was chatting quietly with someone whose dress was as shockingly underdone as theirs was overdone. He was a sinewy, nut-brown young male with a strange, fanatical light in his blue eyes. His fair hair curled around his shoulders, and he wore a long beard. He was dressed in nothing but a leather loincloth and a pair of sandals with crisscrossed laces going up his muscular calves.

Miss LeBeau must have noticed my startled expression, because she whispered to me, "That's the Blessingtons from bungalow six. Mama, Papa and Baby Margaret. They're dress extras."

"Dress extras?" I repeated.

"The studios hire them and their clothes at the same time. For ballroom scenes and such. It pays better than regular extra work. They're a trio of old troupers who've seen better days. Baby was a kid star for a while. Did you ever see *The Happiest Orphan* or *Olive of The Ozarks*?"

"I don't think so. Who's the, um, gentleman with them?" Perhaps he was an *undress* extra who appeared in biblical epics.

"Oh, that's David. Folks around here call him Nature Boy. Kind of a character. Sleeps up in a hollow log in the Hollywood Hills or something, and lives on nuts and berries and what he can sponge off of people. You'd be surprised some of the people he knows. Alice gets tips for her *Movie Mirages* work from him, so we put up with him. Claims to be an English lord." She rolled her eyes skeptically.

"I see," I said, fascinated.

She let me into Blanche's bungalow. Here, in refreshing contrast to the sun's glare, it was cool and dimly lit. There was a small living room with comfortable chairs arranged around a stucco fireplace with wrought-iron andirons, a cheerful, roughly-woven Mexican hearthrug in bright colors, and a low, mission-style table with a matching desk and scarlet geraniums in blue pottery bowls. Beyond this room was a small kitchen in green and white tiles, and a bedroom with more vivid Mexican weaving as a bedspread. The window was covered by a mass of bougainvillea.

"There seems nothing of Blanche Talbot here at all," I said.

"The studio came and took it all away," said Bessie. She peered at me in a knowing way. "*Before* the police had a proper look, if you ask me. Fred Green is a powerful man in this town." Miss LeBeau lowered her voice and leaned toward me, the heavy scent of chypre enveloping us both. "I happen to know he'd written her a couple of mash notes. Pretty hot stuff! I told her to hang on to them. They might come in handy someday, I said. I bet he sent those studio gorillas around to find those notes!"

"Do you think they did find them?" I asked.

She shrugged. "Who knows? It doesn't matter now, I suppose. The thing is, Fred Green is the son-in-law of Julius Fisher."

"Who's Julius Fisher?"

"The head of Corinthian Pictures. And a real family man. If he ever found out that his son-in-law was making a mug of Mrs. Green—that's Julius's daughter Gertrude—Fred Green would be finished in this town."

Baxter Carlson now appeared in the open doorway with my suitcase in one hand and a cocktail glass in the other. "I've taken your typewriter to my bungalow," he said. "I'd like for you to work over there where the manuscript is." He set down the suitcase.

"Shall we begin right away?" I asked.

"No," he said, gazing thoughtfully at his glass. "It's still lunchtime for me. Why don't you have a swim first?"

"That would be wonderful," I said. After the train trip, it would be very refreshing, and I'd get my first crack at some of the people sitting around the pool.

For form's sake, I swam for a little while, and the water was lovely, but my chief interest was to get on with the business at hand, engaging the others in conversation and pumping them for details about Blanche Talbot. Adrian made it easy by introducing me all around.

The Blessingtons and Nature Boy were still there, and Adrian, Baxter Carlson, and Alice Chester were smoking and playing cards.

I had already decided that the washed-out Blessington girl, now changed from her evening clothes and wearing a drab, housedress sort of a garment, would be a good person to start with. She looked as if she would welcome the society of someone her own age, and after my swim I collapsed in the empty chair next to hers. She was reading a book called *Rambles in the Forest with Our Woodland Friends* with a border of squirrels and acorns on the binding, and looked up from it to smile shyly at me. Her mother was on the other side of her, still decked out in a costume suitable for a ball at the Winter Palace before the Bolshevik Revolution, and fiercely knitting what appeared to be a sock.

"Gosh, that felt good," I said. "Really, Miss Blessington,

you are lucky to live here in a place with a swimming pool!"

"Oh, please call me Margaret," she said in a whispery voice. "Yes, I suppose it's pleasant, although a mountain stream dashing over the pebbles as it courses to the sea strikes me as much more exciting."

"I love to swim," I burbled on. Then lowering my voice to a dramatic whisper, I said, "But I understand Blanche Talbot never swam."

"She paddled around a little," said Margaret. "But I don't believe she knew how to swim."

"Did you know her well?" I asked breathlessly.

Margaret shrugged. "She was only interested in show business. We didn't have much in common."

"But I thought you and your family had been in show business for many years," I said.

Margaret's face took on a slightly bitter look. "That's right, I was born in a trunk, but it doesn't mean I have to *like* show business. I'd give anything to get away from it." She turned to me. "I envy you, because you have a real profession and independence."

"Well, surely you could learn to type," I said. "It isn't difficult at all."

"Actually, what I would like to do is start a nature camp for children," said Margaret, sighing. "David and I talk about it all the time."

"David?"

She gestured over at Nature Boy, who seemed to be resting his eyes while Mr. Blessington, still in white tie, droned at him, "The critics compared Mrs. Blessington to Mrs. Patrick Campbell, but of course, that was many years ago. Now our hopes are pinned on Margaret." In the bright afternoon light, his black suit had a decidedly greenish tinge. Up close I also noticed that Nature Boy, despite his very eccentric appearance and state of near nakedness, did look *clean*, which was a blessing.

"Yes," continued Margaret to me, "David has so many ideas about the proper education of children out in the country, with flowers and animals as their textbooks, and the fields and bosky dells as their classrooms. And proper nutrition." She sighed. "If only we had the money to start it, I know it would be a success."

I wasn't quite sure many people would want to turn over their children to Margaret and Nature Boy for any length of time, but I didn't say so. "I guess Blanche Talbot grew up in the country," I said, trying to wrench the conversation back to her. "What a sad thing her death was!"

Margaret's mother now turned to join our conversation. Up close, I could see she was a real battle-ax of a woman, with a pugnacious jaw and a dominating look in her eye. "On the surface, it was a terrible tragedy that Talbot girl died when she did," she announced. "I had just about arranged for Margaret to be her stand-in on her next picture, where I'm sure she would have caught the eye of the producers, and been offered a real part."

Margaret glowered, and I could see that underneath her quiet demeanor she had some of her mother's belligerent quality.

Mrs. Blessington leaned around her daughter to catch my eye, her tiara listing, and said, "But really it's for the best. Actually, Margaret is perfect for the role Blanche was to play. I've been able to arrange for a screen test now that Blanche is, er, unavailable." She dropped her voice down to a whisper and said, as if Margaret weren't there, "Margaret had a great career as a child. Now she's coming out of that awkward age it's time for her to step into ingénue roles, and I will move heaven and earth to see she gets her chance to become the star she deserves to be."

"Oh, Mother! Honestly!" said Margaret with exaspera-tion. Mrs. Blessington ignored this outburst, which led me to believe it was a regular occurrence, like a tic. "Have you met David?" the older woman asked me now. Lowering her voice, she added, "He's really a titled Englishman. Traveling incog-nito, you know." She grew quite pink and happy at the thought. Whether Nature Boy actually had a title, it was clear Mrs. Blessington was thrilled to believe so. I doubted very much she would have tolerated the man otherwise.

Mr. Blessington had apparently stopped talking, and Nature Boy began to hold forth. His accent was English, all right. Perhaps he was an English sailor who had jumped ship and gone native here. "Blackstrap molasses, that's the ticket!" he proclaimed. "This precious food contains all the nutrients and goodness for a completely healthy life. I was talking about this just recently with my dear friend Vera Nadi, and convinced her to give it a go. A week on the stuff and she felt a new woman."

"Vera Nadi, the famous movie star?" I interrupted, acting impressed. I had actually met the legendary screen vamp on a transatlantic crossing, but I didn't say so.

"A wonderful woman," said Nature Boy. "Very receptive to some of my ideas about healthy, wholesome living. A forward-thinking, open-minded sort of woman. In fact, she's invited me to spend some time in her guest house up at Villa Vera."

I supposed it would make a nice change from the hollow log Bessie LeBeau had described. A hollow log sounded not only damp, but as if it would harbor a great many insects.

"But I turned her down, of course," he went on. "My little dwelling beneath a canopy of moon and stars, sheltered by the stately oaks, furnished with the salvaged castoffs of a wasteful and profligate world, is enough for me."

Margaret beamed at him over her book, and he returned her gaze with a rather yearning one of his own, while an oblivious Mrs. Blessington peered at her work, counting stitches and looking for one that had dropped.

It was some time later, after I had dressed and approached Baxter Carlson's bungalow to begin work, that I heard Alice Chester's angry voice coming from within. "Don't pretend, Baxter! You know you were just as besotted as everyone else was with that little tease! You even bought the innocent farm girl act. I saw the way you looked at her with your greedy, depraved eyes. Plus, she was about to become rich!"

"Please, Alice," he said, his voice trembling. "The poor child is *dead!*"

I began to back away, but wasn't fast enough to avoid a collision with Alice, who was flouncing out the front door. "Men are beasts," she snapped at me, elbowing me aside. "I need a drink!"

It seemed to me she had already had plenty. I gingerly approached the front door again.

Baxter Carlson was collapsed against the mantel, one trembling hand on his forehead as he stared downward with a look of pure tragedy.

I cleared my throat and prepared to back out again, but he snapped into an upright position and said, "You must forgive us, Miss Hooper. We're all a little shaken by what happened to poor Blanche. Life is so . . ." he trailed off.

"It's very understandable," I said. "Actually, my name is Cooper."

"Yes. Cooper. Of course."

"Would you like me to begin work immediately?" I asked briskly. "Where is the manuscript?"

"It's all over the place," he said helplessly, looking around. This place was furnished exactly as mine was, but it was untidy and less cheerful. Drawn curtains, and the absence of the gay hearthrug and bright flowers gave it a more austere look. It was cluttered with books, papers, and old gin bottles, and smelled of stale cigarette smoke. I resolved to give the place a thorough airing out as soon as I could.

"Well, the first thing is to put it all together," I said decisively. I turned to the desk and spotted a stack of pages. "Is this part of it?"

"Yes," he said, and began bustling around collecting loose sheets. Apparently, he had already typed up a draft, which was covered with corrections and annotations. Despite the general disorder, the manuscript itself seemed neat and clear and the pages were all numbered.

Alice Chester burst back through the front door, carrying a cocktail glass. "I'm sorry I was cross, Baxter," she said. "Let's make up, shall we? Come over to the pool. Adrian, Nature Boy, and I need a fourth for bridge."

He left, rather like a younger brother being shepherded around by a big sister, and I set about gathering pages, many of which, I couldn't help but notice, bore the rings of highball glasses on them. After a sweep of the place and a lot of shuffling, I realized they all seemed to be there, although I was surprised to find other odds and ends interleaved, all of which I shamelessly read.

There was a letter from a publisher, which said that the manuscript was very late and threatened to cancel the contract, and another from an agent, which pleaded with the author to finish the work and send it; a bill from a bootlegger; a laundry list; and a telegram, signed "FATHER," which spared no expense and read CANNOT JUSTIFY SENDING YOU MONEY UNLESS SURE YOU CAN LEAD

RESPECTABLE LIFE STOP WHAT HAPPENED TO ALL MONEY YOU MADE STOP SUGGEST YOU ABANDON LITERARY FOOLISHNESS STOP MOTHER WORRIED STOP I ON OTHER HAND DISGUSTED STOP CAN GET YOU GOOD JOB IN BANK HERE IN MUNCIE STOP.

The most startling finds, however, were two notes in a mad scrawl on thick, creamy notepaper with the letterhead "Corinthian Pictures."

"Dear Blanche," read the first one, "I am mad with desire. How can you be so cruel? My marriage is an empty vessel. Do I not deserve a little happiness? Your eyes are windows to a soul that is a pool of purity and goodness in which I long to bathe! I ask for a few crumbs of happiness. Is that so much? I am not like other men. My capacity for love is so deep. Your own boy, Freddie."

The second one was along similarly desperate lines, but ended with an invitation for Blanche to come to Palm Springs for the weekend and the assurance that no one need ever know. It included an ominous postscript. "I am desperate! If I can't have you then no one must!"

I stacked all these papers, put them on the mantelpiece, and sat down at the desk and began to type the manuscript. Presently, I abandoned typing and read ahead. The novel was about a sensitive young Easterner who comes to Hollywood and finds everyone there very vulgar, except for a young actress named Madge Mayhew, who senses the young man's superiority and tearfully reveals to him that she was drugged and presumably taken advantage of by an evil studio chief at a wild Hollywood party.

The description of Madge was so much like Blanche Talbot I could only think she had been the inspiration for the character. Baxter described her as "a creature from another, better world, angelic, with the large blue eyes of a wise child, and fair, tousled curls like the petals of some huge alpine wildflower."

This struck me as silly. Aunt Hermione had once taken me to a lecture on alpine gardens at her Flower Club, and none of the species we learned about there looked like tousled curls. In fact, they were mostly quite small and not at all showy. But then, Baxter Carlson seemed to me to be a man unlikely to know about gardens or other domestic matters.

My suspicions about the origins of the character were confirmed in a scene where Madge declares her love for the hero and collapses in tears on his manly chest, telling him how intelligent and perspicacious he is. Here, Carlson had typed her name in as Blanche, then crossed it out and penciled in "Madge." Alice Chester was right. Baxter had fallen for Blanche Talbot in a big way.

There was a rustle at the door and I hastily began typing again.

Baxter Carlson wandered in, clearly in a better mood. "How's everything going, Miss Hooper?" The sounds of laughter and splashing came from the courtyard.

"I've found all the pages as far as I can tell and have made a good start. There were these, um other papers too. Maybe some of them are important." I handed him the stack, watching him carefully.

"God!" he said.

I cleared my throat. I had noted both how easily he had been led around by Alice Chester and the bullying tone his father took with him and had decided he was easily bossed. "I'm afraid I couldn't help but notice those," I said firmly. "Perhaps, considering their nature, the police should see them. That PS could be construed as a threat."

"But Blanche's death was an accident!" he exclaimed.

"Surely you don't think this fiend could have harmed her!"

"I don't know much about it," I said, "but those letters could be important. How did you come to get them?"

In his agitated state, he didn't seem to notice that my question was impertinent. "Poor Blanche gave them to me for safekeeping. She was young and innocent. She came to me asking for advice. Said I was like a big brother to her." I sensed a little bitterness at this last. "I told her I'd hang onto them. She knew they could ruin Fred Green and that he'd do anything to get them back."

"I think we should give them to the police," I said.

"But the scandal!" He gazed down at the telegram from his father. "My family would hate to see my name in the papers connected with some Hollywood scandal. They're horrible, bourgeois little people. And the studio—my work there—I feel I'm just about to be taken seriously there. If Fred Green found out, this would be the end for me!"

"I can say I found them underneath the sofa cushions in my bungalow or something," I said. Of course I had no real intention of lying to the police.

"I must think about all this," he muttered, staring back down again at Fred Green's indiscreet pleas.

As he stood there, weaving a little from side to side, three thoughts occurred to me. The first was that Fred Green, who had clearly made a complete fool of himself over Blanche Talbot, might have been crazy enough to come and confront her, perhaps killing her in a struggle, because he was spurned. Second, if Blanche had intended to blackmail Fred Green—and why else would she keep the letter?—he might have killed her or had her killed to ensure her silence and get his letters back and save himself from the wrath of his father-in-law and professional ruin. Third, Baxter Carlson was clearly at the end of his financial rope. He might be tempted, if he managed to steel his nerves, to parlay those letters into some money or a well-paying job from either Fred Green or his father-in-law.

I cleared my throat. "It might be dangerous to possess those letters," I said.

"You're right," he said, dropping them hastily on the table. "Yes, you should take them to the police. Would you do that for me? Keep my name out of it?"

"Of course," I said. "I have an idea. That Mr. Clancy who recommended me to you seems the kind of person who could handle this discreetly. I'll call him and ask him to get them to the right people."

"Gosh, that's wonderful, Miss Hooper!" he said, and suddenly his melancholy face blossomed into a happy, smiling one. "You're a swell kid." He lurched toward me. "I could kiss you!"

As he lurched, I made an instinctive evasive maneuver and practically fell into the fireplace. "Ouch!" I said, as the wrought-iron andiron poked me in the calf.

He looked horrified as I inspected my silk stocking. There was a hole in it, and when I turned my ankle and looked over my shoulder for a better view, the hole predictably took off in a spectacular run parallel to the seam.

When I looked back up at Baxter Carlson, his happiness had vanished, and he looked like a nerve case once again, apparently horrified at what he had done and clutching his forehead in a dramatic way. Before this volatile man changed his mind, I snatched up the notes and fled.

Outside, it was dusk, and the evening air was cool and heavy with flowery scents, in contrast to Baxter Carlson's oppressive bungalow. As far as I could tell, the man needed a complete rest cure on top of a Swiss mountain, drinking nothing but buttermilk and building up his nerves.

I was pleased with my progress so far. I could hardly wait to tell Jack about the notes, which fit in with his own inquiries. I also wanted to tell him that Baxter Carlson had apparently been in love with Blanche and Alice Chester was extremely jealous, and that Mrs. Blessington seemed to be pleased that Blanche was dead, thinking it would benefit her daughter.

On my way back to the bungalow to change my stocking, I saw a strange figure crouched in the shrubbery. I let out an instinctive gasp, and then realized I was looking at Nature Boy, and that he was stirring around inside a big galvanized garbage can.

Thinking he might be embarrassed to be discovered going through the garbage, I fell back a little, and tried to compose myself, but he looked up and saw me. "Oh! Hullo!" he said cheerfully. "Amazing what one finds in these things. People throw out the most useful things. Why, just last week I found a perfectly good—"

"Hearthrug!" I said suddenly.

"Well, yes, actually," he said. "How did you know?"

I stared at him for a moment. How did I know? Then it all came to me. "Where is it now?" I asked.

"At home," he replied.

"Where is that, exactly?"

"In Griffith Park."

Just then, Jack came up the path, and looked startled to see me chatting with a half-naked man.

"Jack, this is David," I said urgently. "He has something out at Griffith Park that I think might be of interest to *The Globe*."

"I've worked with the press before," said David. "For a consideration, of course. No one can live entirely off the land."

★ ★ ★ ★ ★

It seemed we had been on the trail for half an hour. Crickets chirped as Jack and I followed Nature Boy past stands of oaks and tangles of manzanita. Finally, we reached his lair. It wasn't a hollow log at all. Actually, it was kind of a wooden lean-to in a grove of trees, and not unattractive. In this balmy climate, living outdoors suddenly seemed less eccentric than I had thought. There was a lovely view of Los Angeles by night, the lights twinkling.

David lit a lamp and set it on a nearby stump, where it cast a rosy glow over everything. Inside his shelter was a camp bed, a collection of pillows, an old steamer trunk and, underfoot, a rug that looked identical to the one in my bungalow.

"It was perfectly good. Just some stains on the back," David explained, handing it to me. "I'll make us some tea, shall I?" Presently, he was squatting next to a small tire outside the little hut.

"The rooms were identical," I said. "But his hearthrug wasn't there." Jack and I turned it over. There were stains on it all right, rusty brown stains that certainly looked like blood to me. The police would find out soon enough. If it had come from Baxter's bungalow, he'd have a hard time explaining why he'd thrown it away.

"It was that look in his eye when I fell back against the andiron," I said. "He had been very cheerful, and all of a sudden, he looked horrified, as if it were all coming back to him. I really believe it was an accident. It's clear from his manuscript that he was mad about her. She was confiding in him, showing him those letters. He dramatized the whole thing in his novel, making those mash notes into something much more horrible, and having the girl throw herself at the hero.

"In reality, I think he threw himself at her, maybe drunk-

45

enly and clumsily. He lunged. She slipped on the hearthrug, and hit her head on that pointed andiron. He panicked, thought she was dead, and threw her unconscious body in the pool. Then the hearthrug with her bloodstains on it, went into the garbage. Very stupid, really."

"But why not just say there'd been an accident?"

"That's what poor Fatty Arbuckle said, and neither the police nor that first jury believed him," I replied. "Anyway, even if it was accepted as an accident, it's conceivable Fred Green at Corinthian Pictures, the number two man, would hold it against Baxter for causing the death of the woman he was so fascinated by. I imagine his career in Hollywood would be over. And Baxter's parents were thinking of giving him some money if he managed to avoid scandal. A dead actress in a bathing suit in a bachelor's living room surrounded by empty gin bottles might be considered more than a little risqué in the quiet circles in which the elder Carlsons apparently moved."

"If this is true, it's the greatest story around here since Sister Aimee's kidnapping," said Jack excitedly. "A lust-crazed man's struggle with innocent beauty ends in disaster. East Coast aesthete cold-blooded killer. Lovely breathes last in literary lion's den."

Nature Boy came toward us with some steaming cups on a tray. He looked rather like a half-naked butler. "This all sounds rather important," he said mildly. "I did wonder why Baxter Carlson was throwing it out."

"Are you sure that's who threw it out?" I asked.

"Yes. I saw him. I was taking a little nap nearby, in the branches of a pleasant tree. I often do when I'm visiting Margaret."

I was suddenly overwhelmed by the tragedy of it all. "Oh, it's all so sad," I said to Jack. "Poor Blanche. And Poor

Baxter, too. He's so weak and ruined by drink, his nerves are shot. Your stories never have happy endings!"

"Don't get soft on me," said Jack, setting his tea down on the steamer trunk and taking out his notebook. "Wild man of Hollywood Hills finds bloodstained clue. Cops scooped by modern caveman. Now, before you tell me in your own words how you came across that blood-stained hearthrug cast aside by a cruel and heartless killer, tell me your name, and how it's spelled."

"Oh, I'd prefer not to," said David dreamily. "I belong to no family. I belong to the hills, the wind, the sky, the earth."

I glanced down at the trunk where the teacup sat. Over the lock was a monogram above some kind of a crest, and on the top there was a glued-on label that read very clearly "David Penworthy. The Manor, Little Threadington, Hants."

"Your name wouldn't be David Penworthy, would it?" I asked.

"David Penworthy!" said Jack. "That's the other big story I've been working on. A lot of people have been looking for you. You're famous—David Penworthy, the Vanished Viscount!"

"I'm not a viscount," said David a little petulantly. "I'm just an honorable. My elder brother is a viscount."

"I'm sorry to tell you," said Jack solemnly, "that your brother died in a tragic hunting accident."

"Then I suppose I am a vanished viscount," said David thoughtfully.

"Actually," Jack cleared his throat, "as of the latest dispatches, you are a missing marquess. Your father was also injured in the accident, but he lingered a little longer." Perhaps because David Penworthy seemed to be bearing up so well, in fact he seemed completely unmarked by grief or shock, Jack explained, "Their horses collided and they both fell off and broke their necks."

"Father and Harry broke their necks?" said David, now beaming. "Really? But this is fabulous! We can run our children's nature school in Threadington Manor! Mummy can move into the dower house and Margaret and I can live in the old grotto behind the gazebo. And Margaret can be a real marchioness, with real jewels, not that shabby old paste her mother wears!"

And so it came to be that when Jack's stories ran, side by side, there was one tragic headline, "Blood Found on Andiron. Carlson Confesses: 'I Killed the Thing I Loved,' " next to a happier one, "Real-life Tarzan Weds His Jane; American Girl Finds Hollywood Ending with Rich, Titled Englishman."

# Rule of Law

**My name** is Marius van Houten, and I am a lawyer, just as my father was before me. My grandfather was a lawyer too, so it isn't too surprising that I am able to maintain a businesslike demeanor in the face of any kind of strong emotion. For three generations, we van Houtens have sat quietly across the desk as our clients grew red in the face, made their hands into fists, pounded stacks of papers, swore and shouted. It has been our job to make order out of chaos and conflict, to find legal solutions to human problems. Perhaps it is in our genes, although the line will die out with me.

I was in my office reviewing the will of old Meneer van Dongen. He was a very, very old man, and a very, very rich one. This old pirate had lived in a villa in Aardenhout, and I had handled his business affairs for many years. He had outlived two other lawyers.

He had mentioned, when I first began my association with him, that he had a proper will which left his considerable fortune to one of his nephews.

There were two nephews, he explained. The first emigrated right after the war. "A good lad with the right stuff in him," van Dongen had said, nodding through a cloud of cigar smoke. The other, he had taken reluctantly into business with him, and he had been disappointed.

In fact, he had told me that the second nephew had stolen from him. "I could have gone to the law," he said, "but the

49

little bastard whined and carried on to his mother—my sister. I agreed to drop the matter if he left the country. Last I heard, he was in Australia. A good place for him. All descended from a bunch of criminals anyway."

"I think nowdays they are reasonably law-abiding," I said. "Although they do drive on the wrong side of the road."

This feeble witticism had been met with great glee. Meneer van Dongen, a rough sort who had made his fortune in Indonesia years ago when it was still a Dutch colony, used to tell me that he liked having a dull, boring lawyer handle his affairs. Yet whenever I tried to joke with him a little, he seemed pleased, as if he, somehow, were humanizing me. I had allowed him this pleasure once in a while.

And now van Dongen was dead. A heart attack after a heavy meal. The housekeeper found him in front of the television set the next morning. It was she who had delivered the will I was reading now, and it was just as he had described it.

The fortunate nephew's name and address were there. He lived in Los Angeles, California, and his name was Nicolaas Octavius Overdijk. He got everything, unless he had predeceased his uncle, in which case everything went to the housekeeper.

Octavius! That ridiculous second name! His mother must have been a very foolish woman. That silly name could seal his fate, because it could only be he. My own Nico Overdijk.

I looked up from the will at Anneke, my secretary. She just smiled. She hadn't noticed any reaction, thank goodness. Anneke so often knows what I am thinking.

The poor girl is in love with me, I thought. She'd been my secretary for seven or eight years at that point, and she was in her forties when she arrived, so I suppose she's no longer a girl. Foolish Anneke. Someday, I thought, I must tell her very delicately how hopeless it is to love an old bachelor like me.

There might have been a time when I could have married and had a normal family life. But that time had passed. It probably ended on the night back in 1943 when I was six years old. It ended with that knock on the door.

"He must come to Holland to settle the estate," I said, rousing myself, handing Anneke the will. "Draft a letter. In English, I think. Enclose a copy of the will."

Some weeks later, we received a reply. Mr. Overdijk didn't want to come to Holland. He wanted me to settle everything. He wished me to communicate with his American lawyer and provide a full inventory of his uncle's assets. He would then send instructions on how to liquidate the estate and wanted to receive some kind of bank draft in U.S. funds.

I wrote his American lawyer. Mr. Overdijk's presence in Holland was essential. The estate was very complex. Dutch law was different from American law, and these differences would make things even more complicated. (Here I threw in some irrelevant facts about Dutch taxation, designed to confuse.) Mr. Overdijk's signature would be required on innumerable documents. In addition, the contents of the house had to be gone through. There were many valuable artifacts there, as well as some good pictures. One of them was thought to be a Frans Hals, though its provenance was murky.

Anneke was suspicious. She knew our work would be much easier without Nicolaas Overdijk. He was willing to let us settle things on our own and to allow us to deal with another lawyer.

"No," I said firmly when she brought all this up in her quiet but insistent way. "I want him here. I want him on Dutch soil."

And then the unquestioning Anneke said something she seldom said to me. "Why?" she said. Her face, pale and pinkish, looked hurt. "Is there something you aren't telling me?"

I sighed and turned around to face the wall for a moment. I might as well tell her. She would find out soon enough in any case. Perhaps it was better that I tell her. Perhaps it would even prevent me from acting impulsively.

"The man is a war criminal," I replied. "I intend to talk to the Ministry of Justice about his case." But until Anneke had said, "Why?" I hadn't intended that at all. I didn't know what my plans were. I didn't know whether they included legal measures. Papa had been a great champion of the rule of law, and what had happened to him? The barbarians came and took him, and Mama too, and all because of that silly pamphlet. "The Rule of Law," it had been called.

I turned around again. Anneke was looking worried, and twisting her hair at the side of her face like a little girl. Suddenly I grew impatient. "Oh, don't look at me like that!" I said irritably. I regretted it at once, but she didn't crumple as I expected. She gave me another look—one I'd never seen before. She tilted her head back with her chin up and her eyes narrowed defiantly. "Very well," she said, leaving the room.

It occurred to me that she might leave. I was horrified. All those peaceful years together. And I needed her now, more than ever.

I went into the outer office after her. She seemed to be sorting papers on her desk furiously. An ominous sign. Was she planning to clear out?

"Anneke, I'm sorry," I said. "Let me take you to lunch. Please."

She stopped sorting the papers and looked at me angrily for a moment. Then she sighed in a sulky way and said, "All right." She opened her handbag and took out a lipstick and a mirror and painted her mouth. I was surprised. Anneke always looked neat and presentable, her rather old-fashioned face always subtly made-up, but she had never allowed me to see her actually do anything that reflected any concern with her appearance. Her applying lipstick like this seemed very intimate and blatantly coquettish.

I took her to a very nice restaurant near the office. We had a sherry before lunch. The food hadn't even arrived before she bore down on me. "Marius," she said, "tell me." After she had worked for me for three years, I had asked her to call me by my first name. She had assented, but in actual practice still managed to avoid calling me anything for the subsequent years.

I told her. Who else was there to tell?

"In 1943," I said, leaning back in my chair and putting the tips of my fingers together like the pompous old lawyer I had become, "I was six years old. There was a knock at the door. It was late. My parents had actually forgotten to put me to bed. I played with my big wooden train in the hall while they talked behind the closed glass doors of the parlor.

"I couldn't imagine why they had let me stay up so late. I had just learned to tell time, and there was a big grandfather clock in the hall. An old one with a moon and the sun rotating on a separate dial on the face. It was ten o'clock, and they just kept talking in low, worried tones. I tried to be as quiet as possible so they would forget about me and let me stay up.

"When the knock came, my mother rushed out to me. She picked me up, kissed me, and put me in a big old-fashioned wardrobe that stood there, and tucked me in among coats and galoshes.

" 'Be still,' she said. 'Whatever happens, be still. Papa and I may go away tonight, but we love you. If we are not here in the morning, then go to Mevrouw Huisinga next door.'

"I nodded sleepily and she gently closed the two doors

that closed in the middle, leaving me just a few centimeters to look out."

Anneke began to cry and I looked down at the tablecloth and straightened the silver.

"The Gestapo came. And they brought with them a local member of the NSB. We all knew who he was. Nico Overdijk. Young, tall, blond. A little swaggering baby collaborator. Mama and Papa left. Forever."

"My God," said Anneke. "And you're sure he's the same one?"

I nodded. "I found out later he had that silly second name —Octavius. He was the one who denounced my father. For a little leaflet about the rule of law."

"And you had no idea that Meneer van Dongen was his uncle?" said Anneke now, taking my handkerchief I offered her and drying her tears.

"No. Ironic, isn't it? I've spent years doing everything I can to make sure van Dongen's estate is in fine shape so it can all be handed over to the man who killed my parents. It makes you wonder about justice."

"I had wondered," said Anneke, "about you."

"Well," I said briskly, "it will take some time, but I want us to make inquiries and see if we can arrange to have the little thug brought to justice."

Later, I cursed myself for telling Anneke. Because I knew that nothing would be done about Nico. I had managed only to get a lot of bureaucratic claptrap from the Justice Ministry. The case was too old. It had been put on some sort of inactive status in 1947. Yes, there was an ancient file on Nico Overdijk, now apparently an American citizen, but the Dutch government had no interest in pursuing the case. The young woman I discussed all of this with had been born long after the war.

"You realize he's coming tomorrow," I said to Anneke. "We're going to hand over a fortune to him and he'll leave again."

"There are the Americans," said Anneke, who had become an expert on the case in a period of weeks. "He could have his citizenship revoked. If he lied on his application to go to America, if he said he had never been a Nazi—"

"So what?" I said. "He'll just come back to Holland and live like a king in that villa in Aardenhout. It's the ones they used to want to send back to the old Soviet empire who once had something to fear."

Anneke and I met Overdijk and his wife at Schiphol airport. "Listen," I said to her harshly as we waited. "Not a word. Not a glance. Nothing to indicate we know who he is. I want you to promise that."

"Marius," she said. "I'm afraid. I've never seen you like this."

"There may still be some remedy, and I want him to feel completely safe. Not a word." I seized her arm and squeezed it until she let out a little cry, and then I apologized.

I don't know what I expected to see. A young blond bully, I suppose. The one I'd glimpsed through that cupboard door. Instead, I saw an old man. A fit old man, to be sure. Dark brown skin from the California sun, in strange contrast to the light blue eyes. Gray hair that had the look of having once been blond. And a big, friendly, open American-looking face.

His wife was younger. About fifty-five maybe. She looked like an actress from some American television film. Too much bleached blond hair all puffed up around her head. She was dressed very casually, in a jogging outfit and running shoes, but with little bits of gold and diamond jewelry. She too was all smiles in that American way.

"Hi!" she said.

We exchanged greetings and introductions, while they shifted their suitcases around on their airport cart. I suggested we drive to the hotel in nearby Haarlem where we had reserved a room for them.

"Oh no," said Mrs. Overdijk, evidently speaking for both of them out of habit. "We want to stay at your uncle's place, don't we, honey?"

"Well, yes," he said, just a little uncertain.

"I want to see those pictures," she said. "There'll be a ton of stuff to go through. I've been through it all before when my mother died. These old people never throw away a thing. I bet there are some great antiques."

"It is a big house, full of many old things," said Anneke in her shy English.

"Well, maybe you can give me a hand, dear," said Mrs. Overdijk. "Men aren't any good at that kind of thing, and I need someone who knows the territory."

"I sure hope we can get this business cleared up quickly," said Nico to me, in Dutch. "I don't want to spend a lot of time here."

I bet you don't, I thought to myself. I managed to smile. "Perhaps it would be best if we all moved into Meneer van Dongen's house. Well, your house, actually. We can go over everything there much more quickly than if we have to drive or take the train back and forth to my office. It's a little irregular, of course, but it's a very large house, and the housekeeper is still in residence. I assumed you'd want to keep her on until we close things up."

"What's he saying?" said his wife, and I apologized for speaking Dutch in front of her and translated.

"Sounds good to me," she said.

She turned to Anneke. "You too, I hope. You know, you look like one of those Dutch pictures. Those ladies in rooms with the tile floors. You have such pretty skin."

Anneke blushed a little. "Anneke is a Vermeer," I said, smiling at her. I was sorry I'd squeezed her arm tightly. I hoped she could manage not to tip off Nico when we were all under the same roof. I was counting on her feelings for me.

"I just ruined my skin in the California sun," pouted Mrs. Overdijk. "Years and years I spent tanning, and now they say it's terrible for you." She held out her left arm and pushed up her sleeve. "Look. My driving arm is leathery and you get these little white flecks."

I imagined both of them driving the Los Angeles freeways, arms hanging out of the window, sunglasses on, radios blaring, years and years of aimless driving around while I was growing up alone here in Holland.

"Say, look at that," said Overdijk back in Dutch as we passed a kiosk in the airport. "Salt drops. I loved those when I was a kid. I haven't had one since I left this country. I've got to have some."

"What?" said his wife, obviously irritated at his lapse into his native language. He went over and bought a roll of the things.

"Licorice drops with salt instead of sugar," said Anneke. Her English was really very good. I wouldn't have known the word licorice. Anneke looked over at me. She seemed worried. I hoped she wouldn't fall apart. I patted her hand and smiled at her.

Van Dongen's villa hadn't changed in years. It was a big gloomy place, full of Oriental carpets and Indonesian bric-a-brac. It smelled of an old-fashioned cleaning agent called *spiritus*. After we went into the parlor and they stood there gawking for a minute, I went back out to the car to help

57

Mevrouw Termeulen, the elderly housekeeper, carry in the luggage.

Overdijk didn't think of giving me a hand. He was wandering around, looking pleased. "Place hasn't changed since I was a boy," he exclaimed, shedding his jacket on the sofa. He was wearing a bright striped knit shirt and slacks. The man looked as if he's just wandered off the golf course, hopped on a plane, and come to pick up several millions. He'd probably had a perfectly delightful life. Did he ever wake up at night and think about the boy he'd been? I doubted it. He still seemed like a boy.

"My God," he said in English to his wife. "Nothing's changed." As far as I could tell, it sounded like he still had a strong Dutch accent in English. I couldn't hear that nasal American quality, and he never mastered the devilish "th" sound, so "nothing" came out "nuzzing." "Let me show you around," he said to her. "The kitchen is back here. And the dining room." He led her through some old red velvet curtains that separated the parlor from the dining room.

"And the bedrooms are up the stairs here. The one I used to stay in was right over a big linden tree. I'd climb up and down it when I was supposed to be in bed at night."

"My goodness," said his wife from the hall. "That Oriental runner down the stairs looks real. And look at those brass rods holding it down. They're so shiny. Imagine polishing them. That housekeeper must be a treasure."

"Maybe we should settle some money on her," said Nico.

"Well, maybe," replied his wife. "Was she around in your day?"

"No, but she's done a good job for the old boy over the years."

They went upstairs. Anneke turned to me. "What are you feeling?" she said.

"He's never worried about what he's done. Not for a moment," I said.

"She's very friendly," said Anneke.

"All Americans act like that," I said. "It doesn't mean a thing. She's a greedy woman. Can hardly wait to plow through this house and grab what she can. Mark my words, she'll be counting everything down to the last guilder."

"Marius," she said, "are you sure we should stay here? Is it really a good idea?"

"Why not?" I said. I didn't really have a plan. I just knew that I wanted him to realize that he couldn't get away with what he had done. He had been living on borrowed time for too long.

They came back downstairs, smiling those idiot grins.

"Well," I said. "You must be tired. Perhaps you'd like to rest. The time difference and so forth. Anneke and I will go to our homes and pack and return later this evening. Mrs. Termeulen can make us a meal, then we can all get an early start in the morning."

"Fine," said Overdijk, collapsing into a chair. He pulled his salted licorice drops from his pocket, opened the roll with a childish expression of pleasure, and popped one into his mouth.

"Those horrible salt drops," his wife said. "I have never understood how he can stand them. People are supposed to like sugar, not salt."

"In Holland we like sugar and salt," said Anneke.

"I used to get my hand slapped for poking it into the salt canister in the kitchen," said Overdijk. "Maybe we had poor diets or something."

"During the war we did," I said. "Most of us, anyway."

Overdijk didn't bat an eye. "It was pretty bad," he said to

his wife. "The hunger winter, we called it. People ate tulip bulbs."

Mrs. Overdijk shuddered. "How terrible," she said. There were tears in her eyes. "I had no idea."

"I never talk much about the past," said Overdijk as if by way of explanation. "It's as if the past never happened. That's how it is when you emigrate."

Perhaps if I had emigrated, things would have been different. At one time, I thought I would. After the war the Red Cross took charge of me, and there was some talk of having me adopted by a Canadian couple. They even went so far as to send me pictures of their farm, a huge wheat farm somewhere in Alberta—as flat as Holland but not as crowded. Finally, though, they decided I was too old.

After my night in the wardrobe, I had gone to the neighbors as Mama had told me to do. They kept me for a while, then found some of my family. I moved around among some cousins during the war, always mindful that I shouldn't speak about what happened to my parents. I wasn't really sure what had happened to them, and I dreamed, of course, that they would come back and get me after the war.

An old aunt kept my hopes up, promising that when the Germans left, Mama and Papa would come back from the police station. However, most of the people who cared for me as best they could never spoke of my parents. I began to feel that their being taken away was somehow a shameful thing.

And I was always mindful of the fact that I was another mouth to feed. Boys can get so hungry. To this day I grow irrational when I see people waste food. But it was the silence about my parents that I believe had the most profound effect on my character. That sense of shame at the silence became entwined with a sense of shame at having no one who loved me.

If I had believed in psychiatry, I could have spent a fortune sorting it out, but it all seemed rather pointless. And in any case, plenty of people had suffered during the war.

Miraculously, I got through the next day as if I had had a good night's sleep. We went through the papers, Overdijk and I, and he seemed pleased and delighted to learn he was now a millionaire several times over. In dollars, too. He kept figuring the exchange rate on his pocket calculator.

Anneke followed his wife around the house with a fussy little man from an auction house. At one point, the women bustled into the room where we were working. "You sure there's nothing you want to keep, Nick?" said Mrs. Overdijk.

"We talked about this," he said. "Liquidate it all—strictly cash," he said.

"I know, but those carpets—"

"Forget it." He sounded a little testy. "Take the money and buy new ones in California if you want Oriental rugs."

He stretched out his arms, one brown, one whiter, like his wife's. He reached over with the darker one to the mantelpiece. "I might like this, though. I always loved it when I was a kid." He picked up a curved dagger in a scabbard lying there. "The Moslems used to kill infidels with this back in Indonesia. My uncle said so, anyway. He said they'd slit a man's throat with this and they didn't care if they were caught because they thought they'd go straight to paradise. It scared the hell out of me. Who knows if it's true?" He drew it out of the scabbard. "Still sharp as hell," he said.

I glanced over at Anneke. This was one of the times when she knew just what I was thinking.

After all, I thought. Of what use was I to anyone? Not to

poor Anneke, who was, as far as I knew, the only one who really cared. She would find something better to do with her life than follow me around the office. I would actually be doing her a favor.

To my amazement, I felt quite gay and light-headed at dinner. Mevrouw Termeulen had put on quite a tasty spread. I savored every bite. Maybe it was the wine. We had uncorked a couple of excellent bottles from old van Dongen's cellar. I knew I wasn't thinking clearly from lack of sleep, but I seemed to be running on sheer adrenaline.

Anneke looked drawn but was putting on a good show and making conversation in her excellent English. She and Mrs. Overdijk seemed to have become very chummy. The four of us actually had a rather cozy evening of it. Mrs. Overdijk got a little tipsy and giggled. "Mrs. Termeulen has given us two bedrooms upstairs," she said. "Nick is such a terrible snorer that I take the opportunity to sleep alone whenever I can."

"Should be no problem shortly," I said. Anneke shot me a horrified look and I added, "With your uncle's money you can build a house with separate wings."

"Yes, I have to be honest. It will be fabulous to have all that money," she said, reaching simultaneously for the wine bottle and her husband's hand. Anneke watched them, sitting smugly side by side, their overtanned, veined old hands massaging each other.

"And what about you two? Separate bedrooms for you?" She gave Anneke a vulgar leer.

"I'm afraid so," I said.

Anneke looked me straight in the eye. "Mr. van Houten has always been strictly business," she said.

"Yes, yes, everything by the book. The rule of law and all that," I said, and heard myself laughing rather recklessly. And then I had a wild thought. I had two choices tonight. I could either use this night to seek revenge, or I could turn my back on the past and creep down the corridor to Anneke's room. I imagined her in some kind of white nightdress, waiting for me, warm and soft and pink. Sometimes, in the office, I had stood close enough to her to smell her hair, a nice flowery, springlike smell, and had wanted to reach out and touch it. It was very fine and a golden color, shot through with coarser silver hairs.

Anneke flung down her napkin. "I must speak to you, Marius," she said. "A business matter."

Naturally the Overdijks looked startled.

"Sit down," I said. "It can wait until morning. It's an early night for me." I excused myself and went up to my room.

Later, much later, Anneke knocked on the door. "I've got to talk to you," she whispered urgently through the door.

"Go away," I said firmly.

Finally she did, and I lay in a state of twilight sleep. It was almost dawn and my heart was pounding when I rose. I could hear some birds outside my window, and the sky was a pale purple color.

It was all so easy. I went down to the mantel and picked up the dagger. Then I went back upstairs and let myself into Nico's room. He lay there like a baby, his arms, hands, open defenselessly, lying on the white coverlet. He wasn't snoring now.

I laid the blade on his throat and gave his shoulder a push. He woke up in terror. It took him a second to understand where he was and that it was a blade that touched his throat.

"I'm going to kill you," I said, "but first I will tell you why."

I heard Anneke behind me. "Marius!" she said. She had

63

come into the room, but I couldn't take my eyes off Nico's throat and the blade that lay against it.

"Don't stop me," I said. "I'm going through with it. It makes no difference what you say. I suppose you're going to tell me not to take the law into my own hands. The rule of law and all that."

Even then, I began to wonder if I could go through with it. I was furious with Anneke. I wanted to turn and look at her, but I was afraid I would lose control of Nico if I did. And I thought of my father and his damned pamphlet. But it felt so right—it was only simple justice.

"Marius, you fool," said Anneke. "That's not Nicolaas."

I looked down into my victim's terrified eyes. He was too frightened to speak.

"Look at his driving arm," she shouted.

I looked down at his arms. The right arm was darker than the left.

"Marius," she screamed. "What side of the road do they drive on in Australia?" she demanded.

"The wrong side," I said. "By our lights. And the steering wheel is on the other side. So the right arm would get more sun."

"But in America," said Anneke, walking slowly toward me, her hand extended, "it's like here. His left arm should be darker. Like hers. The wrong arm is brown. It's the wrong nephew."

By now Mrs. Overdijk had crept into the room.

"Jesus," she said. "Oh my God."

"And the salt drops," said Anneke, standing next to me now and speaking very quickly. "He told us in Dutch that he hadn't had any in years. She didn't understand. Later she said she'd never understood how he could stand them, remember?"

I lifted the blade from his neck and I handed the knife to Anneke. The American woman was screaming, "What is she saying? Speak English."

Anneke went over to her and slapped her. "Shut up," she said. "Don't wake the housekeeper and we can all make it out of here."

That slap was the last thing I remember before I collapsed. I suppose I fainted. Later, Anneke told me I'd been asleep for hours. She was sitting in a chair next to Overdijk's bed where I lay on the coverlet, waiting for me to come around.

"I tried to tell you," she said. "But you wouldn't listen. So I waited in the hall just in case you tried—I fell asleep there —but I heard you leave your room. You wouldn't listen, but I had figured it out when I saw them holding hands.

"They've admitted it. Nico died three years ago. They were his widow and his brother, the one from Australia. They wanted the money, naturally. The brothers looked enough alike to manage the deception. No one in Holland had seen them for years."

I began to tremble. "And I almost killed an innocent man." I sat on the side of the bed.

"That's right," she said. "He won't pursue it, though. I put them in a cab back to the airport. Our silence is as important to them as theirs is to us. We'll keep all those papers he signed with his dead brother's name as evidence, just in case."

"And the housekeeper?"

"Mevrouw Termeulen was delighted to hear she'd inherited a fortune. Whatever she heard last night will go with her to her grave."

"Anneke," I said. "You kept your head while I was mad. Thank God for that."

"How do you feel now, Marius?" she said. She looked

65

very tired and relieved.

"I feel as if I were back among the living," I said, reaching for her and wrapping my arms around her and burying my face in her sweet-smelling hair.

# A Romance in the Rockies

*I first* met Ursula Destinoy-Pinchot in August of 1927 on board ship. She was sailing to America with her mother, an old school friend of my aunt Hermione. Gladys Destinoy-Pinchot was an American woman who had married a rich Englishman and gone completely English. My aunt said she even rode to the hounds sidesaddle!

Poor Ursula was a dowdy, horsey sort of girl in clothes that were just all wrong for a girl our age. Whether they were too young for her or too old for her it was hard to say; they were clearly designed to make her seem unattractive. Ursula's mother was afraid of fortune hunters, you see.

So of course, on board ship, Ursula, dowdy clothes and all, fell immediately into the clutches of a bogus French count, which, I must admit, managed to do wonders for her complexion.

In any case, I was surprised to see her exactly a year later in the lobby of the Chateau Lake Louise in the Canadian Rockies. Ursula seemed transformed. I first spotted her striding with confidence across the lobby in fashionably boyish and sporty attire—jodhpurs and a vivid sweater and a felt hat at a clever angle that covered what seemed to be bobbed hair.

"Look," I said to my aunt as we stood before the registration desk. "There's Ursula."

Aunt Hermione fumbled for her pince-nez, which she kept

connected to a brooch on her lapel with a chain. "Where?" she said.

"Over there," I said, remembering not to point. I used my shoulder to indicate a group of sofas situated in front of a stunning picture window, affording a view of the incredible turquoise lake, the dazzling white glacier, and the looming rocky peaks. "See? She's wearing—"

And then I saw something shocking enough to render me speechless.

"Where?" prompted Aunt Hermione, who had now placed her spectacles on her nose.

"Over there," I said, nonplussed. "Slapping that young man."

Ursula—and I was now certain it was she—had bent over the young man who had been sitting with his back to the window reading the paper, and spoken to him, and when he rose, with a courteous but rather bemused expression, she had slapped his face. There wasn't anything playful about that slap. It was a regular wallop.

He looked, quite naturally, shocked, and stood there with one hand on his cheek, as if to see whether she had actually struck him.

"My goodness," said Aunt Hermione. "Slapping him in one of the public rooms." She shook her head slightly. "Not that it would have been all that much better, I suppose, to have slapped him in privacy."

Ursula was now coming toward us at a pretty good clip. Without hesitation, I stepped forward as she passed. I suppose it was rather forward of me to insinuate myself into her little melodrama, but I couldn't help myself.

"Ursula," I said. "Is everything all right?" Which was, of course, a silly thing to ask. Clearly, everything wasn't all right.

She stopped and her eyebrows shot up with surprise. I thought I detected the beginning of tears, and her cheeks had bright spots of color in them. "Iris Cooper," she said, startled. And then she asked rhetorically, "Aren't men beasts?" "Of course they are, dear," said my aunt. "Iris, go with Ursula. Get her a cup of coffee or something. I'll see you later in our room." Aunt Hermione is very kind, and of course she was sincere, but I knew also that she hoped I would get all the grim details about Ursula's little contretemps.

Just then, the object of Ursula's wrath came up to us— rather nervously, of course. Aunt Hermione glared at him and he winced a little, then bowed his head to her slightly and coughed. "I believe, Madame," he said, "that there has been a terrible misunderstanding. Are you this lady's mother?" He indicated Ursula with his now neatly rolled up newspaper. There was something rather defensive about the gesture, as if he were prepared to ward off any further slaps with this makeshift weapon. In fact, he seemed like a perfectly respectable young man: fresh-faced with neat hair parted in the center, a stiff collar, and a sober dark suit. He spoke with an English accent.

"Oh really," said Ursula. "Don't be absurd. You've certainly met Mother. How can you have forgotten!" She took my arm and hustled me away. In full retreat, I looked back over my shoulder and saw the young man take a tentative step after us, then step back and address my aunt. A moment later, Ursula and I were sitting on a rustic bench near the lake's edge. Even up close, it retained its remarkable turquoise color. The lake was a jewel in a setting of startling peaks, blanketed partway up with forests of lodgepole pine, then, above the timberline, reaching to the clouds in sheer masses of opalescent rock. Ursula apparently noticed that the natural beauty of the place had distracted me, for she said a little peevishly, "Yes, yes. I know it's incredibly beautiful. That just makes it all worse somehow."

I patted her hand while the poor thing snuffled herself to a stop, and presently I learned what had happened.

Ursula had been here with her mother for several weeks. She had apparently fallen in love with the young man in the lobby, who was an artist named Hugh Kent. "Not a famous artist or anything," she said rather apologetically, which irritated me, as it implied she thought she deserved a famous one. "In fact, the starving kind. He was living in a tent, in the government tourist park. But we didn't know that right away, because he came up to the hotel in evening clothes one evening, and we assumed he was a guest. Mother said that he was posing as a gentleman, in hopes of meeting some heiress. Mother's always worried that someone will marry me for my money. I believe it's because that's why she married father."

Ursula blew her nose.

"And God knows *they* don't get on. We've been traveling the world for a year now, Iris, and she doesn't seem to miss him in the least. So I suppose I shouldn't let anyone marry me for my money."

"Are you saying you slapped Hugh Kent because he was living in a tent and dressed for dinner?" I said, indignant at such snobbery. "I believe Sargent came here to paint and lived in a tent. I don't know whether he dressed for dinner."

"No," said Ursula, "I slapped Hugh because he stole my pearls. At least, I think he did. He must have. But I haven't told Mother yet. It's all too terrible. I suppose she was right about him. I hate it when she's right."

"You must call the police," I said.

"I can't," said Ursula. "I would have to tell them he was in my room."

"Oh," I said.

"It's not what you think," she replied. "One day we were climbing with the Swiss guides we have here, and then he wanted to change into a lounge suit for the tea dance, and I gave him the key to my room so he could change. My mother found out about it, I'm afraid, and she said he was trying to compromise me. The horrid part is, she also said he could have stolen our jewelry."

"And you think he stole the pearls then?"

"Yes, I do. I hate to believe it, but it's the only explanation. Anyway, the next day he was gone. My mother told me she had offered him money to cease his attentions to me. It was humiliating." She leaned over confidentially. "She did that once before. Do you remember the Comte de la Roche?"

"Yes, but wasn't he engaged to somebody else?"

"Marjorie Klepp, the cotter pin heiress. But Mother offered him money just in case. And he took it. She didn't tell me that until four days ago. She then told me Hugh was also happy to take it. I hate money. It's all anyone ever thinks about. Then, Hugh had the nerve to write me, saying he knew Mummy forbade us to meet but that we should meet secretly and that he wanted to marry me."

"Did you reply?"

"Yes. I didn't tell him I knew he'd taken her money. I told him I never wanted to see him again, that we were from two different worlds, and that surely he could understand that it would be unsuitable for me to be the wife of a starving artist. I was as condescending as I could possibly be."

Ursula began to weep again. "I had to say it, so he wouldn't think I really cared for him. Hugh was wonderful and he did love me. I know it. Underneath it all. But then he allowed Mother to buy him off.

"After I wrote the letter and sent it down the mountain with the bellboy, I discovered the pearls were gone. The cad, pretending to be a pure artist with no thought of crass material things! Oh, Iris, will anybody suitable ever really love me?"

"Of course," I said, patting her on the hand again. I didn't tell her I often wondered the same thing. "But we must get those pearls back. Are they very valuable?"

"Very," said Ursula. "They came from Daddy's family. Three strands of graduated pearls with a diamond and ruby clasp. Oh, Iris, what should I do?"

"Call the Mounties," I said. "Your mother is bound to find out."

"I think I still love him," said Ursula.

I ignored this. "Why weren't they in the safe?" I said.

"I was going to wear them that afternoon. I took them off when we went up the mountain, and Mother asked me about them. I told her that I hid them in the pocket of my peach-colored pajamas in the bottom drawer. The chamber maid would hardly go through all the pockets of my pajamas, would she? The horrible thing is, I had that conversation in front of Hugh."

"Did the room show any sign of having been searched?"

"None. Whoever took them went directly to the pajamas in question and took out the pearls. You see, it had to be Hugh."

"Well, if you won't ask for them back, I will," I said. I actually relished the idea of threatening the louse with the Royal Canadian Mounted Police. I had seen plenty of them, handsome in their scarlet jackets and khaki hats, on the streets of Banff and was sure one or two of them could be summoned to the hotel in short order. Ursula was awfully cavalier about those pearls, I thought. Of course, she'd just said she didn't care about money, but I thought it was horrible to let Hugh steal her jewelry after breaking her heart.

"Oh, Iris," said Ursula, "would you? Do you think you can do it without Mother knowing?"

"Of course I can," I said. It was easier to convince Ursula that I was plucky and clever enough to carry it off than it was to convince myself. "Why don't you go up to your room and bathe your face in cool water. You don't want to get red and blotchy or anything, do you? I'll see if I can corner him and have it out with him and get the pearls back before dinner." It had already occurred to me that he very likely had them on his person. After all, he couldn't exactly sell them in one of the little towns around here—Banff or Lake Louise, or even Calgary—without attracting immediate attention. And surely he wouldn't keep them in a tent.

I went over the phrases in my mind. After confronting him with the theft, I would demand the pearls back immediately, no questions asked. (Not that there were any questions to ask, really.) If he said he had them somewhere else (a hollow log in the forest or something), I would remind him that the Mounties could seal off this place very easily, either by road or rail, and he hadn't a prayer of leaving with the pearls.

I would give him, I decided, no more than a couple of hours to come up with them. The morning train from Banff had already left, and the other wouldn't leave until late tonight.

I also decided to conduct our interview in some public place. If Hugh Kent were a desperate criminal, he'd be perfectly capable of hitting me over the head in order to make good his escape. Which brought up the most obvious question, of course. Why hadn't he made good his escape? Why had he appeared back in the hotel, cool as a cucumber?

I hadn't a moment to lose. After having been slapped, he might be planning to lie low or find some way out by car. I began to wander through the hotel, looking for Hugh Kent.

It is startling to find such a hotel in a pristine, remote spot like Lake Louise. You would expect to find it in the middle of any cosmopolitan city, with its nine stories and its sprawling wings, covering an area the size of several city blocks. Within its large, high-ceilinged rooms, I heard a half dozen languages. Many of the guests were dressed as elegantly and as formally as you would find anywhere, yet others were dressed for alpinism and trail riding. Several examples of the taxidermist's art—heads of buffalo and moose—presided over the rooms where women paraded in beautiful dresses and jewels. And everywhere the spectacular vistas brought into the hotel through huge picture windows dwarfed the mere mortals who had come to worship nature in complete luxury.

When I finally found Mr. Kent, it was outside underneath a gay red-and-white canvas umbrella at a table by the poolside terrace. The pool, which artificially matches the beautifully colored lake, is open to the sky above, but the terrace is enclosed on the sides by elegant arches, where more picture windows keep out the cool mountain breezes but let in the scenery. Mr. Kent, however, seemed oblivious to that scenery. He was having what appeared to be a very friendly tête-à-tête with my aunt Hermione.

When I came to the table, I gave him a cold look, but Aunt Hermione didn't seem to notice. "Iris, dear," she said, "this young man is Mr.—"

"Kent, I believe," I said, narrowing my eyes to let him know I was on to him.

"Yes. Mr. Kent has the most interesting story to tell, and I believe it may shed some light on poor Ursula's curious action just now. This is my niece, Iris," she said to him, and turning back to me she said, "Sit down, dear. We're having tea."

Mr. Kent rose and bowed. "My name," he said, "is Rupert Kent."

"Rupert?" I said, sitting down. "Don't you mean Hugh?"

"That's just it, darling," said my aunt. "Poor Mr. Kent gets mistaken for his brother all the time. They are twins, you see. Just like Charlotte Mannering's adorable babies."

"My brother and I," said Mr. Kent, "are as alike as two peas in a pod." He sighed, as if he weren't particularly pleased about the fact.

"Ursula never mentioned a twin," I said.

"I have only just arrived," said Mr. Kent. "Looking for Hugh, actually. I've been following him all across Canada. I'm afraid Hugh has been a trial to our family, and I'm trying to catch up with him and let him know my father has found him a good position on a coffee plantation in Kenya. We feel it may be just the sort of place where he could find a fresh start for himself."

"Naturally," said my aunt, "Mr. Kent and I are curious as to what made Ursula want to slap him. Not that it is any of our business, actually, but poor Mr. Kent seemed so distressed."

"I'm afraid," said Mr. Kent, "that the resemblance between us has caused all sorts of trouble for me over the years. Stealing fruit from trees, bullying other boys, teasing the girls—so often, I would be blamed." He touched his cheek. "This won't have been the first blow I took for Hugh. But your aunt is wrong. I wouldn't presume to want to know what trouble the young lady may have had. I only hope to have the opportunity to apologize to her on behalf of the family for any ungentlemanly behavior to which she may have been subjected."

"I think you're displaying excessive delicacy of feeling," said my aunt firmly. "You are not responsible for what your brother has done." She turned to me. "What exactly"—she hesitated for a moment, then plunged on—"has he done, Iris? Were you able to find out?"

"Yes," said Mr. Kent, who had abandoned his delicacy quite quickly, at least in the matter of discovering what brought on the slap. "What did he do?"

I didn't reveal all the humiliating details about Ursula's mother having bought him off. I considered telling him about the pearls, but then I stopped. Perhaps it would compromise Ursula somehow to say Hugh had been in her room. "Maybe Ursula will tell you," I said.

He leaned forward eagerly. "Do you think," he said, "you could arrange a meeting?"

"Certainly," said my aunt. "Iris, go find Ursula and make her promise not to strike Mr. Kent again. This one, anyway."

I found Ursula in her room, which was evidently part of a suite she shared with her mother. In fact, that formidable lady was at the open door of the room, snapping at a tall man in striped trousers who appeared to be the hotel manager. "Absolutely absurd," she continued. "I won't hear another thing about it." Gladys Destinoy-Pinchot was up to her old high-handed ways. Aunt Hermione said Gladys had been poor as a young girl, wearing old hand-me-downs, and the bitterness of the experience had shaped her behavior now that she had wealth and position.

Mrs. Destinoy-Pinchot now turned to me, her face still fierce and red. "It's Hermione's niece, isn't it?" she said. "Ursula told me you were here. So nice to know there are respectable people about."

"My aunt was glad to know you were here," I said, trying to inject some warmth into my voice. It occurred to me then that I could use my aunt to decoy Ursula's mother so I could spirit Ursula away to confront Mr. Kent. After a certain amount of maneuvering, I did just that, arranging to go off with Ursula, and telling her mother that my aunt would be up to see her soon.

I told Ursula the story of the Kent twins—one apparently good and the other apparently evil—in the elevator on the way down. She seemed quite taken aback by the whole thing, which is understandable. When we all met again at the table by the pool, she offered Mr. Kent her hand and held his for a while, gazing into his eyes. "It's remarkable," she said.

I explained to my aunt that she must keep Gladys Destinoy-Pinchot occupied for a while, and she agreed. Implied was the understanding that I would fill her in on all that transpired. I knew that *she* knew that I knew all about Ursula and why she had slapped this young man. When I was able to tell her about the stolen pearls and Ursula's mother writing out checks to her daughter's suitors, I knew she'd be even more fascinated.

Ursula, Mr. Kent, and I all sat down rather awkwardly. "I'm sorry if my brother did anything to distress you," he said earnestly. "I am afraid he is often careless. He has the artistic temperament, which I do not have. But he is not really a bad fellow."

Ursula continued to stare at him. "I can't believe you're not Hugh," she said.

He sighed. "I am not," he said. He leaned forward, apparently fascinated by Ursula. "I don't mean to pry, but was my brother paying you attentions that—that is—well, I can understand it, I really can. You're a jolly nice-looking girl."

Ursula gazed right back at him. I cleared my throat to break their mood. "I think you should tell him, Ursula. He may help you get them back."

"Get what back?" said Mr. Kent, looking alarmed.

Ursula gave me a sidelong look. Then she said, "My pearls

are gone and I believe your brother took them."

"But how?" he began, looking so genuinely alarmed that I felt instantly sorry for him.

"It doesn't matter how," I said quickly. "Ursula's mother doesn't know, and I propose that you help me find your brother and get them back before there's any fuss. I'm sure you'll do what you can to help avoid having your name connected with any scandal."

"It's impossible," said Mr. Kent. "Hugh would never steal anything."

"You said he stole fruit as a boy," I said.

"Yes, but he's not a thief. He may have led a rather bohemian life—while I chose a more regulated existence in the family firm. But he's not a thief." He fell silent for a moment and looked down at the ground. He seemed to be thinking. "At least I can't imagine him doing anything like that." He passed a hand over his eyes. "This is terrible."

"I know it is a shock to you," said Ursula. She went around to the side of his chair and put an arm on his shoulder. It seemed such a familiar gesture, but perhaps, having known his brother, she thought she knew him.

Presently he straightened up. "It is remarkable," she said. "You part your hair in the center, and he parts his on the side, but you have the same little counterclockwise cowlick." She began to sniffle a little.

"Please don't distress yourself, Miss Destinoy-Pinchot," said Rupert Kent. He reached for a handkerchief in his breast pocket and handed it to her. "There must be a way to get those pearls back. Are you sure they aren't simply mislaid?"

"Oh, I don't know," said Ursula. "I'm so confused." It was clear Ursula had taken to him. They seemed to be consoling each other about their disappointment in Hugh and didn't notice at all when I excused myself. I was eager to find

Aunt Hermione, but it was some time before we were reunited and were able to compare stories.

As we were unpacking, I told my aunt all about Ursula's pearls.

Aunt Hermione was naturally shocked. "And they haven't called the police?"

"Mrs. Destinoy-Pinchot doesn't even know about it. I told Ursula I'd try and get them back from Hugh Kent, but then he turned out to be Rupert."

"Perhaps Rupert, if he finds his brother, can get them back," she said. "Such a nice young man. How sad that his brother is such a rascal. In any case, Ursula will have to let her mother know eventually." Aunt Hermione looked a little nervous. "I feel that perhaps Gladys would think it my duty to tell her what I know."

"Oh," I said hastily, "Ursula would be devastated. She told me in confidence, not knowing that I confide so much in you, and I told you in confidence—"

"Naturally I won't say a word," she said. "But I wish the pearls could be found. It would be terrible if Ursula made trouble for the maids, knowing that the young man took them."

"There's more," I said, filling her in on how Ursula's mother had bought off two suitors.

"What a dreadful thing for poor Ursula," said Aunt Hermione. "Even if Gladys felt it were necessary to buy off these men, why on earth would she tell the poor girl? It is humiliating.

"To be honest, Iris, I think she would prefer Ursula never marry. I believe that underneath it all she'd like to keep her to herself so that she might have a companion for her travels. Did you know they'd been traveling around for a year, staying first with relatives and now drifting from hotel to hotel?"

"Not much of a life for Ursula," I said. I love travel, but I was also eager to get back to Stanford in the fall.

"I told Gladys that she must make sure Ursula gets to spend some time with young people. I told her I never allow myself to cling to you and prevent you from enjoying yourself with people your age."

"You are a wonderful aunt," I said.

"And you are a wonderful niece. I never need to worry about you. You are so sensible for a girl of twenty."

I hate it when my aunt says that. I am sensible, but I don't like to have it pointed out too much. It doesn't strike me as a particularly charming quality. Aunt Hermione must have noticed my slight displeasure, because she added, "You don't mind being sensible, do you? I used to worry that you had been cheated of a normal girlhood by early responsibilities. Your father hasn't always understood that."

This was a reference to the fact that my mother died when I was young and I have looked out after my brothers and sisters a lot. But Aunt Hermione had insisted I go away to college, and she's taken me all around the world, too.

"You have done lots to make sure I haven't turned into a hopeless domestic drudge," I said, embracing her. "Father would have been perfectly glad to have me manage the house and help him with secretarial work forever."

"And Gladys, I believe, would be perfectly content to have Ursula be her mousy little browbeaten companion forever," replied Aunt Hermione. "I arranged for us all to dine together. I hope you don't mind. That way, we can set an example of how one chaperones the modern girl." Aunt Hermione pinched some waves into her blue marcelled hair.

"If Ursula is running around getting tangled up with lounge lizards and slapping men in hotel lobbies," she went on, "Gladys is partly to blame. Won't it be nice to have a little sherry before dinner? I understand they had Prohibition here in Alberta too, but wisely abandoned the experiment."

In the dining room, the sherry, the magnificent views (there seemed to be one from every point of the hotel, all visible through the startling huge windows), the five-piece orchestra, and the festive buzz of conversation combined to make me almost forget about the Destinoy-Pinchots and their troubles, but soon Ursula and her mother joined us.

Ursula was wearing a girlish white dress, but now that she was hatless I could see she had indeed bobbed her hair, and she was wearing a little light lipstick, too, and had penciled her brows. All in all, it was a vast improvement over the Ursula of a year ago. Maybe her American relatives had had some influence. Her mother, however, looked like one of Queen Victoria's ladies-in-waiting, in stiff corseting and bottle-green damask silk.

"Isn't this a wonderful hotel?" said my aunt when we were all settled in. "We were for a while at the Banff Springs Hotel —also very nice of course, quite luxurious—but the setting here is quite another thing, isn't it? Even more remote and lovely, if such a thing is possible."

"We were there too," said Ursula with a sulky little flounce. "Mother didn't like it. She probably won't like it here, either."

"Cheeky, that's what they were," said Mrs. Destinoy-Pinchot gruffly. I imagined she expected a lot of feudal servants pulling their forelocks. I couldn't imagine anything worse than being her traveling companion.

"Really?" said my aunt. "I have found everything in both hotels to have been absolutely first class. Here, of course, it is rather sportier, which I thought might make a change for Iris." I recognized that she had begun telling her old friend how to behave toward Ursula. "It's so important that young people be allowed some scope. Lots of fresh air and exercise and of course wholesome companionship of others their age—"

Mrs. Destinoy-Pinchot narrowed her eyes. "Have to be on your guard, Hermione. Plenty of adventurers about. People whom one does not know. Riffraff. Ever since the war, standards have slackened."

Aunt Hermione began to speak, but before she had a chance, Mrs. Destinoy-Pinchot, who appeared to be staring fiercely over my shoulder, began to tremble with anger.

"Ursula," she hissed, "there is that Kent person again. You are to cut him dead, do you hear?"

"Oh, for goodness sakes, Gladys," said Aunt Hermione without her usual gentleness. "That isn't Hugh Kent. It's his twin brother Rupert. I met him earlier. They are twins but entirely different people. Whatever quarrel you may have had with his brother—"

Mr. Kent bowed rather stiffly toward us, and Ursula, my aunt, and I all waved gaily at him. He smiled rather sweetly and sat down at a table by himself. He had brought a book.

"Oh, look, he's eating alone," said my sociable aunt. "Let's ask him to join us."

"Absolutely not," said Mrs. Destinoy-Pinchot. "If he is a relative of that odious—"

"I'm sure he'd rather eat alone than be insulted by Mother," said Ursula brusquely. Her mother gave a grim little smile, as if pleased with her powers to repel.

"I don't know what has passed between you and the young man's brother," said my aunt untruthfully but with great dignity nevertheless. "However, there is such a thing, Gladys, as being too exclusive."

Ironically, it was just at this point that a rather flashily dressed couple came up to our table and greeted Mrs.

Destinoy-Pinchot like old friends. Mr. and Mrs. Cutter were Americans in their forties. He wore evening clothes with an exaggerated cut and a lot of brilliantine in his hair, and had a wide and friendly smile. Mrs. Cutter was olive skinned with dark hair arranged in elaborate spit curls, dangling earrings that I supposed were rhinestones, a scarlet dress revealing a lot of décolletage, sheer stockings, and scarlet evening slippers.

To my astonishment, Mrs. Destinoy-Pinchot was actually gracious, introducing them and falling in with their suggestion she and my aunt play bridge with them after dinner.

Ursula gave me a little look of triumph. We could be alone this evening. I hoped to find out more from her about Rupert Kent. Perhaps he could help us find his brother, and the pearls.

"Thank goodness those awful Cutters appeared," she said, when her mother and my aunt had left. "I can't think what she sees in them. They're bridge fiends and she's had them up in our room at all hours playing cards. Now we can talk."

We decided on a stroll by the lake, which was lovely by moonlight. Ursula had plenty to tell me. "Rupert has been so kind. He's appalled at Hugh's behavior and says he can't believe he took the pearls. I also learned more about the Kents. The father is a clergyman and Rupert got a nice job in a bank from his uncle, and I gather he has a pretty solid future." She sighed. "He's just as handsome as his brother, but more respectable."

"Ursula," I said, "it's every girl's dream. A romance with an attractive but unprincipled suitor falls all to pieces, and you get a second chance with a better version of the same man."

She sighed, and fingered the chiffon scarf she wore over

her shoulders. "I rather liked it that Hugh was artistic," she said. It was clear from her wistful tone that the pearls were the last things on Ursula's mind.

"It is rather unsettling," she continued, "that they look so alike. It is hard not to believe they are one person. I think Rupert's face might be a little fuller, but otherwise they are exactly alike."

"Mirror images," I said, thinking of the Mannering twins and their bald, fuzzy heads. "Ursula," I said suddenly, "perhaps they are the same person. What was it you said yesterday about his cowlick?"

But she was unable to answer, as Mr. Kent came up to us just then. Ursula beamed happily at him.

There was no point being subtle with these two. "Ursula says you have the same cowlick as your brother. She said it went counterclockwise. Is that so?"

"It's at the back of my head," he said, startled. "I wouldn't know which way it went."

"Twins," I said, "are mirror images of one another. If one twin's cowlick goes clockwise, the other must go counterclockwise. I noticed that on baby twins I know as they were sitting side by side."

Ursula gazed at him, startled. "But it can't be," she said. "His face is fuller."

"An illusion, caused by the center part," I said. "Ursula," I said firmly, "yesterday Mr. Kent offered you his handkerchief. Do you still have it?"

She blushed. "It's in my bag," she said. "I meant to return it." I imagine she had meant to keep it for sentimental reasons. Poor Ursula had fallen in love with the same man twice.

She began to hand it back to him, but I snatched it. "Let me see that," I said. There, embroidered neatly in the corner, were the initials H.K. I showed it to Ursula, trying to keep the

84

triumph out of my gesture.

"You should have called yourself Harry," I said, flinging his handkerchief at him.

"How could you?" said Ursula, who had begun to sniffle. He handed her the handkerchief she had handed me and I had just handed him, and she started to wipe her eyes, but then she gazed at the monogram and burst into tears.

"I didn't know what else to do," he said. "Your mother told me to leave you alone, and you wrote me that dreadful letter saying I wasn't good enough for you, just a starving artist, so I came back as myself."

"As yourself?" I said.

"Well, in a way. We're perfectly respectable people and I do work in my uncle's bank, or I will soon. I just took a long holiday living outdoors and painting before I settled down into the bank. But you thought I was so disreputable I thought I might have a chance if I came back transformed somewhat. Stiffer collar, a little less of the bohemian. And I checked into the hotel and abandoned the tent."

His voice took on a little anger, and I liked him for it. "I shouldn't have done it. I'm not ashamed of my painting, or of living in a tent. But I fell in love with you, and you've turned me into a liar and a hypocrite. I suppose it's the influence of that mother of yours. Well never mind, I'll go now."

"What about the pearls?" I said.

"I didn't take her wretched pearls. Do you think I'd be such a fool as to come back if I had?"

"No, I don't think you would have," I said.

"I came back," he said, "because I am disgustedly besotted with Ursula. I suppose I shall get over it." He turned to her and said, "You know, Ursula, you never should have slapped me. How could you have thought I took those pearls?"

Ursula's lip trembled a little. "You were the only one who knew where they were. Besides, that isn't why I slapped you."

"Why," he said, exasperated, "did you slap me? Because I proposed?"

"Ursula thinks her mother bought you off," I said bluntly.

"Did she tell you that?" he demanded. "I think I'll go have a word with the old dragon." And with that, he turned on his heel to leave.

But he hadn't gone more than a step before Aunt Hermione joined us. She nodded at Ursula and Mr. Kent, who both tried to wipe away the intensity of feeling from their features. Being English, they succeeded pretty well.

Aunt Hermione was carrying my Chinese shawl. "Iris, I've brought you a wrap. It's so chilly."

"Aren't you playing bridge?" I said.

"I'm dummy," she said, "so I excused myself to bring you this. But I'm really looking for a fourth to replace me. To be quite honest, I had no idea that Gladys was playing for such high stakes," she said. "Out of my league, I'm afraid."

The stakes must have been high for her to have said that. Aunt Hermione was a terrible bridge player, but she didn't know it. She was always overbidding and blaming the resulting shambles on bad cards.

"It was rather awkward, as Gladys and I were going down badly."

"Ursula," I said, "didn't you say your mother's been playing a lot of bridge with the Cutters?"

"Yes. They were at the Banff Springs Hotel and they played there and they turned up here after we did."

"It's all beginning to make sense," I said. "Has she been losing a lot?"

"I don't know," said Ursula. "I hope not. Father said he wouldn't give her more than her allowance to take care of her bridge debts any longer. They had an awful row about it right before we left England. I think that's why we've stayed away so long."

"I saw the manager up in their room today," I told my aunt. "Now that I think about it, he was probably asking for payment."

"It's so awful," said Ursula, putting a hand to her face. "The manager at the Banff Springs came up to our room and demanded we settle the bill too," she said. "Thank goodness Mummy's allowance came through the next day, and we left soon after." She turned to Hugh. "This is so disgraceful. What must you think of us?"

"Never mind that," he said. "I happen to be an excellent bridge player. Do you think your mother would consent to accept me as a fourth?"

"A perfect idea," said Aunt Hermione, arranging my shawl around my shoulders. "Come with me and I shall arrange it."

"Don't," said Ursula. "You may not be able to afford it."

"It sounds as if your mother can't either," he said.

"Mother would never allow it," said Ursula. "Remember how horrid she was at dinner?"

"Listen," I said to my aunt Hermione. "I have an idea. If Mrs. Destinoy-Pinchot seems the least bit reluctant, look her in the eye very firmly and say this: 'I just saw Ursula in that lovely white dress. It would look so nice with pearls.' And then give her a real fish-eye. I think she may just do whatever you say."

Aunt Hermione repeated my phrase. Bless her heart, she had such confidence in my cleverness, she never even asked for an explanation, although I knew she expected one later. She bristled pleasurably at the hint of intrigue and led Mr. Kent away with her.

"Come with me, Ursula," I said.

"Where are we going?" she said. She looked so vague and bemused there was nothing to do but order her around.

"To try and get your pearls," I said.

"Where?"

"Where they should have been all along," I said. "Where your mother said they belonged. The hotel safe."

Ten minutes later, a clerk was handing over a velvet case and Ursula was signing for it. As I had instructed, she said she wanted the pearls her mother had placed there.

"I don't understand quite," she said, opening the case and looking at the pearls. I looked at them too. They were lovely, and if I were Ursula I would never have been so blasé about their disappearance.

"Hugh wasn't the only one who knew the pearls were in the pocket of your peach pajamas. He was there when you told the real thief. Your mother."

"Thank God he didn't take them," she said. It was clear that her mother's treachery wasn't as important to her as Hugh's innocence.

"Your mother was strapped for cash and wanted to bust up your romance. My bet is she decided to kill two birds with one stone. Drive a wedge between you and sell the pearls when she could. She'll deny it, of course." I was probably too blunt, but Ursula may as well know just what her mother was —if she hadn't guessed yet.

"You knew Hugh didn't take them," she said. "I'm so glad."

"Why would he have come back if he had?" I said. "Ursula, I think he cares for you very much. Impersonating himself was the act of a man desperately in love." It irked me a little that someone should do something so thrilling for someone like Ursula, who was nice enough but not terribly bright or anything, but I have noticed that men often fall in love with the dull, helpless sort of girl.

"It is rather thrilling, isn't it?" said Ursula.

"Yes," I said, trying not to appear envious. "I like the idea. The opposite of that Prisoner of Zenda thing. Instead of a double impersonating someone, someone impersonates a double."

"He is awfully clever, isn't he?" she said.

"It wasn't too clever to hand you a monogrammed hand-kerchief," I replied, "but I hope he is clever at cards."

A few days later, Aunt Hermione and I were having lunch, gazing, as usual, out the marvelous picture window. "Look," I said. "There is Ursula."

But this time she wasn't slapping Hugh. She was walking with him hand in hand.

"Such a nice man. And such a good bridge player. I shall never forget that scene when we went into the room after that bridge game." Aunt Hermione's eyes glistened at the memory. Ursula and my aunt and I had gone into the room just as the Cutters were handing over some crisp bills to Mr. Kent and a pile of I.O.U's to Mrs. Destinoy-Pinchot. "The look of relief on her face," said my aunt. "I have no doubt the Cutters would have made it very unpleasant for her if she'd had to make them good. I think they are professional card sharps."

"I rather relished the look on her face when she saw those pearls around her daughter's neck," I said. "I was glad to see her squirm. And that transparent story about simply wanting to teach her daughter not to be careless with valuables! Even Ursula saw through that."

"It is better sometimes to allow foolish people such as Gladys to save face. I think she has been humbled a little, don't you? Her opposition to Mr. Kent seems to have vanished. She should go back home and patch things up with her husband. Besides, I think it's extremely likely she won't have Ursula as her traveling companion for too much longer." We looked out the window again. Hugh and Ursula were embracing, as the sun glinted off the glacier behind them and the turquoise water took on olive glints.

Aunt Hermione added, "Of course, she has a lot more money than he does, but taking his mother-in-law into account, it will come out about even." She smiled happily. Aunt Hermione believes things always work out for the best in the end, and I suppose I do too.

*Peril Under the Palms*

# 1

*A restless* excitement had overtaken me on the third day out from San Francisco. Suddenly the air was balmy and the water a luscious aquamarine. The crew appeared in its white tropical uniforms. Pale linen suits emerged from the steamer trunks of the male passengers, and any gentleman foolish enough to wear a hat, instead of a cap, was forced to walk the deck with one hand on his head to prevent a capricious trade wind from lifting up his straw boater or Panama and sending it gently over the rail.

We ladies blossomed forth in the corals, blues, soft greens, and lavenders so appropriate to southern latitudes. Everywhere on board the *Malolo*, there was a festive sense of anticipation.

Aunt Hermione and I had been in the South Seas a year and a half before, when we'd circumnavigated the globe. We'd stopped then in Honolulu, but our stay had been tantalizingly brief. Even so, we'd had time to cast our leis into the harbor as the *President Cleveland* put out to sea. How thrilled we'd been when the gaudy bands of flowers lapped back up against the beach. Tradition has it that this is a sign the visitor will return to the islands.

We were not, however, returning alone. My classmate at Stanford, Antoinette Caulfield, a Hawaiian sugarcane heiress, was bringing home her fiancé, Walter Carlson, to meet her people. Her grandmother, a very correct old lady, had wanted the couple to sail on separate vessels, but when I told my aunt about them, she volunteered to chaperone.

"Of course, everyone said it was so queer to come in June," she was saying now. It was the last night out, and the four of us sat in the main saloon, listening to the ship's orchestra play plaintive Hawaiian melodies. "But of course, Iris is in school during the season. Except for Christmas, of course, but we must spend that at home with the younger children, and Iris's father refuses to travel with them. Traveling with children can be trying, and Iris's father can be very irritable. He always has been, ever since he was a boy."

She sipped some champagne while Walter and Antoinette listened politely. "Besides," she continued, "the *flowers* will be in bloom. I am sure I was not alone among the ladies at the Town Club who felt that Mrs. Bergstrom's talk about the gardens of Honolulu was shockingly *scant.*"

"Really?" Walter murmured with apparent interest. He was a very attentive young man, who'd been charming to Aunt Hermione during the voyage.

"I'm afraid so. The talk was courteously received, however," she conceded.

Antoinette, fair and pretty with almond-shaped blue eyes and a short, neat little nose, clasped her hands together. "Walter will absolutely adore the gardens of Honolulu," she said. "The flowers are wonderful."

"I'm sure they are," said Walter, turning to her with a radiant face. "Just like you." Traveling with an engaged couple was, to be perfectly frank, becoming rather a trial, and I was glad we'd be arriving the next day.

"It's so important that Walter love Hawaii as I do," Antoinette continued, tearing herself away from his gaze and addressing us, "as we are to live there after we are married."

"It has all been decided, then? Before Walter has even

seen the islands?" asked my aunt rather pointedly.

Antoinette waved her hand. "Walter says my happiness is the chief thing," she said with a contented sigh. "He's agreed to go into the family business. Isn't it wonderful? My grandfather will be so glad to get a clever young man like Walter. His partner, Mr. Spaulding, will just have to go along with it." She wrinkled up her nose. "Mr. Spaulding has wanted to marry me off to his son Charlie for years. It will be grand to show them Walter." She gave a little laugh of triumph.

"Charlie, eh?" said Walter pugnaciously. "Well, I'll let him know what's what." His handsome, rather aquiline features clouded for a second.

When they had excused themselves to dance, Aunt Hermione leaned over to me. "A lovely-looking couple," she said as we watched them fox-trot. "And that boy has perfect manners."

"Yes," I said. "She's very lucky."

Aunt Hermione's dear, round face grew pensive, and she patted a hydrangea-blue marcelled wave. "I suppose so," she said. "Although perfect manners are always a little suspect."

"I shall remember that," I said with a smile. "I shall try very hard never to have perfect manners."

"Oh you don't have to worry about that," she said. Then, laughing, she added, "That is to say, you have perfectly nice manners. Well, imperfectly nice manners, I suppose I must say to be consistent. But you're always so . . . *natural*. Walter is so in love he's straining to make a good impression. I hope it won't be too much of a trial when he meets the family."

"Perhaps he'll go to seed in the tropics," I said. "People do, you know."

Two ladies approached our table. We had played bridge with them on the trip out. They were a pair of middle-aged New England spinsters with graying, shingled hair and fresh complexions. Miss Pomfret, the younger of the two and, we suspected, a paid companion to the elder, waved her finger archly at us. "Going to seed in the tropics? You aren't planning to do that, are you?"

Miss Blodgett, as was often her habit when her friend spoke, snorted. "There, there, Pommy, don't be ridiculous. You're always coming in on the ends of other people's conversations and misconstruing things."

"Please join us," said my aunt.

"Well, we were going to our stateroom," said Miss Blodgett rather ungraciously, "but I know Pommy likes to listen to this horrible dance music, so I suppose we could stay a while longer."

I surveyed the ladies' evening gowns. Miss Pomfret wore a printed chiffon dress that was a little too young for her, but pretty nevertheless. Miss Blodgett wore a severe dress of iron gray satin. Only its rich fabric and the addition of a handsome dog collar of pearls, with a front clasp of yellow diamonds, prevented the dress from looking like the uniform of a Victorian prison matron.

"Have some nice champagne," said my aunt as the ladies seated themselves. "This Prohibition business adds an extra fillip to travel, don't you think?"

"When we are at home," intoned Miss Blodgett, "we always obey the law. However, I do enjoy a glass of something occasionally." She removed the bottle from its ice bucket and gestured imperiously to a waiter for additional glasses. "I've given up domestic consumption as an example to the lower classes."

"Very noble, I'm sure," said Aunt Hermione.

Her tone failed to convey that she herself felt no such constraint. Father's bootlegger's inability to provide us with decent sherry was a source of extreme annoyance to her.

"Here's to going to seed in the tropics," said Miss Pomfret girlishly, raising her full glass and giving Miss Blodgett a rebellious glance.

"It's nothing to joke about," said Miss Blodgett, drinking to the toast anyway. "These islands we're about to visit have cast a wicked spell on many an impressionable soul. 'Don't dwell there too long'—that was my great-great-uncle Josiah's advice."

"Oh yes, your relative, the missionary," I murmured. We had heard all about him at bridge.

"But he didn't take his own advice, did he?" said Miss Pomfret. "He stayed there his whole life."

"A life of Christian service," said Miss Blodgett. "He was an exceptional man with great strength of character. I'm researching his life for a chapter in my history of the Blodgetts of Massachusetts," she added unnecessarily, as she had already told us all about this work at some length.

Walter and Antoinette came back to the table, and Miss Blodgett seemed annoyed to have to stop and greet them before launching into what sounded like a draft of her work.

"Though barely a lad of nineteen when he sailed from Boston in 1833," she began, "he possessed a maturity and discipline unusual for one of such tender years. His fortitude in serving in what was then a land of unspeakable debauchery can only be attributed to his impeccable breeding."

She sipped her champagne thoughtfully. "And his faith in God, too," she added as an afterthought.

"It's very interesting," said Walter brightly. "Miss Blodgett has let me see this fascinating diary. I'm sure a review of Hawaiian history, now that I'm to live there, will be very instructive."

Now that Walter had foolishly shown some interest, I

knew there'd be no stopping the woman. I cursed his kindness to old ladies.

"The family thought he should have come home for the Civil War," interjected Miss Pomfret. "We found that in some old letters, didn't we?"

Miss Blodgett frowned at any implied criticism of Great-Great-Uncle Josiah. "He was much too old to serve," she said sternly.

"His diary said he prayed for guidance," said Miss Pomfret, goggling saucily over the rim of her glass. "And God told him to stay just where he was."

"Beneath the whispering palms," said Aunt Hermione. "Much more pleasant for him than one of those Civil War battlefields, I'm sure." Then, as if she'd implied that Great-Great-Uncle Josiah had been a slacker, she added hastily, "All most interesting, I'm sure. Perhaps, Iris, we shall read the book about the Blodgetts when it is finished."

"Oh, it will be printed privately," said Miss Blodgett with a wintry smile. "Just for our family." She looked over sharply at her companion as the latter poured herself another glass of champagne. "Although I may present some copies to colleges and libraries in New England that were touched in some way by my family."

Miss Pomfret sipped. "You mean your family was touched in some way by the colleges and libraries," she said. "For funds." She burst into a delicious giggle and tried to muffle it behind her hand to no avail.

Miss Blodgett glared at her. "The family has always done its philanthropic duty, without having to be, as you so vulgarly put it, 'touched.' " She sighed. "Oh, Pommy, you look all pink. You shouldn't be having that second glass. You're not used to champagne."

"It's my fifth, actually," said Miss Pomfret. "We had several glasses at our own table, remember?" She looked unrepentant and took another sip. On close inspection, she did seem to be weaving in a manner not consistent with the motions of the *Malolo*.

"Perhaps," said my aunt, "the heat has affected her. The tropical sun can do queer things to the brain."

"I'm a little dizzy," said Miss Pomfret decidedly, "but it's a very pleasant sensation."

"Come, Pommy," said Miss Blodgett, rising. "You'd better lie down." Then she added with a little more indulgence than usual, "I hope it wasn't a mistake bringing you to the tropics. These waters have a reputation for bringing out a general looseness. My great-great-uncle knew all about it. His words should be a warning to you."

"Yes, Viola," said Miss Pomfret, although a defiant gleam in her eye made me wonder if she intended to take the advice of the long-dead missionary.

After they were out of earshot, Antoinette and I caught each other's eye and began to giggle. "I hope Miss Pomfret can lay off the *okolehao* when she gets to Honolulu. It's the local bathtub gin, made from its root," she said.

"She will if Miss Blodgett has anything to say about it," I replied.

Just then, someone rushed into the saloon and announced that the beacon on Makapuu Point had been spotted.

"We've only to sail around Koko Head and we'll see Honolulu!" exclaimed Antoinette.

Land, even after such a short voyage, is a thrilling sight. We went up on deck and stared at the point of light on the horizon, bigger and brighter than the myriad stars above. I felt so impatient.

I felt even more so the next day as we sat at anchor by the channel entrance.

Before us was Diamond Head, dark and jutting. Honolulu was a jumble of piers and warehouses, a strip of brilliant green vegetation, a modern skyline marked here and there by a genuine skyscraper, all set against the furrowed hills. Above was the tropically blue sky, immense when compared to the outcropping of land which was the island of Oahu.

The khaki-clad doctor from Quarantine arrived on his launch, and it was then that I saw the woman in white—a solitary figure strangely at odds with the festive passengers pointing out over the rail at the sight before them.

She wore a very smart white crepe de chine ensemble and a close-fitting white hat with a half veil. It was the hat that made her so conspicuous. It was all wrong for a tropical cruise. Despite the veiling, I had the impression of a neat profile with a short nose and a rounded chin. She had a mature, though trim, figure and elegant stockings and shoes.

The woman in white created a vivid impression of unhappiness at first glance. It wasn't in her features, which were obscured by white tulle, but rather, in the set of her shoulders and the way her small, well-manicured hands gripped the rail. Her whole attitude spoke of such tension, she looked as if she were about to snap.

Later, after we had descended the gangplank, I spotted her again in the crush of the holiday-like crowd that met the ship. The Royal Hawaiian Band played. Leis were thrust about our necks not by the beautiful Polynesian girls with glossy dark hair and slim brown hands of the travel brochures, but by smiling old ladies in straw hats.

Aunt Hermione buried her face in the sweetly scented flowers that encircled her throat. "What lovely people," she said, sighing happily. "So generous. And what a profusion of flowers. I can hardly wait to begin my research into the flora of the place."

I murmured something as my gaze followed the woman in white. She ignored the gay atmosphere on the pier and made her way swiftly, like an apparition, through the crowd. She was still veiled. It was all rather unsettling, and I felt a frisson of excitement, as if the woman were somehow an omen of interesting trouble in paradise.

# 2

*Leaving the* busy streets of the city, we went by taxi to the new Royal Hawaiian at Waikiki. It was a magnificent sight, a palace of coral pink, topped by blue tile and surrounded by century-old coconut palms. A light breeze from the mossy ravines of the Koolau Range gave relief from the heat without. Within, the thick walls seemed to exude coolness, but the bowls of vibrant flowers, cages of vividly plumed birds, gaily designed draperies, and the blue silk pajamas of the lobby boys reminded us that we were indeed in the tropics.

While Aunt Hermione made arrangements about our room and luggage, I crept out to the broad lanai that overlooked the beach. I couldn't imagine a more beautiful sight than that stretch of white beach, with its rounded bay and gentle but insistent foam-crested waves rolling neatly toward shore. Swimmers and surf riders frolicked in the turquoise waters. With a wriggle of anticipation, I turned to go back and get into my bathing suit as quickly as possible.

In the lobby, however, I stopped and bought a postcard, the brightest I could find, with a view of the beach and the hotel. Up in our room, as Aunt Hermione began her exhausting unpacking program, I sat at a small desk and took a letter from my handbag. I'd meant to answer it sooner. It was from Jack Clancy.

*May 28, 1928*

*Dear Iris,*

*Aw, come on, Iris. There's no need to be sore. I wanted to take you to that dance, but how could I leave the game when I was on a winning streak like that? And later, how could I leave the game without giving the other fellows a chance to win back some of it? It wouldn't have been sporting.*

*I think it's pretty low of you not to answer my telephone calls. I thought we were supposed to be pals, and this is no way to treat a pal! I've been in the newspaper business long enough to know when I'm being kidded. Those giggling coeds who answer the phone in that dormitory don't fool me a bit. Not to mention that old dragon of a housemother who didn't even pretend you were out.*

*As Ever,*
*Jack*

*P.S. If you need help solving any more murders, get in touch. I'll drop a poker game for a scoop anytime.*

Shuddering at the memory of that horrible evening when I languished in my dormitory room in a brand-new dress of lavender-and-green changeable silk with a handkerchief hem, feigning an interest in my roommate's orchid corsage and saying brightly that I was sure Jack would arrive soon, I began to write my postcard.

*Waikiki*
*June 15, 1928*

*Jack:*

*I'm sorry I was out when you phoned. Don't distress yourself unduly. It's clear we live wildly different lives. A school dance seems as unimportant to you as a card game in some low*

*den reeking of cigar smoke seems to me. Anyway, none of it
matters, as the school year is over, and I am vacationing with
my aunt before spending the summer at home in Portland, Oregon.*

> *In haste (the surf beckons),*
> *Iris Cooper*

*P.S. I solved those murders by myself.*

I was referring to the two most exciting events of my life
—murder cases that Jack in *The Globe* luridly referred to as
the "death in the deck chair" and the "murder in the mummy
case." Sometimes I thought that my intense excitement at
solving baffling crimes was not entirely wholesome. I told
myself, however, that I had not committed those crimes,
merely solved them, with a little help from Jack.

I told Aunt Hermione I was going swimming immediately.

"How many hours has it been since you've eaten?" she
said with a worried look.

"Hours and hours," I said impatiently. I mailed the postcard to care of the *San Francisco Globe* in the lobby, then went
immediately to a dressing room on the beach, changed into
my bathing suit, ran to the water's edge, and plunged into the
refreshing surf.

I swam out over the buoyant waves, feeling free and mar-
velously alone. I floated on my back for a while and gazed up
at the blue sky. A rainbow appeared above me, and a light
shower, the kind they call "liquid sunshine" in the islands,
scattered refreshing droplets on my face for a few seconds.

Nothing, I thought to myself, will ever be better than this.

I felt completely relieved of any responsibility—there were
no exams to study for, no brothers and sisters to care for, no
silly school dance to worry about. I was all by myself, under a

blue sky and a hot sun, being rocked by the waves as their coolness massaged my body deliciously.

Later, however, when I'd returned to shore and was reclining lazily in a canvas beach chair, my carefree mood was shattered. Aunt Hermione had come out to find me.

"You must call your friend Antoinette at once," she said. "She seems so agitated and wants to speak to you."

I sighed. I'd hoped to relax and enjoy the beach before launching into any social program.

I didn't bother to dress, I just threw on my beach coat, for the hotel is wonderfully informal. In the lobby I telephoned the number my aunt had given me.

"Iris," said Antoinette, "I must speak with you. Something very mysterious is going on at home, and you're so good at mysteries. Everyone at school knows all about your adventures."

"Antoinette," I said, "what is it?"

"I mustn't speak about it on the telephone," she said. "Come with your aunt to tea tomorrow. I've arranged it with my grandmother, and we can speak privately. I can't even talk to Walter. But I must know just what is—"

Here her tone changed abruptly. "Yes, and bring your aunt by all means," she said. It was apparent someone had come into the room. "Tell her our chief gardener, Mr. Takahashi, will show her around the garden. Around three then? We'll send a car. Bye-bye."

Before I had a chance to question her further, she'd replaced the receiver.

# 3

*I returned* to the beach to find Aunt Hermione supervising an attendant as he arranged a large umbrella for us over two canvas chairs. When he'd finished that, she ordered two large lemonades to be brought to us.

Aunt Hermione looked very gay in a brightly printed cotton beach pajama, a scarf tied around her hair.

Naturally, she wanted to hear all about my conversation with Antoinette, but by the time we were all settled in, the Misses Pomfret and Blodgett joined us.

I watched their progress up the beach. Miss Blodgett wore a strange hat that looked like a pith helmet and trudged purposefully through the sand, while Miss Pomfret, in a dainty frock, darted barefoot along the wet sand, letting the waves lap over her toes.

The attendant rustled up some more chairs for the ladies, who told us they had rented a small house farther down the beach.

"I need quiet for my work," Miss Blodgett explained. "I was afraid a hotel would be too busy, and although the house is small, it will suit us well. A maid comes in the mornings."

"At night we shall hear the surf lapping up on the sands," said Miss Pomfret with a sigh. "It will be like a lullaby."

To my surprise, Miss Blodgett's eyes took on a dreamy cast, too. "And the breezes in the whispering palms . . ." she began, then seemed to catch herself up short. "That is, these islands are certainly beguiling, but I must remember how they first appeared to Great-Great-Uncle Josiah. 'Unspeakably hot and damp, a climate with a bad effect on the health and the morals of the dirty, wretched, unclothed natives.' "

"Yes," mused Aunt Hermione. "I imagine he was eager to get them all fitted out in frock coats and Mother Hubbards."

"Oh, look," said Miss Pomfret, observing a handsome young Hawaiian, the descendant of one of the natives Great-Great-Uncle Josiah had described so unflatteringly. Far from wearing a frock coat, he was wearing a one-piece bathing suit, and his smooth, coppery torso gleamed in the sun. He was instructing a large, middle-aged lady in bathing suit and cap, in the art of surf riding and had one well-formed arm around her shoulders as he demonstrated the proper stance to assume on the heavy wooden board. I had been dying to try that myself.

Miss Pomfret clasped her hands in front of her. "Oh, they give lessons. I'd love to learn."

"Nonsense," said Miss Blodgett. "It isn't possible to remain erect on a piece of wood that is being tossed by the waves."

Miss Blodgett, if she had bothered to turn and see that it was possible and that a score of people were doing just that some yards from us on the water, would probably have continued to deny it.

"Oh, but it would be so thrilling," said her companion. "Viola, I am determined to give it a try. You know how athletic I am." She turned to us. "I have dozens of cups at home from my field-hockey days."

"Don't be conceited, Pommy," said Miss Blodgett.

We watched the Hawaiian instructor and his pupil carry their boards to the shore and plunge into the water, kneeling on them and paddling determinedly out to sea.

"Perhaps later, after we have made some progress with our work," said Miss Blodgett. "Now, we really should be going," she added. "It isn't wise to spend so much time in the sun."

"Maybe I'll just sit in the shade of a palm tree this afternoon," said Miss Pomfret. "If you really want to work. You won't need me just yet, will you?"

"Pommy! I'm surprised at you." Miss Blodgett sounded exasperated. "Didn't you *read* Great-Great-Uncle Josiah's diary? It is full of good advice for the unwary traveler to these parts. *Never* sit beneath a coconut palm. The heavy fruit can fall on you."

"Oh, yes," said Miss Pomfret, explaining to us with a little giggle. "Apparently a drunken sea captain from New Bedford was beaned by one of the things and died, right here at Waikiki. Great-Great-Uncle Josiah thought it the intervention of Divine Providence."

"Always unwise to second-guess God, I think," said Aunt Hermione. "But, being a clerical man, perhaps it was a professional hazard." She smiled mildly.

"Do come and see us soon," said Miss Pomfret as she was led away. "We're quite alone in our little bungalow." She pointed down the beach. "It's just past the Halekulani Hotel, beyond the sea wall."

"We should be delighted," said Aunt Hermione. "Maybe we can get in a little bridge?"

I groaned inwardly. I found the company of these ladies rather difficult. I was always tempted to defend Miss Pomfret against the tyranny of Miss Blodgett, whose rigid views were a trial to me. It's so hard sometimes not to criticize one's elders, especially when they are as idiotically self-righteous as Viola Blodgett.

"Well," said Aunt Hermione as soon as they had gone, "what did Antoinette say? I'm dying to know."

"Not very much, I'm afraid," I replied. "Something is troubling her, and she seemed to think that if I solved some mystery for her, it would help."

"A mystery? How fascinating!"

"She says that she wants to get me alone tomorrow when we go there to tea, and she will tell me all about it."

Aunt Hermione looked conspiratorial. "I'll do my best to leave you girls alone. Although I don't see how you can shed Walter. He never lets her out of his sight."

"She said she couldn't even tell Walter about it," I said.

"Aha! Then the mystery concerns him in some way. Very interesting. What could it be? Perhaps she's come to suspect his intentions in some fashion. I wondered if that boy was after her money." She looked thoughtful. "Which is not always as bad a thing as you might think. I think there are some perfectly respectable people who marry for money and keep up their end of the bargain through the years. Still, it is not the ideal way for two young people to start their lives."

I was shocked. "Aunt Hermione! What a terrible thing to say! I shall marry for love or not at all," I said with a toss of my head.

"Well, it's a moot point in your case, dear," said my aunt. "You aren't as rich as that Caulfield girl, and you're twice as lovable."

The following afternoon, Lee, the Caulfield chauffeur, called for us. The drive through the Nuuanu valley, away from the heat of the beach and into the cooler hills, was lovely, offering vistas of thick vegetation interlaced with rainbows. Aunt Hermione had already begun her study of horticulture, remarking on a particularly fine row of banyan trees, all snarly roots and sinister canopies of foliage, as we went along the Pali Road.

Passing through iron gates in a high wall of volcanic rock, we approached the house, an imposing white structure with a tile roof, surrounded by a magnificent garden. I had no idea what the profusion of flowers were, other than a magnificent crimson bougainvillea that seemed to have engulfed the carriage house. It was so different from the neat little garden at our house on Madison and Ardmore back in Portland.

We saw a rather shabby old Ford parked on the circular drive—rather out of place in this luxurious setting. On the large, shaded porch, we encountered two people waiting at the door, presumably the owners of the car. A short, neat Japanese man in a somber suit, who appeared to be in his twenties, gave us a small bow. With him was a woman about the same age, but her features looked more Polynesian, with a coppery cast to her skin. She wore a demure office dress with an immaculate white collar and a small black straw hat. Her dark hair was neatly waved.

"Oh, are you Mr. Takahashi?" said Aunt Hermione with animation. Aunt Hermione gave a puzzled glance at his business suit. He was carrying a small attaché case. Unless it contained a trowel, I doubted very much that the young man was the head gardener.

"Mr. Yamagamuchi," he corrected her with a puzzled little frown.

It struck me that these two looked ill at ease. I wondered if they were selling something, in which case they were at the wrong door, as there was doubtless a servants' entrance somewhere.

Just then the door in question opened, and a parlor maid stood there. The Japanese gentleman and his companion drew back as we introduced ourselves and were shown into the hall.

"We have an appointment with Mr. Caulfield," he said to

110

the parlor maid in a rather uncertain voice, and handed her a card.

Why hadn't they parked closer to the house? I wondered. Odd little details such as these generally pique my interest. I could only imagine that they were somehow ashamed of their shabby little car. I found it a disquieting thought and somehow blamed the Caulfields.

The parlor maid asked the couple to wait while she led us into a spacious living room. As we passed a tall mirror, I caught a glimpse of the woman brushing off the man's coat with a nervous, almost motherly little gesture. Whoever these people were, they were determined to make a respectable impression.

"Iris!" exclaimed Antoinette, rising from a low sofa and coming toward us.

She'd never greeted me so effusively before. I could only imagine it was because she wanted me to solve her mystery for her. Walter, who'd been sitting next to her, rose and greeted us cordially. Mrs. Caulfield, seated in a throne-like wing chair, remained seated.

"How kind of you to come," she said, consulting an old-fashioned watch on a long chain about her neck. "And punctual, too. We always serve tea at four."

Any compliment on our punctuality was superfluous, I thought, as her driver had been sent to fetch us.

"You must take tea," she continued. "Although it is hot, it is very beneficial in the tropics."

I for one would have loved some lemonade, but Mrs. Caulfield's manner was so imperious that I wouldn't have dared turned down tea, which arrived with cucumber sandwiches and little cakes. As we began to partake of it, Mrs. Caulfield thanked Aunt Hermione for chaperoning her granddaughter.

"So kind of you, and although it is most irregular to ask a perfect stranger to take on such a task, I felt sure you would be very suitable, having a young niece of your own."

"I'm so glad to have helped," said Aunt Hermione. "It would be a shame to have separated a young, engaged couple and sent them on different ships, as I understand was the original plan."

"Engaged!" said Mrs. Caulfield. "Indeed. There has been no announcement."

"Well, Antoinette led us to believe . . ." began Aunt Hermione. I wondered if Antoinette had been afraid to tell her grandmother they were engaged.

"I'm afraid it's no secret at Stanford," I said lightly.

"A little premature, don't you think?" said Mrs. Caulfield to Antoinette. She attempted to mask her evident displeasure with a frigid little smile. "After all, we have only just met Walter, and we haven't met his people at all."

She raised up her hands in a carefully controlled gesture of exasperation and addressed Aunt Hermione. "These young people today are so hasty. There is plenty of time to make sure these things are wise. I myself was engaged to Mr. Caulfield for seven years."

"I think such long engagements are too difficult for young people," said Aunt Hermione firmly.

"Oh, but I was on the mainland while Mr. Caulfield was setting himself up in business here," she replied. "We wrote letters every week."

Her explanation was intended to convey, no doubt, that all proprieties were maintained by an expanse of ocean. It sounded like a perfectly hideous arrangement to me. Yet, Mrs. Caulfield seemed to be holding it up as the best way to proceed.

Antoinette jumped up from the sofa. "I promised Iris I'd

show her my new dress," she announced. "We won't be long.
Come on, Iris." She took my hand and led me from the room.
As soon as we were out in the hall, she leaned against the wall,
closed her large blue eyes, and sighed. "I'm afraid they don't
like Walter. I can't imagine why. He's perfect."

I didn't know what to say, and Antoinette continued, "Oh,
Iris, it's all so difficult, it's so hard keeping it from Walter,
this awful thing hanging over me, this mystery you must help
me solve."

"Antoinette, what is it?" I said.

"Come upstairs," she said. "They think I'm showing you a
dress."

Antoinette led me up to her room. It looked like a princess's room, with a canopied bed swathed in mosquito netting, some fine old French furniture, and heavy draperies of
pink and gold. A large dressing table with a flouncy skirt was
covered with perfume bottles. On a small bookshelf was a collection of fussy-looking china dolls in Victorian dresses. She
led me to a little chintz-covered sofa and we sat down.

"Iris, it's so horrible. You must never tell a soul what I'm
about to tell you. I probably *shouldn't* tell you, it's just that,
well, if it weren't for Walter . . ." 

Antoinette began to cry. She produced a small cambric
handkerchief from a pocket and dabbed at her eyes.

"What is it?" I said firmly.

"I think I may be insane."

"What?"

"Do you believe in ghosts?"

"Maybe," I said. "I've never seen one, though. Have
you?"

"I don't think so. I don't know."

"Antoinette," I said, becoming annoyed. "Get to the
point."

"All right. All right. I was in the library yesterday, all by myself. I looked at the window, and there was a woman standing in the garden. Staring at me."

"What makes you think she was a ghost?" I said.

"Well, I gave a little shriek. She was staring at me so intently. I turned away, just as Grandmother came in the room. I told her to look out the window, but she didn't see a thing. It took me another minute to get the courage to turn and look myself, and when I did she was gone."

"Why do you think she was a ghost?" I said. "It must have been some real person wandering on the grounds."

"But Grandmother didn't see her. She said, 'There's no one there.' And the view from the library is of a great sweep of lawn. The woman couldn't have run off in that second I turned away."

"Then your grandmother must have been lying," I said. It was the only explanation, although it sounded a little harsh, so I added, "Perhaps she didn't want you to be frightened."

"But I'm more frightened now. Iris, if I'm insane, then I can't marry Walter."

"Don't be ridiculous," I said. "Besides, if you're truly insane, then you wouldn't wonder about it." I wasn't sure on this point, but it seemed sensible. "Why, we had a neighbor in Portland who thought Jesus lived in her laundry room. She didn't worry that she was insane. She thought the rest of us were off our onions."

"But Iris," Antoinette continued in a whisper, "there's insanity in the family!" She burst into tears again.

"Everyone has some distant relative who's a little off," I said, trying to sound jocular. "Why, Father's talked for years about his cousin Etta. She used to knit little sweaters for her parakeets."

Personally, I found the idea of Aunt Etta and her parakeets hilarious, but Antoinette didn't seem to think it was so funny.

Instead she said, "My mother . . . before she died. She was in a hospital on the mainland. I've always thought . . . I never dared ask. Grandmother scarcely speaks of her."

"Well if you're really worried about it, you must ask her," I said. "You're all grown up now, Antoinette. Ready to marry. You deserve to know the truth."

"I don't remember my mother," said Antoinette. "I was just a baby when she went away. I don't even remember them telling me she died. I just always knew she was dead. But I always imagined her watching me from heaven." She had a strange, faraway look in her eyes that frightened me a little.

I put my arms around her. "I know," I said.

I had been ten when my own mother died during the Spanish influenza epidemic. I never really had a chance to say good-bye. She just went to bed and died. I often think she's watching me, somehow.

"I feel the same way about my mother," I said.

"That's why," said Antoinette slowly, "I wondered if I, I'd seen a ghost. Maybe it was Mother. Would that make me insane?"

"Did it look like a ghost?" I said.

"Oh no. She was a very flesh-and-blood sort of person."

"Then she probably wasn't a ghost," I said. "I believe they are rather filmy."

Poor Antoinette was in a horrible state. "Except that she was wearing white," she said. "Ghosts do, don't they? And she was wearing a veil. That's filmy."

I released her and leapt back. "White crepe de chine? A two-piece dress with a row of box pleats from a band at the hip? A snug little cap and a half veil of white tulle?"

"Yes!" exclaimed Antoinette. "Exactly."

"If that was a ghost," I said, "it sailed with us on the *Malolo*."

# 4

*Iris,"* said Antoinette intensely, "can you find her for me? I have to know where she's staying."

Her tone had changed as soon as I had told her I'd seen the same woman. Now, rather than sounding frightened, Antoinette sounded determined.

"But why? Do you know who she is?"

"I can't talk about it now," she said. "It's all too horrible. You know how I feel about Walter, don't you? I'd die if we couldn't get married. He's so, well, he's so correct. I couldn't burden him with this. Please, just say you'll find the woman. I'll tell you about it after we're married. I promise."

"I suppose we could check the passenger list," I said, puzzled.

Antoinette had some horrible secret, a secret she wanted to keep from Walter, and she wanted me to become involved. Whatever it was, it must have been important for the naturally cheerful Antoinette to be taking it so seriously. Her merry little face was drawn and pale, with a queer expression there I'd never seen before.

"I'll try to help you," I said.

"Oh, thank goodness. Now remember, not a word to anyone."

I assured her of my discretion, but any promise I made naturally excluded my keeping anything from my aunt. She and I discussed everything, and a mystery like this would fascinate her. Besides, I wanted her opinion on the matter.

"Let's go back with the others," I said. "I'm sure there's a logical explanation for all this. We can arrive at the facts, I'm sure of it."

Antoinette seemed cheered by my assurances. She dried her eyes, pulled herself together, and followed me meekly back downstairs.

We found ourselves in the hall, just as Mr. Yamagamuchi and his female companion were leaving. No one was bothering to see them out, which seemed odd.

The woman, obviously thinking they were unobserved, remarked, "All right, maybe it is a weird setup, but so what? We know his credit's good."

"I don't know," mused Mr. Yamagamuchi fussily. "It just doesn't seem right."

Antoinette and I exchanged glances. What an odd conversation! After they had left, she rapped on the door they'd closed behind them.

"Grandfather?"

"Is that you, Antoinette?" called out a querulous male voice.

She opened the door, and I saw an old, distinguished-looking gentleman in a wheelchair. The room looked like an office. It was lined with books, and he was sitting at a large oak desk.

"Those ladies gone yet?" he demanded. "I wish I had my old office back. No ladies coming to tea there."

He caught sight of me. "Oh, there's one of 'em now. Well, at least it's a young lady, and a pretty one."

Antoinette introduced me, and she seemed a little embarrassed by her eccentric grandfather.

"How do you do?" he said. "Can't get up. They've got me in this silly chair. Not that I really need it . . ."

"Grandfather's heart mustn't be strained," explained Antoinette.

"They're always fussing at me," he complained. "I feel fine. Just tired all the time, but my mind's still sharp. Thank God for that."

"Who were those people I just saw leaving?" said Antoinette.

"Never mind about them. Say! Take a look at this." He held up a newspaper. "An airplane's going to land right here on Oahu from the mainland. What do you think of that? Why, if I were a young fellow nowadays, I'd look into this aviation business."

"Yes," said Antoinette. "Walter read that to me. He wants to go out there and see the plane come in. Doesn't that sound fun?" She turned to me. "Oh, you must come, too, Iris."

"Go out there and see it," urged the old man. "I'd be there if I could, but I'm a prisoner in this house. Trapped!"

"Oh, Grandfather," said Antoinette in a reasonable tone of voice. "You know it's for your own good." She turned to me. "His secretary comes every day, and he runs the business from the house. It's much better for him."

"For all I know," said her grandfather, "that junior partner of mine is stealing me blind. How'd you like that, Antoinette?"

"Oh, don't worry about that," said Antoinette. "After I'm married, Walter will look out for our interests."

"Walter, eh?" Mr. Caulfield sounded dubious.

"You met this Walter?" he asked me.

"Yes," I said. "Antoinette is a lucky girl. Walter is devoted to her happiness."

"My granddaughter'll be a rich woman one day," he said. "Hate to see it all go up in smoke because of some fool of a husband. Why, when I came out to this place, there was nothing here. Hardly anything, anyway. It was the crossroads of the Pacific, and no one could see the potential. I got into the China trade just at the right time. That's why we're so rich, young lady. Then I picked up the sugarcane fields and later the pineapple acreage. I'd *hate* to see Antoinette throw it all away on the wrong young man. Now if she'd just marry Charlie Spaulding, my partner's boy . . ."

I found this rather odd, as he'd just accused his partner of trying to steal him blind. Antoinette must have thought so, too, for she added with spirit, "But you're always complaining about Charlie's father. You just said he was probably stealing from you."

"That's right," her grandfather said. "If he's anything like his father, my original partner, he must be. Never can catch him, though." He laughed. "If he were at home in a wheelchair, why, I might try to outmaneuver him. That's what you need in business, a little of the plundering spirit. Has Walter got it?"

"Certainly not," said Antoinette. "He's a perfect gentleman."

"Too bad," said Mr. Caulfield.

He turned to me. "You look like my sister Mary. She has red hair. A very sensible girl she was. Dead now. Wonder if I'll see her. You look like a sensible person, too."

"Iris is very sensible," Antoinette said.

"Well, what does she think of Walter?"

"Walter loves Antoinette. Antoinette loves Walter," I said. "That's the chief thing, isn't it?" Something about the old man's brutal frankness made it seem permissible for me to be frank, too. "And if he's not a cutthroat businessman, well, maybe that's all right. It's the founder of an empire who has to be remorseless, not the heirs who are to maintain it."

"You've got a point there," he conceded.

Antoinette looked annoyed. "Really, Grandfather, you do go on so. You mustn't put poor Iris in the position of having to defend Walter. You're not yourself today, are you?"

"Ha! Is that what you think?" He laughed a little. "My dear, I'm more myself than I ever was. When the end's coming," he said, "there seems less and less point beating around the bush."

"Oh, don't say that," she replied.

"What? That the end is near? That's what they tell me. You two run along now, I've got plenty to do. If Miss Cooper here wants to come visit me, she can," he added. "She seems like a sensible person. God knows there's not enough of them around. Besides, she's pretty. But keep that Walter out of here. He's too damned respectful."

"Poor Grandfather," said Antoinette in hushed tones on the stairs as we went down. "He seems to blurt out whatever he's thinking. I know it's a trial to my grandmother."

I could well imagine that it was. Antoinette's grandmother had struck me as a proud, rigid woman who had no countenance for frankness.

In the living room, Aunt Hermione turned and regarded our entrance with interest. She knew I'd listened to Antoinette's problem and, of course, was dying to hear all about it. She managed, however, not to look too curious. I reflected that as we were going back with the Caulfields' chauffeur, we wouldn't be able to discuss matters until we were back at the hotel. I knew Aunt Hermione would be fairly bursting with curiosity.

"Tell us about the dress, dear," she said mildly. "What color is it?"

"Blue," I said, at the same time Antoinette said, "Red."

"That is," I added with a smile, "Antoinette has such a lot of dresses."

120

"How delightful," said Aunt Hermione.

"Your aunt, Miss Cooper, has told me about her talk at the Town Club," said Mrs. Caulfield.

"Yes," said Aunt Hermione. "Mrs. Caulfield has very kindly offered to let me photograph her magnificent garden. What a treat that will be for the ladies."

"Mr. Takahashi can show you around now," said Mrs. Caulfield.

"How fortunate that I have my Brownie with me," said my aunt, who had, I knew, brought it along with just this purpose in mind.

Walter consulted his watch. "If we're to see that airplane land," he said, "we should get out there soon, Antoinette. It's been sighted above the main shipping lanes on schedule. Better to be early than late," he added solemnly.

"Oh, what fun," said Antoinette, sounding her usual enthusiastic self or a good imitation of it anyway. "I hope Iris can come, too. We can take the roadster and a picnic."

I glanced at Aunt Hermione, and Antoinette added, "I thought while your aunt was here taking pictures—"

"Yes," I said, "but my aunt has promised two ladies we met on the boat that we would play bridge this afternoon. Remember the Misses Blodgett and Pomfret?"

"Bridge, you say?" said Mrs. Caulfield sharply, leaning forward with a gleam in her eye. "Are they good players?"

"Quite good, I would say," said Aunt Hermione. "Miss Blodgett is a very shrewd and intelligent player. Miss Pomfret can be a little uncertain."

If the truth were to be known, Aunt Hermione could use a little of that uncertainty herself, especially where bidding was concerned.

"Well, I would be glad to send a car around for the ladies," said Mrs. Caulfield. "Then Iris can go along with Antoinette and Walter, and I'll take her place.

"If Antoinette is to go gadding about chasing after airplanes, I'd prefer she do it in the company of Iris, who seems like such a sensible young lady." She gave me a wintry smile, ostensibly of approval, but succeeded only in giving the impression she didn't trust Antoinette and Walter.

And so it was that we found ourselves presently sitting in some rather dusty grass waiting for an airplane. Antoinette had rounded up some of her old friends from Punahou School, and we ate chicken with our fingers and fresh fruit and tiny sandwiches while craning our necks skyward at intervals.

We had about given up hope when, as dusk was beginning to fall, we heard a low throbbing noise. There was a fair-sized crowd, and everyone rose and scanned the horizon. Presently, the plane did arrive, a dot at first, then a magnificent soaring thing, swooping toward the field. I was thrilled when the craft tipped its wings then circled for a landing.

We all broke into applause, and then, as the craft rolled to a halt, we all rushed forward to greet the heroic pilot who'd flown across the ocean.

"He isn't the first, of course," said Walter. "That was done last year, but it's still quite a feat. And if he's shaved some time off the old record . . ."

The pilot emerged, clad in brown leather helmet and jacket, stripped off his goggles, and waved to the crowd. We all cheered again. Then a second man emerged. He shook his head impatiently, as if glad to be out of the confined space of the ship. When he pulled off his goggles and then his leather helmet, I gasped. It was Jack Clancy.

Presumably he'd been covering the flight for *The Globe*, but he waved and smiled and acknowledged the crowd's applause as if he were somehow responsible for the whole thing. It was very irritating, and typical of Jack.

Both men bounded to the ground. Jack lit up a cigar and posed theatrically next to the airplane, and then with his arm around the pilot for press photographers.

"What daring men." Antoinette sighed.

"One of them's Jack Clancy," I said. "A reporter. I know him."

"Oh, but isn't he the one . . ." began Antoinette.

"Yes," I said icily. And then, because some of the other people in our party seemed fascinated that I knew Jack, I tried to put a jaded and world-weary gloss on the facts. "In fact," I said, "he's a perfect rat who stood me up at the homecoming dance. Got bogged down in a poker game. You know how men are. Especially newspapermen."

Everyone looked impressed with my nonchalant cynicism and by the fact that I had such a raffish acquaintance.

I heard Jack's voice above the crowd. "Okay, boys, that's enough. I've got to get to the telegraph office to wire in my story. *The Globe*'ll be happy to pick up some of those pictures, you can depend on it."

As he made his way through the admiring crowd, I turned to avoid him. I was sure he thought he looked awfully dashing in those aviator clothes. What I saw when I turned away startled me. There she was again, the mysterious woman in white. I think I was disappointed, however, that she was no longer in white. She wore a shiny black dress, and she was staring at Antoinette from a point in the crowd behind us.

"Look," I said, tugging on Antoinette's sleeve. "There she is."

"Who?" demanded Walter.

"Where?" demanded Antoinette, ignoring him.

Just then, the crowd surged backward to allow Jack and the pilot to leave the field, and we lost sight of her again. I began to walk quickly in her direction and heard Antoinette lying to Walter.

"Just an old school friend; stay here with the others, darling, I'll be right back."

I trotted in the direction the woman had gone, and Antoinette caught up with me. I weaved back and forth a little, looking between shoulders and heads, until I caught just a glimpse of black, then I set out after that flash of fabric.

Darting around a portly man in a gaudy shirt, I careened into the arms of none other than Jack, who had stopped to chat with some simpering, admiring girls.

"Iris!" he exclaimed with a ready smile. "I knew I might run into you over here, but I'd no idea you'd be out to meet my plane. Quite a sight it must have been, our landing. Wait till I write it up for *The Globe*. What an adventure."

"I'd no idea you were on that plane," I said. "Excuse me, but I've got to go."

"Wait a second, Iris," he began, but I ran on, free of the crowd now and with the woman in plain sight. She was walking briskly to a waiting car.

"Iris . . ." Now it was Antoinette calling. She caught up and said breathlessly, "Don't go after her now. Walter's curious. Let's pretend we just came to talk to Jack."

"Jack," I said, "this is Antoinette Caulfield. Jack Clancy. Hello. Now, would you please do me a great favor and follow that woman in black."

"Another mystery, eh?" said Jack enthusiastically. "Okay, I guess I can take care of that for you before I wire in my story. I don't know what this is about, but if you're involved, it just might be something big."

Antoinette looked pale, and I called after him as he took off across the field, "I'm at the Royal Hawaiian."

I turned to Antoinette. "Did you get a look at her?" I said.

"That's the woman I saw on board the *Malolo*. Is it the same one you saw in your garden?"

"I think so," she said. "I'd like to know her name and where she's staying."

"There's more to this story than you're telling me," I said. "What is it about?"

She shook her head just a little. "I can't talk about it now, Iris. Just help me."

"Very well," I said, a theory about the woman forming in my mind.

I glanced over at Jack, who was jumping on the running board of another automobile and pointing at the car in which the mysterious woman was speeding away.

"Jack will find out what we need to know," I said. "You can count on it."

# 5

**When I** arrived back at the hotel that evening, Aunt Hermione was rummaging in a steamer trunk. "Oh, there you are, Iris. I want to hear all about the airplane. And about Antoinette's mystery, too." Before I had a chance to answer, she went on. "Have you had enough to eat? I was so tired after tramping through the garden—a magnificent garden, by the way, very large and affording many fine vistas—that I had dinner sent up to the room. But I thought we could go down to the lanai for coffee. There's an orchestra, you know. It should be festive."

She frowned. "I'm looking for my gray evening dress, I can't find anything."

"Let me help you," I said. "I can't think why the maid didn't arrange all this properly in the closet."

"I forgot to leave the trunk key," she said. "Actually, it wasn't the garden that tired me out, now that I think of it. I find flowers very invigorating. I think it was the bridge. Mrs. Caulfield and Miss Blodgett are both so competitive. They were actually sniping away at each other."

"I can imagine that," I said. "They are both quite domineering and egocentric."

"Yes. Miss Blodgett went on about her family—you know, the Reverend Josiah and all that—and said some rather snobbish things about Hawaii, and got Mrs. Caulfield's dander up."

"Here's your gray dress," I said, shaking it loose from a cloud of tissue paper. Aunt Hermione always uses reams of it when she packs. "I almost wish I had seen Caulfield versus Blodgett," I said.

"Oh, thank you, Iris. Mrs. Caulfield said Hawaii had many fine old families, and Miss Blodgett smiled rather wickedly and asked if the Caulfields had any half-castes in their family tree. She really is a most impertinent woman."

She paused for a moment and I said, belatedly, "Yes, I've had enough to eat."

Aunt Hermione and I have developed our own style of conversation. Because she manages to talk about a half-dozen topics at once and doesn't always wait for an answer to a question, I have to get in my replies when I can.

"Oh, good. Well, tell me all about your day, dear."

"The airplane landed safely," I said. "It was very exciting. And you'd never guess who was on board. Jack Clancy."

"How thrilling! Such an interesting young man. So brash and brusque, just like a newspaperman in a stage play."

"Yes. I sent him off to help solve Antoinette's mystery."

"Tell me all about it," she said from inside the dress, which she was pulling over her head.

So I did, and then I told her some of my theories.

"It's almost too horrible to think about," I said, "but it did occur to me that the strange woman may have been her mother."

"But her mother's dead."

"So she thinks. Or so she says. What if, instead of being locked in an asylum, as Antoinette suspects, and dying there, she lived? The Caulfields are a proud family; they might have passed her off as dead, and now, she's been released."

"Or even escaped," said my aunt, her eyes growing round.

"I hadn't thought of that. My goodness, I thought my own version was melodramatic."

"Why, it's just like one of those sensational Victorian novels we read when I was a girl. The plots often turned upon madwomen locked up for years and missing parents."

"Antoinette was so queer about it. At first she seemed frightened, fearful for her own sanity. But then, when I convinced her that the ghost was flesh and blood and that we'd seen her on the *Malolo*, her demeanor changed. She wanted to find the woman. And she's most adamant that Walter be kept in the dark."

"Interesting," mused my aunt as she powdered her nose. "If the woman is her mother, why doesn't she just come forward?"

I shrugged as Aunt Hermione fastened the back buttons on my mauve dress. "Maybe she thinks that finding out her mother is alive would unsettle her daughter."

"It might very well do just that. But there is more to consider here. A great deal of money is at stake. In my Victorian novels, the plots often hinged on inheritances and legacies."

"Yes. Antoinette was the sole heiress. But if her mother is alive . . ."

"What happened to her father?"

"He died several years ago. Antoinette often speaks of him. He was a sporting type, a clubman."

When we were properly dressed, we went downstairs, refraining from speculating in front of the elevator boy about any horrible family secrets the Caulfields might have.

On the lanai, however, I forgot completely about it.

The sky was so brilliant with stars, the company so gaily dressed and festive, the scent of the flowers so heady, and the strains of Hawaiian music so sweet and melancholy that I was rather overcome with the feeling of intensity one can get when visiting strange, beautiful places. From the darkness beyond, I could hear the waves lapping up on the beach.

"Oh, look," said my aunt when we had settled in at our table. "Here's your nice Mr. Clancy."

"Good," I said, my mood vanishing. "Maybe he can tell us about the mystery woman."

Jack was wearing a white dinner jacket and looking extremely pleased with himself. He came right over to our table and renewed his acquaintance with my aunt, whom he had met in mid-Atlantic when he and I had solved the deck chair murder aboard the *Irenia*.

"Iris tells me you flew all across the Pacific," said Aunt Hermione enthusiastically, in a tone that seemed to convey I'd been gushing on about him. "I hope you can join us."

He sat down. "Glad to. Say, what a trip that was. I've just finished wiring *The Globe*. It'll make a swell story. 'Your reporter conquers the air. Two men against the vast Pacific. A tiny plane against the tropical night sky. America's outpost comes nearer after feat of aviation.' "

"Very interesting, I'm sure," I said. "Did you follow that woman?"

"Yes, I did. And I got a good address on her." He smiled confidently. "Tell me what gives, Iris. I'm counting on you to give me a swell story. If I don't come up with one, my editor will expect me to take the first ship home, and to tell you the truth, I kind of like it here."

"Counting on *me?*" I couldn't help but recall the evening I'd counted on him to take me to the school dance.

Just then, the Davidsons from Portland came to our table. Dr. Davidson and his wife, who served with my aunt on the altar guild, were old friends. Introductions were made, the Davidsons joined us, and Jack asked me to dance. I was glad of that, since we couldn't discuss the mystery woman in front of the Davidsons.

"You remember what a great dancer I am, don't you?" he

said as we began to fox-trot.

"You tell me that every time we dance," I replied.

"Which reminds me," he said. "You aren't still sore about that college dance, are you?"

"Not at all," I lied. "I can't expect you to take an interest in something like that. After all, you're flying around the world and carrying on."

"Glad to see you're still sensible," he said.

"Where does the woman live," I said. "Who is she?"

"Who wants to know?"

"I do."

"What about that little blonde you were with? She isn't Antoinette Caulfield, the sugarcane heiress, by any chance?"

"Well, yes, she is. A friend from school."

"Okay. This could be a big story. She's news. Or could be with the right angle."

The last thing I wanted was for the Caulfields to be embarrassed by one of Jack's sensational stories in *The Globe.*

"Well, what's the connection? She seemed mighty interested in the woman," he continued.

"Oh, please don't ask me. I just wanted to know where she lived."

"Why should I tell you if you're holding out on me?"

"Tell me where she's staying, Jack. If there's a story there, I'll check with the people concerned and see if it's all right with them, and then—"

"Iris, you're driving me nuts. That's not the way the newspaper business works. I'm not a society reporter." Then he relaxed and smiled. "What am I worried about? I'll get it out of you sooner or later."

Jack's confidence in his ability to worm things out of people was irritating, but I just smiled.

"Then you'll tell me?"

"Sure. We can go there now. It's just up the beach."

I glanced over at my aunt's table, where she was chatting animatedly with the Davidsons, and gestured to her above the dancers that I was leaving for a little while.

Jack looked down at my satin slippers and said, "We'd better take the street."

On the way over, he told me about his activities since I'd seen him leave the airfield. "I caught a ride with some nice fellow who drove me into town right behind the woman. Naturally, he was impressed with my flight, and he kept asking me about it, so he did a lousy job of tailing the car. I got the license number, though, before we lost it.

"A pal of mine at the *Star-Bulletin* found out who owned the car. It was a hired machine, and the driver told me about his passenger. Seems this woman wanted him to park in front of the Caulfield place this afternoon, then they followed the girl's roadster out to the airfield.

"Cost twenty bucks of *The Globe*'s money, but I got the woman's address. A little bungalow covered with vines and eaten up by termites. That's the trouble with the tropics, too many bugs."

We passed the Halekulani Hotel, then went farther along, past the little bungalow where the Misses Pomfret and Blodgett were staying.

"Here's the place," said Jack, leading me down a narrow lane toward the beach. It was a small brown structure covered with bougainvillea. We saw a light at one of the windows and crept closer. The woman was seated at a table, writing furiously. One hand twisted her fair hair, the other pushed the pen rapidly along.

"She's got something on her mind all right," whispered Jack.

"Shh!" I said.

131

"Let's knock on the door."

"No!" I hissed.

If we had stumbled on some dreadful secret I didn't want Jack involved. Besides, I'd only promised Antoinette I'd find the woman, not speak to her.

"Why not? We'll say we have the wrong address."

"She saw me at the airfield," I replied. "She'll know it's a ruse."

Just then a car pulled up. I was afraid its lights would catch us. Jack took my hand and pulled me into some foliage.

"Let's go," I said. "We can walk back the beach way. I'll carry my shoes."

It was clear that if we left the way we came, the occupant of the car would spot us.

"Just a minute," said Jack as I bent down and took off my slippers and stockings.

"Come on," I said, pulling at him.

"Got a look at the fellow. Little man with a mustache," said Jack. "Looked angry. Rapped on the door pretty hard."

I just wanted to get away and avoid detection. We managed to thrash our way out of the foliage and onto the beach. It was heavy going in the sand, so we went toward the shore and walked where it was firm and wet. It felt delicious and cool between my toes.

"All right, Iris," began Jack. "If there's a story here and you're not coming out with it . . ."

Why Jack thought I owed him a story, I don't know. But then, Jack thinks everyone owed him a story. I'd seen him convince plenty of people of it, but in the past I'd slaked his deep thirst for a scoop only when I had to, to get him to help me detect. I didn't need his help now. I was simply going to give Antoinette the address and let her do what she wanted with the information.

Presently, as we passed the cottage Miss Blodgett and Miss Pomfret had rented, I glanced toward it, and Jack followed my glance. Curiously, two wooden surfboards were propped against the wall. I smiled. Miss Blodgett must have given in and allowed her companion to take instruction.

Then, to my amazement, I made out two figures in the moonlight. They were clasped in a passionate embrace. They parted for just an instant, and I recognized the handsome Hawaiian surf instructor we'd seen earlier on the beach.

"Oh, my," I said.

"Happens all the time around here," Jack remarked. "The place is a real hotbed of passion, they tell me."

"But the lady is a very correct middle-aged lady from Boston," I replied. "We met her on board the *Malolo*."

Miss Pomfret had wasted no time going to seed in the tropics.

# 6

*The Caulfields'* garden being so vast, and Aunt Hermione's interest in it so extensive, she had arranged to go back the following day and photograph it some more. I thought I'd go along. It would give me the chance to tell Antoinette that I'd found her mystery woman. While I knew my part was just to find her, I looked forward to seeing Antoinette's reaction to the information. The whole story was so curious. We arrived by taxi, and an Oriental houseboy took us immediately out to the garden.

"Mrs. Caulfield says she hopes she can meet with you after your tour," he said stiffly.

"Oh, how nice, I can get started right away," said Aunt Hermione, then added for the servant's benefit, "that is, it will be lovely to see her afterward so I can thank her properly, rather than before."

"Is Miss Caulfield at home?" I asked.

Just then Antoinette, in a tennis dress, came bounding down the stairs into the front hall.

"Hello," she said, with all her usual sparkle. "More of the garden tour?"

"Why don't you girls chat by yourselves awhile," said my aunt, allowing herself to be led toward the garden by the houseboy. She knew I wanted a private interview with my friend.

"What did your friend Jack find out?" Antoinette asked

134

me as soon as we were alone.

"The woman's staying in a little bungalow at Waikiki," I replied, adding the address.

She repeated it, then went over to a little telephone table and wrote it on a scrap of paper. "Oh I knew I could count on you," she said intensely.

Just then, Walter appeared on the stairs in white flannels, carrying a racket. Antoinette stuffed the scrap of paper in the pocket of her dress.

"We're playing tennis," she said unnecessarily. "Maybe you want to come along. We've a court just out beyond the poinciana trees. We could take turns."

"Tennis is for two," I said. "I'll join my aunt. Perhaps I'll see you later."

"Fine," said Walter, who was probably looking forward to a little time alone with his fiancée, but just then Mrs. Caulfield came into the hall from the large living room.

"Perhaps Charlie Spaulding will make a fourth, and you can play doubles," she said. "I invited him over, now that you're home from school."

"Oh, Grandmother," said Antoinette petulantly. "It will be so awkward."

"I don't see why," her grandmother said with a steely glare. "He is your childhood friend, and the man who may run Caulfield and Spaulding one day. You cannot cut him." Then, as if she'd said too much, she allowed her features to soften. "You young people run along, and I'll direct him to you when he arrives. Shall I have some cool drinks sent out later?"

I went out with Antoinette and Walter. "I'll lend you some tennis things," she said. "And don't pay any attention to Grandmother, Walter. If I have anything to say about it, *you'll* run Caulfield and Spaulding one day. After all, I shall inherit sixty percent. Charlie will only get forty." She permitted herself a small smile.

We walked along the terrace and I glanced through French windows into a rather inviting-looking library. The house, full of dark furniture and heavy ornaments, was at odds with its surroundings. It could have been a large house in New England but for the riotous flowers that grew around it. On a sideboard I noticed a large, old-fashioned book that looked as if it might be a family album.

"You two go ahead and play a few sets by yourselves," I said. "I'll stay with my aunt. When Charlie arrives, you can fetch me and I'll change into tennis things and play doubles, if you want."

Again Walter agreed with alacrity. "Fine," he said, taking Antoinette's arm and hustling her off.

When they'd turned a corner, I went over to the French doors and was delighted to find them unlocked. Quickly, I stepped into the library, went over to that book, and lifted the heavy, gilt-embossed cover.

I had been right. It did contain photographs. I knew that what I was doing wasn't right, exactly, but I told myself that if an album of this kind were left lying around, then it must be meant for public perusal.

The pictures seemed to be in chronological order. There were old daguerreotypes of the previous century, in which everyone had a grim, beady-eyed look from sitting so long before the camera. There was a wedding photograph of Antoinette's grandparents with the date inscribed beneath in brownish ink, showing the bride, straight-backed and handsome, certainly not a young, blushing bride, in a sumptuous lace dress.

I flipped ahead and found christening pictures, but that couldn't have been Antoinette's mother. After all, her name was Caulfield. Her mother would be the Caulfield's daughter-in-law, and would, presumably, not show up until later. I was surprised to see that there was no Caulfield son. In fact, there were many pictures of the elder Caulfields and one child—a little girl. All of a sudden, I remembered that Antoinette once told me she had taken her mother's maiden name after she was orphaned, as her grandparents were raising her.

Then I saw what I had been looking for. It was a portrait of a young girl, probably at her debut. She wore white and pearls, and had a great deal of fair hair piled on her head in the fin de siècle style. The features resembled Antoinette's, although they were somehow coarser. This girl had a heavier mouth and stronger brows. It could easily have been Antoinette's mother.

It wasn't until I'd seen another photograph of the same girl, in an old-fashioned pose with one hand on a pedestal, the other holding a fan, the head in profile, that I wondered if it could possibly be the same woman I'd seen on board the *Malolo*, at the airfield, and later, in profile, through the window of that beach cottage. It was hard to tell. The veiling made it difficult, as did the smudgy cottage window. Still, it did seem that this could have been that same woman, but, of course, much younger.

Now that I had found what I wanted, I felt suddenly guilty. I slammed the book shut and prepared to leave, but I heard voices from the next room, which, I suspected, was the living room.

"It is the sort of thing a discreet family lawyer is for," said a voice, obviously Mrs. Caulfield's. "It must be taken care of swiftly."

"Why not a detective?" replied the second voice. I stepped closer to the wall. Antoinette's grandfather was speaking. "I've got an excellent man. He's taken care of a lot of dirty work for me in the sugarcane fields when that troublesome union business came up."

"We need someone discreet," she said. "It is a matter of extreme delicacy."

"He's done that, too," said Mr. Caulfield.

I think I heard him chuckle.

"What?"

"You'll find out soon enough," he said.

"I abhor secrets," said Mrs. Caulfield. "You've been so strange lately."

"If you didn't like secrets," he replied, "you wouldn't be looking for a lawyer or a detective right now."

"You are insufferable." The cold fury in her voice was evident even through the thick walls.

Then she apparently swept out of the room, because the door to the library opened and she stood there facing me, her face flushed.

"Hello," I said mildly.

She gave me a sharp look and glanced at the book in front of me. "I hope you don't mind," I said, as it was clear she knew I had seen or was about to see the family photographs. "I do adore family albums. I thought I'd let Antoinette and Walter play a little before the other young man arrived."

"I see," she said. Her face froze into a little smile.

"I expect I'll go find my aunt," I said. "She's in the garden."

Mrs. Caulfield walked in a slow circle around to the album, then interposed herself between me and it, waiting while I made my way back out the doors. I heard a squeaky sound, which proved to be the sound of Mr. Caulfield's wheelchair.

"Oh, there you are," he said brightly. "That nice girl who looks like Mary."

"She was looking at the photograph album," said Mrs. Caulfield, "but now she's going to find her aunt in the garden."

He glanced over at the album. "That's just the half of it," he said, then began to cackle merrily.

"You must rest, dear," said Mrs. Caulfield to her husband. "You've been taxing yourself too much lately."

"I don't get any peace," said Mr. Caulfield. "I want this nice young lady to take me out for a turn in the garden. That'll be nice and peaceful."

"You mustn't impose on Miss Cooper," said his wife with a nervous look masked by jocularity, as if she were amused at his eccentricity.

"I'd be delighted," I said. "I imagine your chair isn't too difficult to push, and I've noticed there are some smooth paths."

Mrs. Caulfield looked clearly furious, but I managed to wheel the old man out onto the terrace, and we set out down one of the paths.

"A prisoner in my own house," he mused. "Never let it happen to you. Don't know how to prevent it, though. I'm as helpless as a baby. I get so tired. My heart's working double time just keeping me alive. Doesn't give me much strength for anything beyond staying alive a little longer."

"What a lovely garden," I said, thinking that he must wonder how much longer he would see it.

"Yes, I'll miss it," he said, as if he'd read my thoughts. "Wonder if there's a better one in heaven, or if I'll end up there. Who knows?"

"I guess we'll all find out eventually," I said.

"That's right," he said. "You seem to understand. No one around here wants to talk about it. They know I'm going soon, but when I talk about it they just cut me off, change the subject. It's damned irritating."

"Perhaps some clergymen . . ." I began lamely, realizing that it was with his nearest and dearest that he wished to talk about his impending death.

"Never could stand the breed," he said. "Suitable company for women, that's all."

After a moment he gestured to a bench. "Park me over there and sit down a moment before we go back," he said. "Can't see you when I'm in that chair and you're pushing. Always like to look at a pretty girl. I'll be sorry if I can't look at pretty girls afterward. Won't be much of a heaven without 'em."

"Perhaps heaven is whatever we want it to be," I said. "There couldn't be one heaven that was suitable for everyone."

"Or one hell," he said. "But I intend to go up, not down. I've been plenty wicked in my life, but I figure if I do what I can to get everything in order before I go, why, then I'll have a pretty good chance. I'd like to see my sister Mary again. She died young. I got everything else I ever wanted," he said with confidence.

It was clear that the old man had never been spurned or defeated in business, and he didn't think God was any more difficult an opponent than anyone else he'd ever dealt with.

"I'm going to get it all straightened out," he said. "No matter what anyone else thinks. I'll be gone to a far better place. They'll just have to live with it." He laughed again, then glanced sharply at me. "I'm rambling on, aren't I? Why don't you take me back to the house?" He consulted a little pocket watch. "I've got an appointment with a Mr. Yamagamuchi and his secretary."

I wheeled him back to the house, puzzling over his conversation. Was his mind going? There was a strange craftiness to his manner as he'd spoken about settling his affairs. I wondered if he meant what he said in a literal sense or symbolic sense. Whatever was on his mind, he seemed to be enjoying some huge private joke.

Mrs. Caulfield was waiting for us back on the terrace. With her was a big, rather blustery-looking fellow in an open shirt and khaki trousers. I assumed he must be Charlie.

"So kind of you to take Mr. Caulfield out for a turn," she said sweetly. "I hope he didn't ramble on and bore you," she continued, wagging a finger.

Mrs. Caulfield, trying to be arch, presented a rather ludicrous picture. She introduced me to Charlie, who muttered that he was amenable to playing tennis. Some tennis shoes of Antoinette's were fetched. They were rather tight, but I could manage, and I was presented with a racket. My light blue linen dress was sufficiently loose to allow me to play.

Charlie led the way to the courts with easy familiarity, striding ahead of me impatiently. "Can't imagine why Antoinette didn't call me as soon as she got to Honolulu," he complained. "And who's this Walter Mrs. Caulfield's told me about? Who is he?"

"He goes to Stanford with us," I said, scrambling to keep up.

I wasn't about to break it to him that Antoinette was engaged, but Antoinette made short work of that task. As soon as we arrived at the courts, she introduced the two men.

"Walter is my fiancé," she said. "It isn't official yet, of course."

Charlie gave Walter a fierce glare. "Fiancé, huh," he said. "Oh yeah?"

"That's right," said Walter. "She's going to make me a very happy man."

"Let's play tennis," I said.

I ended up playing with Charlie. Antoinette and I might as well not have been in the game. The two men practically pushed us aside in their attempts to return each other's shots with as much power as possible.

"Mine," I cried when a particularly good chance came along for me to use my backhand, but Charlie careened toward me, smashed the ball wildly over the net and off to one side, and lost the match for us.

I had to admire Walter. He kept calm and played consistently, so that although Charlie may have been the stronger player, he hadn't a chance. I was pleased for Walter.

# 7

*I was* rather relieved to depart from the Caulfields' house when Aunt Hermione finished taking her photographs. She insisted that we not stay for lunch, although Mrs. Caulfield had extended a half-hearted invitation.

"No, no, I wouldn't dream of taking further advantage of your marvelous Hawaiian hospitality," she said. "And I do thank you so much for allowing me to photograph the garden. I shall tint all the photographs, so I made notes on the exquisite colors. That marvelous hedge of yellow oleander, for instance, such an interesting counterpoint to the blue flowers in the border. Magnificent."

"I'm sure your talk will be a great success," said Mrs. Caulfield.

Antoinette, Walter, and Charlie had come down with me to the house. "I'll call you later," said Antoinette. "Maybe we can all go dancing tonight? At the Moana? I'll arrange something."

"I'd be glad to come," said Charlie grimly. It was clear he wasn't giving up Antoinette without a fight, but his attitude seemed boorish.

"I'm not sure I can," I said, wishing I had a more definite excuse.

Watching Charlie lock horns with Walter had been rather painful. Antoinette seemed unable to shed him, and I couldn't help but remember her grandmother's words. The old lady was right. She and Charlie were inextricably linked through Caulfield and Spaulding.

Aunt Hermione talked about the garden on the way back, but I only murmured politely as my mind wandered. The Caulfields' house had such an oppressive atmosphere that I was glad to be away from it. The overheard snatch of conversation, the evidence in the photograph album that Antoinette's mother might still be alive, the grandfather's strange mood, and then the almost frightening jealousy exhibited by Charlie Spaulding all seemed too much.

I decided a swim would be the best cure for my mood. When we arrived back at the hotel, I put on my bathing suit and beach coat and went out toward the waves.

On the way, however, I caught sight of Jack Clancy, wearing a white suit and a Panama hat. I could only imagine he'd refurbished his wardrobe at *The Globe*'s expense, as he'd carried only a small satchel from the airplane.

Jack was sitting at a table full of men, all of whom were leaning forward and listening to him while he talked and gestured with a tall glass of some fruity drink.

"Now that my story's been filed, I'll be glad to let you boys in on some of the details," he said. "I tell you, it was a thrill, relying only on the stars and good luck to lead us to a small speck of land, a rocky outcropping in a vast ocean. Beneath us there was nothing but a shark-infested sea. Above us . . ." He saw me and rose, removing his hat.

"Hello, Iris. Come on over here and meet some of the local gentlemen of the press." He turned to the men with him. "And see that you act like gentlemen, too. Miss Cooper here is the source of some of my best stories. Great yarns." He waved at a chair. "Sit down, Iris, and listen to my adventure in the air."

"I'm going swimming," I said. "If I want to hear about

your adventures, I'll read about them in the newspaper."

"Miss Cooper and I are working on a little mystery of our own right now," Jack explained as I gave him a severe look. He *wouldn't* tell them any of Antoinette's secrets, I trusted. "There just might be a swell story there. I'll give you the details after I've got the scoop."

"I'm surprised you gentlemen don't want to interview the man who flew the plane," I said. "Mr. Clancy was simply a passenger."

"Ace has gone on to Tahiti on the second leg of his journey," said Jack. "I could have gone with him, but I don't speak French."

The idea of spending some time in the company of a lot of colorful newspapermen was certainly appealing, but it seemed to me that Jack was already getting too much attention, so I smiled, kept walking, and swam.

A little later, when I emerged dripping from the water, Jack stood at the water's edge, just far enough away to avoid getting his black-and-white shoes wet. He threw me a towel.

"Ready to get to work, Iris?"

"What do you mean?"

"I made a few inquiries about that mystery woman. She's flown the coop."

"What?"

"You heard me. She turned in the key of that bungalow, and she's gone with no forwarding address."

"Oh." I frowned. What could this mean? She'd just arrived.

"You're still interested in learning more about this, aren't you?" said Jack, eyeing me carefully.

I tossed my head and tried to look nonchalant. I'd told myself to forget about the matter, but I realized that I hadn't really helped Antoinette. The address I'd given her wasn't correct anymore. I made my way up the beach to my chair, not answering.

"If you're *not* interested," said Jack, "I'll just drop it. But I did make arrangements for the two of us to search the place. Tonight."

"You did?" My eyes widened and I couldn't help smiling.

"That's right. The landlord's meeting us there. Thinks we're prospective tenants. Said he hadn't time to clean the place up, but I said we wanted to see it immediately."

"Much better," I said.

Jack smiled. "That's the old Iris I remember. I knew you'd look forward to the prospect of rummaging in a few wastebaskets. A girl after my own heart. I'll come and get you at your hotel at nine o'clock. That's the earliest I can get the key."

"All right," I said, then added hastily, "but you know I can't tell you what this concerns."

"I know, I know. I already heard all that. A fine thing, I must say. Here I am, trying to earn an honest dollar, and you're stalling me with a lot of scruples about the Caulfields. Listen, with their loot, a little scandal once in a while is just part of the cost of doing business."

"What makes you think there's some scandal involved?"

Jack shrugged. "The way you're acting, for one. You're onto something, and you won't tell me about it. If it were illegal, a nice girl like you would call the cops. So it must just be embarrassing." He laughed. "But confidentially, Iris, if there's no story here, that's all right, too. Because this little expedition tonight gives me the right to tell my editor I'm working over here and I can't make the next boat home." He looked at his wristwatch. "In fact, I just missed it." He smiled happily. "See you at nine," he said over his shoulder as he thrust his hands into his pockets and walked away whistling.

By night the little bungalow looked dark and sinister.

Vines engulfed it with a tropical vengeance, and a porch swing creaked ominously.

"I don't know why I'm doing this," I said to Jack. Even though we had the landlord's permission, I felt very sneaky and was whispering. "I could be out dancing."

"Well," said Jack as he fumbled with the key, "I passed up a Filipino cockfight. Probably a good thing, too. I might not have had the stomach for it."

The door swung open and Jack switched on the light, flooding the room with a sickly light from a dim bulb. There was a mildewy smell and lots of rattan furniture with vivid cushions. The whole thing gave a rather shabby impression after my luxurious suite at the Royal Hawaiian, but it was simply a rather down-at-the-heels beach cottage. There was no sign of the previous occupant other than a full ashtray. Whoever had smoked all those cigarettes wore a light red lipstick.

In the kitchen a lizard startled me by scuttling across the ceiling. In the sink were discarded coffee grounds, bread crusts, and eggshells. There was a dirty dish on the table.

In the bedroom the coverlet had been hastily drawn up over rumpled sheets. There was a glass-topped dresser with face powder in a startling white and a bobby pin or two spilled on its surface.

"Pretty sloppy," said Jack. "Not exactly the kind to be hanging around with the Caulfields, I'd think."

"Sometimes people who've grown up with servants leave a mess like this," I mused.

Jack gave me a sharp glance and I fell silent. I didn't want him to suspect this strange woman was Antoinette's long-lost mother.

"Well, here's something," he said, rummaging in the wastebasket by the dresser.

He pulled out a *Honolulu Star-Bulletin*, folded out so the society page showed. I took it and skimmed the right-hand column, which was circled in red lipstick.

> *The charming and pretty Miss Antoinette Caulfield is back in the islands, along with many other of Honolulu's young collegians. She arrived aboard the* Malolo. *Also aboard was Mr. Walter Carlson of Stockton, California, who will be staying with Miss Caulfield's grandparents, Mr. and Mrs. Abner P. Caulfield at their Nuuanu valley home.*

I showed the paragraph to Jack, who eyed it with interest. He shook the paper open and something else fell out. It was a letter from a Boston bank.

> *Dear Mrs. Montesquieu:*
>
> *We are happy to forward this letter of credit as you requested, to be presented to the Bank of Honolulu.*
>
> *While we understand that your Hawaiian interests necessitate your visiting the islands and that you must have funds for such a voyage, it is with the strict understanding that the visit is necessary to conclude certain business arrangements and that you will, upon your return, be in a position to cover the rather large overdraft in your account.*
>
> *Believe me dear Mrs. Montesquieu, it is with regret that I bring this matter to your attention, but I feel it my duty to make the bank's position clear. If there is anything I can do to help you regularize your affairs, please call upon me.*
>
> *Yours faithfully,*
> *Cornelius W. Montgomery*

"Well," said Jack, "it looks like she had money troubles. Maybe she's trying to put the squeeze on the Caulfields in some way. Wonder what she's got on 'em.

"Oh, really, Jack," I said, turning away.

The picture was looking bleaker and bleaker for Antoinette. Now it appeared her mother may have returned, not to be reunited with her daughter but simply to get money from the family. And the letter didn't sound like a letter someone in a lunatic asylum would receive.

Where had the woman gone? It was very mysterious.

Jack slipped the letter into his pocket. "Oh, Jack," I said. "Should you?"

"Anything in the wastebasket is fair game," he said with dignity. He glanced around the room one more time. "Well, if we hurry, you can still go dancing and I can make that cockfight." He shuddered. "Sounds gruesome, but it might be a colorful piece for *The Globe*."

"Jack," I said earnestly, touching his sleeve. "You won't bother the Caulfields, will you? Poor Antoinette. Oh, I never should have allowed you to be involved."

He gave me a steady, level gaze. "You know how I make my living, Iris. I've never pretended I wasn't always after a scoop."

"But it would be awful if I were the cause of their unhappiness."

"I can keep you out of it," he said. "Anyway, you said there's no story here. Aw, come on, Iris, why don't you just come clean. You have my word of honor I'd never violate a confidence."

I wasn't sure that was so. We stepped out of the front door and were surprised to see a small man in a blue suit standing there. In fact, he was the same man who'd rapped so smartly on the door of the bungalow when we'd observed it the night before.

"Well," he said, rubbing his hands in anticipation, "did

you and Mrs. Clancy decide to take it?"

Jack handed back the key. "My wife saw a lizard in the kitchen," he said. "Scared the daylights out of her. Won't stay here. You know how women are."

The landlord, a precise-looking fellow with a small mustache, glared at me. "This is Hawaii," he said. "There are geckos here."

I resented having been accused of being frightened by a lizard. "Oh, it's not that," I said. "I just don't think it's suitable."

I hadn't meant to insult the place, but the landlord, a testy little man, took umbrage.

"Oh, it isn't, eh!" He glanced at Jack and then back at me. "And this is Mrs. Clancy, you say. I don't see a ring on her finger. I don't rent out love nests, you know."

"Watch what you're saying," Jack said indignantly. "Are you insulting my wife?" He stepped forward, his hands in fists.

The landlord took a step back. "If I do rent you the place," he said prissily, "I'll have to ask to see your marriage license."

"Well, we're not interested," said Jack. "And I'd thank you to lay off. Mrs. Clancy's not used to this kind of insinuation."

"Oh, really?" he said, smirking at me. "And I suppose you're friends of the previous tenant. Tell her I still expect her to make that check good. I can't abide some of the low-life types that are coming to these shores nowadays."

"Come along, dear," said Jack, taking my hand and leading me away.

We went around by the beach, perhaps through force of habit, as that was how we'd left the night before.

A little farther away, Jack turned to me. "The nerve of that guy," he said. "I should have popped him one. He had it coming."

"But Jack," I explained patiently, "he was right. We're not married."

Jack released my hand. "That's not the point," he said. "I told him we were, and who's he to question my word?"

I sighed. Jack's convoluted moral code was too much to fathom. Instead I concentrated on the beauty of the place.

It was hard to believe that the year was 1928 and that bustling, modern Honolulu was nearby, or that the beach was normally teeming with tourists. For a moment it seemed as if I had been transported back to old Hawaii.

All was silent, except for the rhythmic, gentle insistence of the surf and the musical breezes among the lofty tops of the coconut palms. The sky was clear, the unfamiliar stars of more southern latitudes standing out like jewels against the inky sky. There was a full moon that night. It hung out over the Pacific with a strange, cool beauty, casting a rippled silver path on the bay before it.

I turned to Jack's profile in the moonlight. "It's all so beautiful," I said. "I don't know if I can bear it."

We stopped walking, and he turned toward me. His eyes had a shiny look in them, and his mouth was curved in a little smile I'd never seen before.

"I know," he said in a low voice. "It pretty nearly breaks your heart."

Then, before I knew what was happening, he took me in his arms and kissed me slowly and more passionately than I had ever been kissed before. I found myself returning that kiss with a strange urgency. Afterward, with my head on his shoulder to steady myself, I clung to him with almost a sense of relief. I felt as if I belonged in his arms on that beach beneath that moon forever.

"Jack," I murmured.

"Iris," he whispered into my hair. "Iris, I'm sorry."

I smiled. "Don't be," I said.

He took me by the shoulders and held me away from him. "No, I mean—" His face was suddenly serious.

"What is it?" I said, startled.

"That dance," he began.

"Who cares about that dance," I replied, tilting my head and preparing to kiss him again. I felt suddenly very giddy and happy.

"Iris, we've got to talk," he said. "I guess I owe you an explanation. There's a reason I didn't take you to that dance. There's a reason I can't—" His face clouded over. "Iris, you're so beautiful. I'm so crazy about you, Iris, but it's all wrong."

"Jack," I said softly, frightened by his intensity.

"Listen, Iris," he said. He was holding me at arm's length now, and I longed to cling to him again. "You're young and fresh. You come from a nice family and you're going to Stanford. You don't want to get mixed up with a guy like me. I've knocked around a lot, Iris. I've seen and done plenty you'll never do."

"What does any of that matter?" I said.

"You don't understand, Iris."

He let go of me now, and I felt a pang of separation. He raked his fingers through his hair, and I watched his hand and longed to run my own fingers through his hair.

"You don't understand," he repeated impatiently. "A girl like you and a fellow like me—you should find yourself a nice college boy."

"Why? You're just a few years older than I am," I said.

Paradoxically, Jack had never looked younger than he did just then, his smooth forehead and his strong jaw and cheekbones shining in the moonlight, and his usually confident face now somehow unsure.

"Because, because"—he stretched his hands out toward me and let them hover above my shoulders and then outlined the shape of my arms—"because I would want all of you. I couldn't settle for less, and it wouldn't be fair to you, because I couldn't offer enough in return. I don't expect you to understand."

Angrily, I turned away from him and looked at the distance, farther up the beach. "Very noble, I'm sure," I said, trying to sound light and feeling very young and foolish and inexperienced.

"Yeah, and I'll hate myself for it later," said Jack, "but I guess you bring out the better instincts in me as well as—"

"Jack, look!" I exclaimed. I pointed farther up the beach. There, huddled under a palm tree, was the unmistakable form of a human being. "Do you see it, there, under that palm tree!"

"Looks like a body," he said eagerly, adding, "or maybe they're just hurt. We'd better go and see."

We ran toward the palm tree. It felt good to run after the heavy, languid feeling I'd had ever since Jack kissed me.

I wondered if the figure were asleep or drunk, but we rushed toward the palm tree and the figure never stirred. When we got to the base of the tree, it was clear that we were looking at a corpse. Sprawled awkwardly on the sand, slumped to one side, the head hanging over the chest, the corpse had a huge, bloody wound on the back of its head.

A quick glance nearby told the story. A large, bloodied coconut lay not far away.

"My God," I said. "I know her."

"What a terrible accident," said Jack. "Conked on the head by a falling coconut while resting beneath a palm tree."

I wasn't thinking clearly. I put my hand to my forehead and stepped back. "But it couldn't have been an accident," I said.

# 8

*Who is* she?" said Jack.

"It's Miss Blodgett," I replied. "How very odd. I wonder what she was doing out there."

Jack raised an eyebrow and gestured toward the bungalow. "Maybe she had a rendezvous with that beachboy. Isn't this the place we spotted them last night?"

"Oh, but that woman was her companion, Miss Pomfret," I said. "I'd better tell her. And Jack, we must call the police, too."

We went to the door of the bungalow, and Jack knocked loudly. I knew it was cowardly, but I wished someone else had the job of telling Miss Pomfret.

She finally came to the door. "Is that you, Viola?" she said through the door in a nervous voice. "Where've you been, Viola? I was so worried."

"It's Iris Cooper, Miss Pomfret. I'm afraid there's been a terrible accident."

We waited while we heard the sounds of a bolt being slid back. Miss Pomfret appeared behind the screened door. She wore a limp silk kimono over an old-fashioned nightdress.

"Viola?" she began.

"I'm so sorry, but there's nothing to be done," I said simply, taking her hand. "Mr. Clancy and I were walking along the beach and we found her beneath a palm tree. No one can help her now, I'm afraid."

"Oh, Viola," said Miss Pomfret with a pathetic little quiver. "I must see her."

Jack stopped her as she tried to rush past us. "I don't think you should," he said. He managed to hand the poor woman over to me. "Stay here while I telephone," he said. "There is a phone, isn't there?"

Miss Pomfret nodded and pointed. He picked up the instrument from a low table, glancing nervously over at me while I tried to restrain Miss Pomfret without seeming too intrusive.

"No, no," she whispered. "It can't be. My God, it can't be." Then, just after I felt her weaken and fall against me, she seemed to summon all her strength. Snuffling, she pushed me aside and ran out into the night. I hurried after the wild figure as it raced like mad across the sand, the moonlight illuminating the pale, flapping kimono.

"Where is she, where is she?" she screamed, and then, practically stumbling over the body, she fell to her knees beside it. Breathless, I caught up with her as she was taking Miss Blodgett's lifeless form in her arms. I stepped back a little as Jack came up beside me.

"Maybe we'd better get her inside," he said with a worried look.

"Just let her be," I replied.

After what seemed like forever, we heard male voices and saw the beams of flashlights playing along the sand.

"Over here," Jack shouted.

I went to Miss Pomfret. "The police are here," I said, as if this would somehow make a difference, which, of course, it wouldn't.

It did seem, however, that with their arrival, life would begin to take on a more regulated and ordinary course once again. Miss Pomfret rose and stepped back a pace or two from the body. Her kimono was smeared with blood.

Two uniformed policemen arrived, and Jack explained how we had come upon the body as we walked up the beach. I told them Miss Blodgett's name and that she came from Boston.

"This," I continued with my arm around Miss Pomfret, "is her companion. She's very upset, as you can imagine."

"Gee," said one of the policemen as he played his flashlight over Miss Blodgett. "I've heard about it, but I've never seen it. A coconut fell on her head."

Miss Pomfret let out a little squeak, and I glared at the policeman.

"Poor Miss Pomfret is very distraught," I said. "You mustn't stay here," I said to her. "I'll call my aunt. You can stay with us."

"I guess that would be best," she said feebly.

It occurred to me that now that Miss Blodgett wasn't here to tell her what to do, Miss Pomfret needed someone to tell her what to do.

I led her back to the lanai and arranged her on a wicker settee there. She needed something—a glass of brandy, perhaps —but then I remembered how giddy she'd become after champagne on the *Malolo*. Gesturing to Jack to keep an eye on her, I went back into the bungalow and telephoned the hotel.

Aunt Hermione listened as I sketched out the facts, and said she'd be right over to bring Miss Pomfret back to the Royal Hawaiian.

"I'll call the house doctor," she added. "She may need something to help her sleep. She mustn't be alone tonight, in any case.

"How shocking to think that Miss Blodgett is dead. Do you think she'd like to be buried next to her great-great-uncle?" She sounded rather apologetic for jumping ahead, but she rather enjoyed funeral arrangements. "I know it's too soon to think of this, but Miss Pomfret won't be able to. Don't you think transporting the body back to Boston would be rather awkward?"

"Well, for heaven's sake," I said, "don't discuss any of this with her yet. The poor woman needs rest."

"Oh, of course not, Iris. I wouldn't dream of burdening the bereaved. That's why you and I are the ideal people to make some suitable arrangements. We're not really connected, but the two ladies knew no one else here."

When I went back outside, I saw that one of the policemen was questioning Miss Pomfret while Jack listened. When he spotted me, however, he came quickly to my side.

"Iris," he said in an urgent whisper, his eyes glittering with a green light, "it just struck me. What you said when we found the body. You said it couldn't be an accident. Why did you say that, Iris?"

I put my hand to my hair and frowned. "I did? Why, yes, Jack, I did say that. With all the shock, and worrying about Miss Pomfret, I haven't been thinking clearly." I took hold of his sleeve and pulled him toward me and away from Miss Pomfret. "Jack," I said, "it couldn't have been an accident, because Miss Blodgett was talking just the other day about the dangers of sitting beneath coconut palms. She had some old missionary relative, and he'd described a similar tragedy in his diary. Miss Pomfret said something about sitting beneath a palm, and Miss Blodgett was very short with her about it—and most definite. Jack, she never would have sat beneath that tree on her own!"

"Then you think—" began Jack. "Boy, what a story!"

I didn't know quite what to think, but I knew we had to tell the policemen. I took one of them aside and explained that

Miss Blodgett was fully aware of the dangers of sitting beneath a coconut palm.

"In fact," I explained, "she held very strong views on the subject."

"Hmm. I guess we'd better call in a detective," he replied, casting an eye over the scene. "And the doctor, too."

Before either of them arrived, Aunt Hermione came in a taxi. She and I gathered up some things for Miss Pomfret, although it was hard to know which dresses belonged to which lady. They had been about the same size.

"Come along with me, dear," said my aunt to Miss Pomfret. When one of the policemen suggested that she stay until the detective arrived, Aunt Hermione was very firm. "She's in no state to do that now," she said. "It will have to wait until morning. My niece here can help you, I'm sure. She's very experienced in these matters."

The policemen looked at me with interest. No doubt they thought I was some kind of criminal. Neither of them seemed ready to tackle Aunt Hermione, so she left, guiding the passive Miss Pomfret to the waiting taxi. I stood at the curb, watching them, when a dark sedan arrived.

Two men got out. The first was a small man with a light, tropical suit and a Panama hat with a vivid band. His necktie was equally florid, depicting birds in flight over a lagoon. He introduced himself as Detective Dietrich, and his companion, a somber Chinese in a black suit, as Dr. Lu.

"I found the body," said Jack. "With Miss Cooper here. We have reason to believe there's been foul play."

Miss Pomfret, one foot on the curb, the other hovering over the running board, turned, and her face went white with fury. "If anyone's harmed Viola," she said in a voice steely with a resolve I never suspected she possessed, "I'll kill them."

"And who might this be," said Detective Dietrich, with a mildness that contrasted strikingly with Miss Pomfret's vehemence.

"My name is Lily Pomfret," she said. "And I was Viola's dearest friend. If anyone has dared—" She paused, took in her breath sharply, and brought her knuckles to her lips in a gesture of helplessness. "My God, it must have been that man!"

"Man?" said the detective with a raised eyebrow.

"Mr. Kawena. Kimo Kawena. He's my surf instructor," said Miss Pomfret. "He, well, he and Viola . . ." She began to weep and fell on Aunt Hermione's shoulder.

Jack and I exchanged glances.

"I suppose it doesn't matter now," she said. "I don't know what came over Viola. How she could have allowed that man to become such an intimate friend?" She shuddered. "It was so uncharacteristic of Viola."

Jack and I exchanged another sharp glance. I had assumed it was Miss Pomfret who'd fallen prey to the surf instructor's charms. Now we seemed to be learning that it was Miss Blodgett. Both women were about the same size, with shingled dark gray hair, and it would have been easy to mix them up in the dark, as I apparently had. I had assumed that I was watching Miss Pomfret because she seemed, quite frankly, the more feminine of the two.

Suddenly she was racked with sobbing. Aunt Hermione looked at the policeman as if he'd grilled her mercilessly, and bundled her into the taxi. "She needs to be under a doctor's care," she said firmly. "You may speak to her in the morning. She'll be at the Royal Hawaiian."

Before the detective had a chance to say another word, Aunt Hermione had closed the taxicab door and rapped on the glass.

"You're letting them go?" queried one of the uniformed

policemen who had now joined us on the curb.

"*No pilikia,*" said the detective, shrugging. "We can find her again. This is an island, after all. Where's the body? A coconut, you say?"

"*No pilikia* means no trouble," supplied Jack with a knowledgeable air. "They all say it out here."

We followed the two men and the uniformed policeman back out to the palm tree, where the other policeman stood sentinel over the pathetic, huddled shape.

"What a story!" exclaimed Jack, sotto voce. "Boston Brahmin swoons in sturdy brown arms of surfside sheikh."

The Reverend Josiah Blodgett, in a grave somewhere on this island, was no doubt turning in it at that very moment.

The doctor knelt by the body, examining it carefully and blinking slowly behind steel-rimmed spectacles. "Interesting," murmured Dr. Lu.

"That coconut do the job?" asked the detective.

"The head wound is consistent with a heavy object of that size and shape falling upon the cranium," was the reply.

"Looks like an accident, right?" continued Detective Dietrich.

"Looks like it, but appearances can be deceiving. My final report must wait until I've had a chance to examine the wound more carefully back at the morgue."

The doctor stepped back and lit a cigarette. "It's hard to tell much with the blood on the wound, but it does appear, superficially at least, that there may have been two blows. As a coconut does not bounce and land back on the human head with equal force, I would say it is unlikely that this lady met her end by the falling fruit of this palm tree."

"Besides," interrupted Jack, "this young lady here says she heard the Blodgett woman warn her friend about ever sitting underneath one of these things." He glanced over at the corpse and winced. "And believe me, I'll never do it myself."

"You don't say?" said the detective with that casual air I found so unsettling. I knew the pace was different in the islands, but Detective Dietrich seemed casual to the point of negligence.

"I'll have my men come and take the body away," said the doctor, smoking thoughtfully. He walked back across the lanai, and we all followed him.

"Take a look at that," he said to the detective. He pointed down to the ground before him. We followed his gaze and observed a waxy yellow flower on a short, woody stem.

"Yellow oleander," he said.

"Yeah. So what," replied the detective.

The doctor went over and stooped down, touching it lightly with his tapering fingers. "It's been picked."

"The tourists are always doing that," said one of the policemen. "They don't know any better."

"I believe the deceased may have been wearing it behind her left ear," said Dr. Lu. "Interesting."

"How do you know that?" said Jack.

The doctor smiled. "Yellow oleander is one of the most toxic plants around. It acts just like your foxglove. Stops the heart. But it's much more powerful. If you cook meat over its branches, the smoke can poison the food. Merely handling it can give you a rash. It was just such a rash that I observed over the left ear of the corpse."

The thought of Miss Blodgett coquettishly placing that blossom behind her ear and awaiting Kimo Kawena was rather pathetic. The fact that it was now on the lanai was even more unsettling. Had she been taken outside against her will, and did the flower fall off in some sort of a struggle? Whatever had happened to Viola Blodgett on her last evening on earth, it had not been at all what she had expected.

# 9

**The detective** seemed to have the same thought. I watched his eyes follow the path Miss Blodgett might have taken from the bungalow to the palm tree beyond the lanai. He removed his hat, ran his fingers through his hair, replaced his hat, and sighed elaborately.

"All right," he said, gesturing to me and Jack. "I guess we'll need statements from you two."

"There's not much to tell," I began, explaining how we were walking along the beach and happened to see the huddled form of Miss Blodgett. "I knew who she was. My aunt and I sailed with her and her companion Miss Pomfret just recently."

"Would you say the ladies got along well?" he asked.

"Oh, yes," I replied. I hesitated to tell him about what Jack and I had seen the night before, but he had overheard Miss Pomfret talking about Kimo Kawena, so I shouldn't have been surprised when he said, "What about this man Miss Pomfret says was in the picture?"

"We saw 'em in a clinch, just last night," said Jack cheerfully.

Detective Dietrich sighed again. "I guess we'd better talk to Kimo," he said to one of the policemen. "He's never given us any trouble before. We'll probably be able to find him over at Shipwreck Harry's—that is, if he's not showing some *wahine malihini* the sights."

"Well," said Jack affably, "we've told you everything we know. Can we go now?"

I was a little surprised at this. I had assumed Jack would want to hang around, getting underfoot and learning all about the police investigation.

"Not so fast," said Detective Dietrich.

"Say, did I tell you I was a reporter?" countered Jack, taking out his pigskin-covered notebook. "Clancy of *The San Francisco Globe*. How do you spell your name? And is there really a Charlie Chan on the Honolulu police force?"

"A reporter, eh?" Detective Dietrich scowled. "Why don't you two run along? I'll need to know where I can get ahold of you, though."

"Miss Cooper is staying at the Royal Hawaiian," said Jack. "And I think I'll be moving in there, too. I'm leaving that cheap hotel *The Globe* put me up in."

"Okay, okay," said Dietrich, wandering over to where the doctor's assistants, who had just arrived, were moving the body.

Jack turned to me and continued. "If I'm going to be covering the swells, I'd better stay at a ritzier spot."

"Miss Blodgett came from an old, proud family, but she was hardly a member of any smart set," I said.

"Well, there's still the Montesquieu dame and the Caulfield angle. There's plenty to keep me busy. Let's get out of here right away. Don't you want to go to Shipwreck Harry's? That's where this Kawena character hangs out."

"Well, I don't know if Aunt Hermione would want me to," I began.

"Suit yourself," said Jack. "But I can't walk you back home. I'm going out there as fast as I can before the police do. I think I know the spot. The local newsboys showed me some of the hot spots, and all we have to do is catch a streetcar on Kalakaua Avenue."

"I'll call my aunt," I said, trying to sound casual about accompanying Jack to a low dive and questioning a murder suspect.

Shipwreck Harry's proved to be a disreputable-looking speak with nautical decor. There were Japanese fishing floats caught up in nets over the bar, a worm-eaten figurehead looming out from the wall, and other bits of brass and teak. A few grizzled-looking sailors and beachcombers gave the place authentic atmosphere; but it was clear to me, from the many fashionably dressed young people in attendance, that the place had become a favorite slumming spot.

"Whatever you do," Jack said to me as we entered, "stay away from the local swill."

*"Okolehao?"* I said, trying to sound knowledgeable.

"That's right," Jack said grimly. "It packs a wallop. Let's just step up to the bar and ask for our man."

Suiting the action to the word, Jack approached the bartender, a red-haired man with glasses, and said, "Kimo been in tonight?"

The bartender curled his lip and said, "Half the fellows on this island are named Kimo."

"Kimo Kawena," said Jack, and the bartender pointed with his thumb toward a small table near the bar. "Oh, there he is," said Jack, although why he had to pretend to know the man, I don't know. The bartender didn't care. I sometimes think Jack likes to fool people even when it isn't necessary.

Kimo Kawena, whom I had half expected to be wearing the one-piece bathing suit in which I had first seen him, had on a loose, open shirt with a pattern of hibiscus flowers, and was drinking some frothy, tropical drink and smoking. He had a smooth, pleasant rather blandly handsome face and crisp, dark, perfectly groomed hair. When Jack and I approached, he smiled, showing beautiful strong, white teeth.

"Hello," said Jack. "Kimo Kawena, right?"

"That's right," he said easily.

"You're a friend of Viola Blodgett, aren't you?" Jack continued after he had introduced me and himself.

A slight cloud came over Kawena's handsome face, and his soft brown eyes grew wary. I suspected that he thought we were Miss Blodgett's relatives, sent to give him his congé, or something. He tapped the ash from his cigarette rather elaborately.

"Yes," he said. "A charming lady."

I would never have described Miss Blodgett that way, but perhaps he'd seen something I hadn't.

"We have some sad news, I'm afraid," Jack went on. "Viola Blodgett is dead."

Kawena stood up. "Oh, no," he said. "I had an engagement with her this evening, and she wasn't there. I wondered —that is to say, I didn't know what could have happened. I thought maybe she'd changed her mind or something."

I wondered how many middle-aged lady tourists accepted invitations from him, then lost their nerve.

"What happened to her?" he asked, his brow wrinkled now. He waved at two chairs opposite him and sat down rather heavily.

"Looks like someone crushed her skull," said Jack flatly.

He scanned Kawena's face for a reaction to this blunt approach. When there seemed to be none, Jack continued, describing the palm tree, the coconut, the doctor's opinion that her death had been no accident.

The Hawaiian's face registered shock, and he gazed at his glass. "That's horrible," he said. "I hadn't known Viola long, but she was a marvelous lady. Very distinguished, very intelligent. Her great-great-uncle was a famous missionary here in the islands," he added, conjuring up the rather odd picture of Miss Blodgett murmuring facts about the career of tedious old Uncle Josiah between caresses in the tropical moonlight.

He looked up at us with a rather pleasant, childlike expression. "We had a lot in common," he said. "Viola came from an important old family back on the mainland. I"—he tapped his chest proudly—"am descended from King Kamehameha I, the founder of our own royal family here in Hawaii. Viola was very impressed when I told her all about it."

"Real interesting," said Jack. "Say, do you think the cops will want to know all about you and Viola? They're bound to wonder who killed her."

"I can't imagine what happened. Who would have wanted to hurt her?" He shook his head in disbelief.

"You say you had a date with her?" persisted Jack.

"That's right, but when I went over to her house, she wasn't home. I was surprised."

"What time was that?" I wondered if Mr. Kawena would resent Jack's sharp questioning, but he answered eagerly, as if he wanted to please us.

"Seven o'clock," he said. "I was right on time. She wasn't there, as I said, so I went for a little walk on the beach, stopped in at the Moana for a while, and then came over here."

"You're a surf instructor, aren't you?" said Jack.

"That's right. I teach the ancient royal art to many visitors."

"I guess a lot of 'em are ladies," said Jack. "Lonely ladies," he added meaningfully.

"Oh, yes," said Kawena guilelessly. "I try to show them the islands and make them feel at home. They are always very kind."

"I imagine they are—to a good-looking guy like you," continued Jack.

Kimo Kawena smiled. "Yes," he said. "I'm a pretty fine-looking man. A lot of my mainland friends tell me so."

He turned his face slightly to one side, as if to demonstrate from several angles how handsome he was. The idea of this vain, simple man bashing in Miss Blodgett's head seemed ludicrous.

"But, please," he said politely, "won't you let me buy you a drink? If you are friends of Viola's, it would be an honor." He hailed the bartender with a suave little gesture. "I can't tell you what a shock it is to learn of her sudden death. Such a sad thing."

When the drinks arrived, he added musingly, "Her companion, Miss Pomfret, must be very sad. Perhaps I should pay a call and offer her some sympathy."

Jack rolled his eyes cynically, no doubt speculating, as I was, that Mr. Kawena planned to salvage the situation as best he could and peddle his charms to the surviving spinster.

Remembering Miss Pomfret's reaction to him, I said hastily, "Miss Pomfret is grieving deeply. I don't think she's in any state to receive anyone."

He shrugged. "Yes," he said, "I didn't know Viola long, but she was a good friend. In fact," he added with a big smile, "she gave me a present—this shirt. Do you like it?"

We were still admiring the shirt when the two policemen we'd met earlier on the beach came in and walked right over to our table.

"Come on, Kimo," one of them said. "Detective Dietrich wants to talk to you. Seems one of your mainland lady friends got herself killed tonight. There's getting to be some pretty tough Kanakas hanging around Waikiki these days. Hope you aren't one of them."

With dignity, Kimo rose, nodded to us, and left in the company of the two uniformed policemen. A little later Jack was presented with a bill for our drinks.

"Well, he timed that right," said Jack. "Finished his drink and got out without the check."

"He really is rather sweet, isn't he?" I said. "Not the predatory sort of creature I had imagined."

"He's got a nice strong back," said Jack contemptuously. "There's no reason he needs to live off women like he does.

"Say, Iris. Your friend Antoinette just walked in."

I waved at Antoinette, who was with a large party, including Walter, of course, in correct evening clothes, and a scowling Charlie Spaulding, wearing old white flannels and an open shirt. She came over to greet us, and soon we were all ensconced at one big table. Introductions were made, drinks were ordered, a noisy cabaret, featuring hula dancers in grass skirts and lots of ukuleles, began, and Antoinette began to speak urgently to me, our conversation masked by the loud music.

"Oh, Iris, I'm so glad I ran into you. But what are you doing here? I left a message for you that we'd be dancing at the Moana, but you'd left. There was a whole crowd of us, and you would have enjoyed it, except"—she glanced around to see if she were overheard—"except I've had a horrible evening. Charlie was at the Moana and he attached himself to our group. He danced with me, then he got me all by myself out on the lanai and proposed."

"He did?" I glanced over at Charlie, who was peering morosely into a cocktail glass.

"He's taken it so badly. All this scheming our families have been doing together over the years has made him think he can have me. He was most forceful about it. I tried to explain to him about Walter, but he just laughed."

"Do you really owe him an explanation, Antoinette?"

"Well, there was a time, when we were younger—anyway, Walter came out looking for me just as Charlie was kissing me. I meant it to be a sort of sisterly kiss. I do feel sorry for Charlie. He seems awfully cut up about the whole thing.

"Walter just took in the scene and withdrew, with a great deal of dignity. He's really wonderful, Iris." She paused for breath and glanced nervously over at Walter, who favored her with a small, sweet smile. "So I told Charlie what was what, and he promised not to kiss me again, and not to propose either, but he says he's not sure he can keep his promise. It's so awkward, Iris, because we're yoked together for life, Charlie and I, because of Caulfield and Spaulding. Oh, it's all too terrible."

"Calm down," I said. "Walter will understand."

"He seems to, but I was afraid he might want to break it off. He was gone for the longest time. I finally found him again and apologized, and we danced and I tried to explain about Charlie. He was wonderful about it, but I know he was hurt, too."

"All right, you two," said Jack heartily from across the table. "Stop that girlish whispering." It was clear he wanted the attention of the entire table. "Iris and I found a body on the beach tonight. Can you beat that!"

A couple of the girls shrieked—not without delight—and a young man whose name was Ditheringham or something said, "Washed up on shore?"

"Nope," said Jack, enjoying the revelation. "Conked on the head with a coconut."

"It was very tragic," I interrupted, feeling that Jack was relishing the whole thing rather too much. "Miss Blodgett, a lady from Boston with whom we'd sailed on the *Malolo*."

Next to me, Antoinette turned pale and clutched my arm.

"That wasn't the name—" she began. "I mean, the woman in white—is she?"

I assured her that Miss Blodgett was an entirely different person as Jack launched into an enthusiastic précis of the earlier events of the evening, right down to the yellow oleander blossom and the rash behind Miss Blodgett's ear. I filled Antoinette in on what we had learned about Mrs. Montesquieu at her little cottage. She nodded, looking nervously over at Walter as she took in the fact that Mrs. Montesquieu had recently left the premises. We weren't really free to talk, so I just gave her the sketchiest of details. Throughout the brief conversation, it was hard not to forget the expression on Antoinette's face when she'd thought the victim beneath the palm tree had been her mysterious apparition. It was hard to tell whether she wanted or feared the death of the woman in white.

# 10

*It was* very late when I got back, and Aunt Hermione was waiting up. "My goodness, Iris," she said. "Where have you been? Have the police been questioning you all this time?"

"Well," I said, trying to sound casual, "as a matter of fact, Jack and I did a little sleuthing on our own. He took me to a rather disreputable speak, and we talked to some sort of beach gigolo with whom Miss Blodgett was involved."

I outlined to her how I suspected Miss Blodgett may have been the victim of foul play. She agreed with me that it wouldn't have been characteristic of Miss Blodgett to sit under a palm tree. We'd both heard her views on the subject.

"How extraordinary!" said my aunt. "And how thrilling! Of course, I'm glad you went under the protection of Mr. Clancy. I'm sure he wouldn't have taken you there if the place was really awful."

I wasn't so sure on this point, but I was glad Aunt Hermione was.

"Beach gigolo? Miss Blodgett! How fascinating." She looked conspiratorial and gestured to a door in the hotel room. "I've arranged for Miss Pomfret to be put up in that adjoining room. She's heavily sedated, so we can speak freely."

I sat down and put up my feet. All of a sudden I was very tired. A great deal had happened since Aunt Hermione and I went down to have a cup of coffee on the lanai many hours ago.

"Yes," I said. "Apparently Miss Blodgett and this fellow —he's that handsome surf instructor we saw on the beach the other day—"

"Yes," interrupted my aunt. "With the well-built arms and torso. It must be all the swimming these people do."

"Anyway," I continued, "it's hard to believe, but apparently he and Miss Blodgett—well, the other night I saw him clasped in an embrace outside the ladies' cottage, and I'd assumed it was Miss Pomfret. After all, she'd been the one talking about going wild in the tropics."

"That it should have been Miss Blodgett instead is not inconsistent with my views of human nature," said Aunt Hermione, her eyes narrowing.

"Poor Miss Pomfret seemed rather cut up about it. I suppose she was jealous."

Aunt Hermione cleared her throat and looked me straight in the eye. "You know, dear," she said, "sometimes these maiden ladies who spend a great many years together become very attached. It can begin in girlhood, with an intense friendship. Some people might call it abnormal."

"Oh," I said. "Do you think Misses Pomfret and Blodgett were . . . abnormal?"

" 'Abnormal' sounds a little harsh," she replied. "I think perhaps they are simply a different type of woman. You needn't concern yourself with such things, my dear. It's just that, well, for Miss Pomfret, her companion's carrying on with this good-looking young man may have been seen as a betrayal of the most profound sort.

"What did this person say when you questioned him?"

"Simply that he had arranged to meet Miss Blodgett, but when he presented himself at her bungalow, she wasn't there.

He didn't think much of it and proceeded to the place where we found him."

"Did you think he could have killed her?" said my aunt.

"I can't think why. She had a handsome yellow diamond ring on her finger. Unless, of course, there was some passionate reason. . . ."

I trailed off, not quite knowing what it might be. As I understood it, Kimo Kawena's interests were purely of a business nature. "Besides," I said, "he seemed rather a gentle soul.

"What did you get out of Miss Pomfret?"

"Nothing. She was very distraught. She seemed to think it was all her fault somehow. A natural reaction, I suppose, in a tragedy of this sort. Still . . ."

She left the thought unspoken, but we both knew what she was thinking. Could Miss Pomfret have killed Miss Blodgett in a jealous rage? It seemed hard to believe.

"In any case," she continued, "the doctor gave her a heavy dose of veronal and said she would sleep heavily. It seemed the best thing. I think you should sleep, too, dear," she continued with a firm tone. "My goodness, you've been racing around all day, solving the mystery of the woman in white and then this murder—Oh! But before you sleep, tell me what you found out about that!"

"Just that the woman has decamped," I said. "And that she appears to be some kind of adventuress."

"My, what fascinating things are happening on these strange shores," mused Aunt Hermione. "If I didn't have such an interesting niece, I wouldn't know a thing about them."

The next morning Miss Pomfret awoke groggily. She joined us for breakfast on the balcony overlooking the beach. The beautiful scene before us, the gentle breezes, and the warm air seemed almost cruelly beautiful when contrasted with the woman's grief. She had been wild and distraught the night before. Now, she seemed listless and defeated.

She picked gently at a papaya and thanked us for taking her in. "It's so confusing for me," she said. "Viola and I had been together for so long. It's hard for anyone else to imagine, I know."

"We know how you must feel," said my aunt. "Naturally, it's been such a terrible shock."

Miss Pomfret gazed out at the Pacific. "We should never have come to this place," she said with some vehemence. "Viola's horrible old ancestor was right. It's corrupt and wicked. Like the flowers here, all waxy and thick and too heavily scented. Viola . . . and that, that man." She put her face in her hands for a moment, then seemed to pull herself together. "I shouldn't have gone," she said. "No matter what she said, I shouldn't have left her."

"Gone where," I asked as gently as possible, buttering my toast slowly and keeping my eyes on her face.

"To Miss Carlmont's," she replied. "The typist Viola had hired. She packed me off to Miss Carlmont's and told me to see how the work was coming. Then she insisted I take Miss Carlmont out to dinner. 'Poor thing, she doesn't get out much,' she said. 'I know a meal with you would be a treat for her, and she seems like such a nice girl.' Miss Carlmont, you see," explained Miss Pomfret, sniffing, "has rather a drab life. She lives at a women's residence and seldom goes out. Respectable, but quite impoverished. She's the daughter of some reprobate sea captain and ended up here through no fault of her own. Practically stranded. She's from New England, and a lovely girl."

Miss Pomfret, by now, was letting forth a torrent of words, as if exhaustive conversation would distract her from her sorrow. "I couldn't help but think that Viola was almost forcing me together with Miss Carlmont—Rose Carlmont her name is—so that she could be together with this horrible swarthy man. She never said as much, but there was a rather horrid gleam in her eye as she sent me out around five. There really wasn't anything to check, as far as the work went. Rose was making good progress."

Miss Pomfret fished in her sleeve and produced a handkerchief. "I wasn't in the habit of questioning Viola. We were dear friends, of course, but I was also—very few people knew this—a paid companion. Viola was, in the strictest sense, my employer. I seldom questioned her. Oh, if only I had last night."

"Please don't distress yourself," said my aunt. "These things are not completely in our hands, you know."

There was little doubt in my mind that Miss Pomfret was genuinely grieving. It also seemed as if she had an alibi. That, of course, depended on Miss Rose Carlmont.

"Perhaps," continued my aunt, "you'd like to rest after breakfast. Iris and I could go down to your little bungalow and pack up the rest of your things, and, Miss—well, all the things there—and have them sent around to the hotel. Wouldn't that be better? I don't think you'll want to go back there, will you?"

"You're very kind," said Miss Pomfret. "Really, I don't know what I would have done without you."

Aunt Hermione beamed. She loves to feel useful.

"Perhaps you'd like us to wire Miss Blodgett's relatives," I added, although it occurred to me that besides offering to take care of Miss Pomfret, we should be giving her something to do herself, since it is generally best to keep busy at times like this.

After breakfast the police arrived to question Miss

Pomfret. She was alone with them during the interview, so I learned nothing new. Later they talked to me. I had answered most of their questions the night before, but I did note that Detective Dietrich seemed eager to learn if Miss Pomfret appeared to have any guilty knowledge of the crime.

"Do you think she knows who did this?" was the way he put it.

"Oh," I said, "then you think she was actually—murdered."

He sighed. "Looks that way."

"Miss Pomfret seems genuinely grief stricken," I replied. "In fact," I continued, "I wonder if I might go over to her cottage and pack some things for her. She doesn't want to stay there anymore, as you can imagine."

"Go ahead," he said. "We've been over the place thoroughly. Nothing out of the ordinary, just a tray with a pitcher of cocktails and two clean glasses. Kind of sad, really."

Later, Miss Pomfret telephoned Rose Carlmont, the typist who'd been working on the late Miss Blodgett's manuscript. When Miss Pomfret hung up the phone, a small smile animated her pale face.

"Rose is coming to see me. Such a comfort, she really is a very good girl. I do wish you two would go out and enjoy yourselves. I'll be fine, I really will. I just need a little rest and quiet, and I wouldn't want to spoil your vacation."

We both murmured our protests but, with relief, we realized she really meant it. Tiptoeing around as solemnly as possible, Aunt Hermione gathered up her beach things and prepared for a swim. I planned to join her later, but first I had decided to go back to the cottage and do a quick packing. In the lobby I ran into Jack Clancy.

"Well, well," he said. "Miss Cooper on the case, I presume. No swim? Plan on doing a little sleuthing? I've wired in my first dispatch, and I'd better come up with more soon."

"I was just going over to gather up poor Miss Pomfret's things. And Miss Blodgett's, too, of course."

"Fine," said Jack. "I'll walk with you. You can fill me in on what Miss Pomfret said."

"Oh, Jack, I don't know. I'm not sure I should—"

"And I'll tell you what I learned at the police station last night," he concluded, with a gleam in his eye.

Jack knew just how to get to me. "Come on," I said. "You can tell me what you found out on the way."

"Not too much. Just that the old girl hadn't been dead long when we found her, and that she was probably conked on the head at some distance and then dragged over to the palm tree. Her heel marks made little furrows in the sand."

"Would it have required a great deal of strength?" I asked.

"Not really. A coconut is a pretty heavy object. She would have had to turn her back on whoever did it, though."

"There was bound to have been some spattered blood, too, I should have thought," I said, as we arrived at the little bungalow.

It looked quite charming by day, and not at all as if some horrible tragedy had taken place there.

But the serenity outside proved to be deceptive. Inside, the place had been torn apart, twisted clothing flung around. A pile of books and papers were in a mad jumble on the floor; cupboard doors yawned open, revealing shelves of dishes on their sides, as if some giant paw had stirred them all up.

"Ransacked!" exclaimed Jack with relish. "And they didn't find what they were looking for, either, did they?"

"Why do you say that?" I said, staring at the devastation around us.

Strangely, the sight of that bungalow, torn all apart, was almost more frightening than the body of poor Miss Blodgett.

That poor lady had an air of serenity about her, despite her horrible death. These ransacked rooms spoke of terrible rage and desperation.

"It looks like they kept looking and looking," said Jack. "Nothing could have been hidden that well, so I'm guessing they never found it."

"Jack," I said as a sudden inspiration came to me. "Have you noticed how similar this bungalow is to the one that had that Mrs. Montesquieu in it? These ladies from Boston hardly seem the type to get murdered and then have somebody ransacking their bungalow. I mean, they weren't exactly gangsters or anything, were they? Do you think someone made some horrible mistake?"

Jack looked pensive. "Well, they weren't perfect angels," he said. "What about Kimo Kawena?"

"You don't think he had anything to do with it, do you?" I really couldn't see it.

"I don't know what I think," said Jack, narrowing his eyes. "But you've given me something to think about. I think we'd better find the mystery dame again. And no more fooling around. We ought to have a little talk with her, right away."

# 11

*How are* you going to do that, Jack?" I said.

"It shouldn't be hard. This burg isn't too big for Jack Clancy to find his way around." His features took on a grim cast.

"I suppose we'd better tell the police about this," I said, gesturing helplessly at the disheveled interior.

"You do that. Then break it to Miss Pomfret that someone's been through her things. I'll check back with you at the hotel later." Before he left, he gave me a serious look and lowered his voice. "Iris," he said, "I may have to talk to your friend Antoinette. I've got a job to do, you know."

He turned on his heel and left, before I had a chance to protest. Suddenly, despite the heat, I felt a strange chill. I wanted to get out of this little house. The pathetic scattered belongings, the memory of Miss Blodgett slumped beneath the palm outside, the bloody wound. It was all too much. I was overcome with the feeling that nothing in this strange tropical landscape was predictable or orderly, and I fled from the premises.

Once outside, I began to think more clearly. I needed to warn Antoinette and be honest with her about Jack's interest in Mrs. Montesquieu. She would have to know that he would be trying to find out what she was up to, and that there might even be some link with the murder of Miss Blodgett. This was a rather wild theory, I knew. It was just that the two houses

179

were so similar, and next to each other. Both ladies were from Boston, and the Blodgett-Pomfret ménage seemed so entirely blameless, while Mrs. Montesquieu, from what little we had learned of her, could well have been part of some demi-monde.

I wasted no time finding a public telephone booth. I left a message with Aunt Hermione to call the police and tell them that Miss Pomfret's bungalow had been ransacked. Then I took a deep breath and telephoned Antoinette. Fortunately she was home, and I could talk to her without Walter around.

"Antoinette," I said firmly. "There are some things I must tell you, privately and confidentially, about the woman-in-white business." I took a deep breath. "I'm afraid I made a mistake in having Mr. Clancy follow her. He's very curious about her, you know." I took another deep breath. "He may try and ask you some questions for his newspaper."

Antoinette arranged for us to meet at the Liberty House tearoom immediately. I looked forward to discussing the whole thing with her in a frank and open manner. When she arrived, she looked chic as usual in a green linen dress, but there were telltale signs of worry on her face. Her skin, which normally glowed with a light suntan, was pale, and there were lavender shadows under her eyes.

We sat at a quiet corner table behind a potted palm and ordered tea. I came straight to the point.

"Antoinette," I explained, "has it occurred to you that this strange woman may be your mother?"

"That's exactly who she is," said Antoinette with a deep sigh. "For years I was told she was dead, but then I learned differently. And to tell you the truth, I wish she were."

She sipped her tea and then rummaged in her bag for a cigarette. She lit it, inhaled deeply, and her face took on a hardened aspect. I felt a deep stab of pity for her, and curiosity, too.

"I don't want Walter to know," she said. "My mother left when I was a baby. She must have been a bad woman, Iris. My grandparents abhor scandal—at least my grandmother does, and she came up with some story about a hospital stay, followed by a death. I thought it was a mental hospital, the way no one ever talked about it. They just said she needed a rest cure.

"But lately I've learned that she was in—" Antoinette closed her eyes with distaste and pronounced the word— "prison. Grandfather is very powerful, and he managed to keep it all hushed up. They raised me and called me by their name after Papa died."

"How did you find out?"

"She wrote me a letter. A sentimental sort of thing about having left with another man and wanting to see me now, but that she'd been in prison and didn't know if my grandparents had told me or not. How could she leave a baby? It's horrible."

"Oh, Antoinette," I said. "I am sorry. Tragedies occur in all kinds of families," I added in an attempt to be of some comfort.

"I haven't told a soul about this, Iris. Not a soul. Promise you won't?" Antoinette looked small and pinched and frightened.

"I promise," I said.

"She's depraved, Iris," continued Antoinette. "She's done dreadful things. She's been in prison. Can't you see how Walter must never know?"

"What did she do?" I said, my eyes growing round. I couldn't imagine.

"I don't know. But whatever it was, it can't be more

shameful than leaving me. Iris, I could forgive her for being in prison, but to have been left when you were a baby, it makes me so ashamed. Ashamed. That's how I feel."

"But it wasn't your fault," I said.

"I know, I know. But I can't help feeling this way. I don't want Walter to know. I want to have a happy family life with him." She paused and smoothed out her brow with her fingertips. "Yet she seems to be stalking me. I can't think why, but I mean to find her and beg her to leave me alone. Just when I have a chance at happiness." The hard eyes softened and filled with tears, which made me more comfortable, somehow.

"What did the letter say?" I asked.

"It was a horrible thing, full of cheap affection and apologies. She said she had been in prison and used the name Montesquieu. She said she wanted to see me and hoped I'd turned into a nice young woman. Well, it was too late for her to worry about that, wasn't it? If she'd cared, she would have raised me herself. I wrote her back, telling her I didn't want to see her."

Antoinette paused and wiped her eyes with the side of her hand. The gesture made her look like a small child. "But Iris," she said, her voice thick with tears, "I did so want to see her. I really did. I wanted us to fall into each other's arms and be great friends. I wanted it all to be perfect. I even kept the letter. I put it in my jewel box with Walter's letters, and then I found I hadn't the courage to read it again. How can I forgive her?"

"You probably cannot," I said.

I knew it was un-Christian not to forgive but decided that sometimes it is simply impossible. Even if my own mother hadn't died, I can't imagine I would ever be able to have too much sympathy for a woman who could leave her child.

"Iris, why is she here in Honolulu? There are people here who will recognize her."

"That must be the reason behind that veiling," I said. "Although, after all these years, not everyone would recognize her."

"Is she following me?" said Antoinette. "What do you think she wants?"

"Money, no doubt," I said. It was harsh, but there was no point in putting a gloss on the facts. I told her about the letter Jack and I had discovered, the letter from that Boston bank. "It's perfectly plausible that she's come to the islands to blackmail your family. Perhaps she's learned about your engagement, somehow."

"I must contact her. I must speak with her. If she has any feelings for me at all—" Antoinette broke off. "But how could she?" she said bitterly.

"If she's here to try to get some money from your family," I said, "she may well have contacted your grandparents already."

"I can't bear to ask them about it," said Antoinette. "Poor Grandmother. And Grandfather, too. She broke their hearts. It's better if I never mention any of it. You see, they don't realize I know she's alive." Antoinette crushed out her cigarette. "And with Grandfather's weak heart—Oh, if only I could rely on Walter. But I don't want him to know. I'm so ashamed of my family."

"I can't imagine Walter would love you less," I began, but then I stopped.

To tell the truth, I thought it perfectly possible that Walter would cancel their engagement if he learned that his future mother-in-law had been to prison. He seemed to be such a correct young man. I sighed. Was it proper to withhold information like this from a prospective fiancé? I wasn't sure a future husband had to know *everything*. Was it reasonable to expect a girl in love to throw away her happiness for the sake of perfect honesty?

"It will all come out at some point," I said. "Don't you think . . . I mean, secrets like these cannot be kept forever."

"Just until the wedding," she said rather desperately. "Help me, Iris, will you? Help me hide this horrible secret at least until the wedding."

"It seems to me," I said, "that we must find your moth— this woman and see what she wants. If she wants to be bought off in some way, could you do it?"

Antoinette's small hands curled into fists. "I have some jewelry. Nothing too elaborate. Grandmother says I'm too young for cut stones. And once I marry, I know I'll receive a generous settlement. My grandparents wouldn't want me dependent on any husband's salary."

"That might be a problem," I said.

"Of course, I have some expectations. I mean, I will be a rich woman someday, after Grandfather dies." She shrugged. "Even if he never gets around to drawing up a will, I should inherit."

"What? Your grandfather has no will?"

"No, he's very stubborn about it. He's been putting it off for years."

"Well, I'm no lawyer, but if he dies intestate, don't you think your mother will inherit, instead of you? Your grandmother would get something, I imagine. I don't know what the law says about widows."

"Iris, I never thought of that. My mother *will* inherit!"

I found it startling that Antoinette hadn't figured that out, but then the very rich may be so nonchalant about money as to never think of it. In my experience, however, they are just the opposite.

"The first order of business is to find this woman and discover what she wants. Jack Clancy is already looking for her. He wonders if there's some connection between her and that killing on the beach."

"What?" Antoinette grew even paler. "You don't think she's involved somehow? Oh, Iris, I can't bear another scandal."

"No, no, it's just a theory. You see, Mrs. Montesquieu's bungalow looks just like Miss Blodgett and Miss Pomfret's bungalow. And they were all from Boston. I wondered if there was some kind of mix-up somehow. After all, Mrs. Montesquieu was absconding—from her landlord perhaps. Maybe she was in some other kind of trouble as well. Maybe gangsters were pursuing her." I experienced a tremor of excitement as all sorts of sordid possibilities came to mind, but a glance at Antoinette's worried face reminded me that I was dealing with a real human tragedy. "Oh, let's forget about it," I said. "If you're to have any peace of mind at all, we must find the woman. Perhaps you'd like to arrange some kind of a meeting."

"Maybe you could go with me, Iris," she said, taking my hand in hers and holding on tightly.

"I'll be glad to do whatever I can to help you," I said simply.

"I must be getting back," she said. "Walter will wonder where I am."

We embraced as we parted outside the store. Poor Antoinette. I hoped Walter was worth all the agony she was going through. I doubted he could ever suspect that his vivacious fiancée carried such a tremendous burden.

# 12

**Miss Cooper,** I'd like to present Miss Carlmont—Miss Rose Carlmont."

I had run into Miss Pomfret in the lobby at the Royal Hawaiian and was pleased to see that she was looking a little less peaked.

"How do you do," I said, turning to her alibi, a pleasant, well-scrubbed-looking woman of indeterminate age. Miss Carlmont had a genial but rather shy manner and wore an extremely unbecoming hat. She struck me as that rare kind of woman who doesn't know or care a bit how she looks.

"Your aunt told me that someone had searched the bungalow," said Miss Pomfret. "I was terrified to hear about it. It must have been that horrible Kimo Kawena. At least that's what I told the police."

"It's frightening, I know," I replied, reflecting that the ransacking of the bungalow, unpleasant as it may have been for Miss Pomfret, nevertheless made it appear less likely that she had killed Miss Blodgett in a jealous fit. "I didn't touch anything, in case the police wanted to investigate further, but when they say it's all right, I'll be glad to go back and gather up your things."

"How kind," said Miss Pomfret, blinking back tears. "I can't think why everyone is being so kind."

Rose Carlmont took her hand. "You've been through so much," she murmured.

Feeling that Miss Pomfret was being properly looked after, I excused myself and went to the desk. There I found a message from Aunt Hermione—"Am on the beach. Come see me"—and another from Jack, which said, "New developments. I'll be in touch."

It was rather refreshing to spend some time on the beach. After all, that's what we had planned to do when we came to Hawaii in the first place. After a whole afternoon of swimming, cool drinks, napping in the shade, and pleasant conversation with my aunt, I had almost forgotten about all the mysteries that seemed to be cropping up.

Then Jack came out to find me, looking incongruous as usual in his business suit on the beach. It occurred to me that even here in Hawaii he was always dressed as if he were in a newspaper office.

"Hello, Iris," he said. "Thought I'd stop by and see if you were anywhere around. Got a line on that mystery woman. Want to come along?" He managed to tip his hat to my aunt while he talked.

"Oh, do go, Iris," she said. "I want to hear all about it."

I scrambled to my feet. "Just let me get dressed," I said.

"By all means," said Jack, "although the way people are wandering all over this town in bathing suits, nobody would mind, I'm sure, if you didn't."

"Have you been in the water at all?" I said as we walked back to the hotel.

"Haven't had time," said Jack. "You know me, Iris. All work and no play. It makes me nervous when I'm not working. Speaking of which, let me tell you about the swell lead I've got going here. I went down to the newspaper office, see, to place a little advertisement. You know the kind of thing: 'If Mrs. Montesquieu, formerly of such and such an address, will reply to box number such and such, she will hear

187

something to her advantage.' I figured it was worth a try."

"What a wonderful idea," I said, finding it all quite thrilling.

"Yeah, well, someone else already had it. Seems there was another advertisement in there along similar lines. I poked around a little and found out who placed it. A private detective."

"Oh, Jack!" I said, even more thrilled.

"I arranged to meet him and thought maybe you'd come along. He might be kind of hard to pump. I figure having a charming young girl along might help."

I ignored the compliment, which didn't sound like one the way Jack said it. Sometimes it seemed all Jack ever cared about was getting people to tell him things they shouldn't or wouldn't.

"I'll hurry," I said, leaving him in the lobby as I went toward the elevator. "I've never met a private detective. How interesting."

"They're okay, I guess, if you overlook the fact they make their living snooping around hotel corridors," said Jack, settling in with a newspaper on a blue banquette beneath a huge potted palm.

Hugo Sprague looked like just the sort of man who'd have no objection to making a living that way. Jack had arranged to meet him in a gaudy Chinese restaurant downtown. He sat at a small corner table, dwarfed by giant scarlet pillars entwined with gilt dragons. He was a small, sallow man in a limp tropical-weight suit that hung from gaunt shoulders. The yellowish cast of his skin was repeated in his queer eyes, rather a golden color, and curiously flat.

"Well, hello there," said Jack, in a manner I judged too hearty and blustery for the wary-looking detective.

We introduced ourselves, and Jack shook hands with Mr.

Sprague so enthusiastically that it looked as though the thin, limp-looking creature would flop like a rag doll at the end of Jack's arm.

"The noodles are excellent here," said Hugo Sprague laconically. "They do a real nice job on 'em."

"Glad to hear it," said Jack. "Guess I'll have some myself. Now, let's get to the point, Mr. Sprague. It appears we're both looking for the same party."

Mr. Sprague didn't fill in the pause Jack had left hanging between them. Instead he twirled his noodles expertly on his chopsticks, regarding us all the while with his strange, golden eyes.

"Maybe we can pool our efforts here," Jack persisted. "You know. Share what we all know."

I felt a little stab just then, as I knew who Mrs. Montesquieu actually was and certainly didn't plan to share that knowledge. I covered my guilt with a very nice smile for Mr. Sprague, but he didn't smile back.

"What do you say?" said Jack.

"Why are you interested in Mrs. Montesquieu?" he replied after a pause.

"Well, maybe for the same reason you are," said Jack. I could tell from his expression that he was extemporizing and that he expected Mr. Sprague to volunteer his own motivations for placing the newspaper advertisement. Mr. Sprague didn't oblige, so Jack blundered on. "Um, I suppose you know she wrote her landlord a bad check. We said we'd try to recover it for him. He's by way of being a pal of ours."

"Oh, really?" said Mr. Sprague.

"I suppose you're working for a client," said Jack.

"That's right."

"Well, what's wrong with taking on a second one? After

all, we both want the same thing. We want to find Mrs. Montesquieu."

"Honolulu's not such a big place," said Mr. Sprague. "You'll probably find her on your own."

"Well, if you're in a position to turn down business," said Jack rather huffily. "I mean, we'd make it worth your while."

"I doubt that," said Mr. Sprague. "You're certainly not willing to spend more than the amount of the bad check you're talking about."

"All right, all right, pal. You got us. We'll level with you. There's more to it than that."

"Is that a fact?" said Mr. Sprague. "Just what is your interest in this lady?"

"Well," said Jack, taking a deep breath. "Why don't you tell him, Iris?"

He had obviously run out of lies and found it impossible to tell the truth. I, on the other hand, find telling the truth usually works as well as anything else; and it's easier to keep the facts straight. Not that I was about to reveal Antoinette's secret.

"It's simple, really," I said. "Jack here is a reporter for *The San Francisco Globe*, and he's covering a murder case here in Honolulu. A woman I knew was killed in the bungalow next door to Mrs. Montesquieu's. We wondered if she'd seen anything or was connected somehow with the case."

The detective gave me a long look. You could hardly call it searching. Those strange eyes remained flat, but I had the uncomfortable feeling that I was being studied by a keen, cold mind.

"I wouldn't pursue it if I were you," he replied. "Let the police handle that sort of thing."

"Suppose there's any way of knowing who that client of yours is?" said Jack, leaning forward in an insinuating manner. "Now that you know who I am, there's no point being coy. *The Globe* does have an expense account, you know. We'd be glad to help any public-spirited citizen who helps us do our job—telling the public what it wants to hear."

Hugo Sprague gave him a thick-lidded look of contempt. "You're out of your league, Clancy," he said. "Now why don't you just drop the whole thing." He turned to me. "I don't see what your interest in this matter is, unless it's him you're interested in." He shrugged toward Jack. "But take my advice, sister, and stay out of it."

"I suppose you think this cheap, tough-guy sort of thing is going to intimidate us," said Jack, leaning menacingly forward.

"There's nothing cheap about it," said Mr. Sprague. "My client has a lot of pull in these islands. You can take me on, but I don't advise you to take on my client. You're not rich enough, and you're not powerful enough." His features relaxed for a moment. "Come on, kids, just stop playing detectives, will you? Last time I worked for this client, things got kind of messy. I don't want to see anyone hurt."

Jack had made his hands into fists and was using them to prop himself upright and lean across the table. Mr. Sprague continued eating his noodles. Suddenly I remembered the conversation I'd overheard at the Caulfields' house the day I'd come across that photo album in the library.

"Let me guess," I said coolly, putting out a restraining hand and placing it on Jack's sleeve. "Don't tell me you did some union-busting work in the cane fields for him? And now you're working on a domestic matter? That client of yours isn't so tough. He's a sweet old man in a wheelchair, and he thinks I look like his sister, Mary, so you'd better not make any threats like that."

Mr. Sprague still registered no emotion. He did, however,

stop chewing his noodles to stare at me. After a while, he resumed chewing and stared at Jack.

"Well, if you are a friend of my client," Mr. Sprague said, "you'll want to remain one. There's plenty of people in these islands who can tell you what good advice that is."

# 13

*Well,"* said Jack huffily, "I suppose there's not much more to say."

Mr. Sprague didn't even bother to reply.

"Come on, Iris," said Jack, taking my hand and leading me away.

I actually had to trot to keep up with him as we crossed the room between tables covered with crimson cloths. As soon as we had left the restaurant, however, Jack slowed down and gave me a superior little smile.

"I think we handled that pretty well," he said.

"Oh, really, Jack," I said, disgusted. "The man thought we were idiots, or at least that you were."

"That's right. Just what I wanted him to think."

I gave him a look of scorn, hoping to tell by a corresponding flinch whether or not Jack had actually intended being taken for a fool, but he was consulting his wrist-watch.

"A pal of mine is going to come by any minute now and lend me his car. We have to go up to Punchbowl."

"We do? What for?"

"Well," said Jack smugly, squinting into the sun, "when I found out that classified ad ran in the paper, I managed to get a gander at the reply. Please don't ask me how, except that a reporter friend of mine is engaged to one of the girls who files the box replies. Anyway, Mrs. Montesquieu is meeting this Sprague character at an address up there in about half an hour."

A moment later a thin little man with thick spectacles turned over a dark blue coupe to Jack. We piled in and drove up Punchbowl Hill. Despite the excitement of our errand, I was still able to appreciate the view of Honolulu spilling across the foothills below us and the turquoise Pacific lapping at her shore.

The address we were looking for proved to be a small clapboard house surrounded by a stand of bamboo. Jack drove by slowly, then parked the car some distance away and we approached on foot.

"The way I see it," he said, "we might be able to overhear something, especially if they indulge in a Hawaiian habit and sit outdoors. But in any case, we'll get a good look at our mystery woman and follow her, so we can find out where she's staying. By the way," he added, "that was quick work, figuring out who that shifty Sprague's client was. Sounds like Antoinette's grandfather. Am I right?"

I ignored the question and cast an eye over the small frame house, its white paint peeling under the hot sun. It was surrounded by a patch of dry-looking, neglected garden. There was a "For Sale" sign planted in the front lawn.

"Interesting," said Jack. "I guess she's not staying here. She wanted to meet on neutral ground—and private." He checked his watch again. "Let's see if we can get in. If the Montesquieu woman hasn't arrived yet, we can pop into a closet or something. What do you say?"

"I don't know, Jack. That Sprague seemed like a dangerous man. I'd hate to have him find us."

"Don't worry about a thing," said Jack as we turned up the walk and approached the house. "We can revert to our old pose —the nice young married couple looking for a place to live."

"It was hardly successful last time we tried it," I said, recalling the suspicious landlord at the bungalow.

"It's a good thing we're only up to some wholesome detecting and aren't trying to live in sin, then," said Jack trying the front door. "You must look guilty or something."

Finding the door locked, he trooped around the house to a screened entrance that opened onto a sleeping porch. He rattled at the handle and then shook the door violently. Finally, the single hook and eye fastening gave way.

"There's no one here," he said with confidence. "They would have heard all that racket by now."

The door made an ominous sound as he opened it and we found ourselves in a small kitchen. The place had the sad feeling an empty house always does.

"Maybe we could hide in the coat closet," said Jack, walking into the living room. There wasn't one, however.

"I guess they don't wear coats much in the tropics," I said, although Antoinette had told me there was a small but intense fur season observed by Honolulu ladies.

Jack strode over to French windows that opened onto a lanai. "Maybe we should stay outside and place ourselves next to these doors." He opened them a crack. "They'll probably choose this room for their little chat."

Suddenly, I heard a car pull up and I touched his sleeve. We hurried back out through the kitchen just as we heard a key in the front door. We stepped behind a piece of lattice covered with vines just as Sprague came out the kitchen door into the yard. He looked sharply around before going back inside. I stood as still as I could, watching him, trying not to breathe, hoping the play of light and shadow through the lattice and onto my face didn't catch his eye.

When he'd gone back in, Jack took me by the elbow and dragged me around the house. A minute or so later we were poised on the lanai against the side of the house just next to the French doors. We heard Sprague pacing, then a knock at the front door as Mrs. Montesquieu arrived.

"Mr. Sprague?" Her voice was hard and flat.

"That's right. Come on in."

"Did the Caulfields send you?" she said.

"That's right. What's the pitch?"

"What do you mean?" She had a suspicious edge to her voice.

"Come on, let's get straight to the point. Three months ago you wrote a letter to the Caulfields asking for money. They took a pass. Now you're here in Honolulu, and you've written them a note asking for a meeting. What's the deal, Mrs. Montesquieu?"

"Edna—that's their daughter—she always told me I could come to her family if I ever needed help."

"Yeah?"

"And besides, there's the child. Antoinette."

"What about the kid?"

"I kind of wanted to talk to her about her mother."

"The Caulfields don't think that's such a hot idea," said Sprague.

"Well, why not? After all, I was with Edna at the end. Where were they?"

He didn't reply, and she added, "It was the damp that got her. She couldn't take the damp, having been raised up here. I was working in the infirmary. Poor dear Edna. She'd cough and cough, and ask for that baby."

"You haven't written the kid, have you?" said Sprague.

"Matter of fact, I did. Back on the mainland. I felt an obligation to Edna." Mrs. Montesquieu sounded defiant and also defensive. "I wrote her at school. She never answered. I was afraid she wouldn't, that's why I—" She paused. "Got a light?"

There was silence for a moment, then cigarette smoke

drifted out through the crack in the door. "I told her I was her mother."

"You what?"

"I wanted her to answer me. I didn't want her to think I was just some confidence trickster. The girl needed a mother." She sounded breathless and perhaps a little mad.

"Edna told me what her own mother had done. The child had already been told Edna was dead. Edna wanted to get back and see that baby so badly, but that man wouldn't let her. And then, well, after that, she couldn't."

"Pretty rough, weren't you," said Sprague harshly, "telling her you were her mother? Sounds like fraud to me. Why, I've half a mind to tell my clients not to make any arrangements with you at all."

"Yeah?" Suddenly Mrs. Montesquieu sounded less cultivated. "Well, how would they like the world to hear about Edna's troubles?"

"If you were a real pal to Edna, you wouldn't tell the world."

"Edna didn't have anything to be ashamed of. It's her family that should be ashamed. That man just swept her off her feet. It's not the first time that happened. And then later, when she was arrested, well, it was self-defense, and if she'd had the right lawyer, she could have proved it. The kid deserves to hear that," said Mrs. Montesquieu more firmly. "Any kid deserves to hear about its mother's last days."

"That's not the way the Caulfields see it," said Sprague. "As far as the kid and anyone else knows, Edna went to the mainland for a rest cure and died in the hospital. We've booked a passage for you on the Wednesday boat. When you get to San Francisco, there'll be ten thousand waiting for you."

"Ten! They can afford a lot more than that."

"Maybe, but that's all they want to spend on you, Mrs. Montesquieu. Take it or leave it. And I wouldn't suggest you leave it. The Caulfields have a lot of pull. Pull only money can buy. Not just on these islands, either. There've been people who tried to cross them and they were sorry. A hophead moocher like you is no match for the Caulfields. They could have you arrested tomorrow, and how'd you like it in jail without your happy dust?"

"There's no need to talk to me that way. I'm going. I just wanted to do right by the kid."

"And gouge her grandparents," said Sprague.

"I don't see why they can't help me out. Edna would have wanted it. She and I were—well, we were both respectable once. We understood better than the others. We'd lost more. But she, poor thing, she lost that baby."

"Real touching, sister," said Sprague. "Tell me where you're staying and I'll have that ticket sent around. And if I hear you've bothered the girl—well, I'm not even going to tell you what kind of measures we're prepared to take. Let's just say no one would miss you."

"You tell her for me," said Mrs. Montesquieu, her voice slightly agitated. "Tell her Edna wanted to come get her. Tell her Edna talked about her at the very end. 'I'm going to get well,' she said, 'and go back and get my baby.' "

"Where are you staying?" said Sprague in a bored-sounding monotone.

"A little place on Hotel Street. The LaGrande."

"Your ticket will be there. And the money will be in San Francisco."

"I've had expenses," she said now, a little whine creeping into her voice. "If I could have a little in advance—to pay the hotel bill?"

"Here's fifty," said Sprague.

"You're no better than I am," said Mrs. Montesquieu after a pause, during which, I presumed, he'd handed over some cash. "Just a big goon, trying to scare me. I was Edna's friend when no one else was."

"Okay, okay," said Sprague. "Why don't you just beat it. And don't miss that boat on Wednesday, either. I'll be there to make sure you're on it."

"You'll tell her, won't you?" said Mrs. Montesquieu in a muffled voice that seemed to indicate she was making her way toward the front door. If Mr. Sprague bothered to answer, we didn't hear his reply.

# 14

*Jack!*" *I* said as soon as Sprague had left and we dared to emerge from our hiding place on the lanai. "I want to talk to Antoinette right away. We've learned things about her mother she has a right to know."

"You mean you bought the whole story the dame told?" Jack looked dubious.

"I think she was basically truthful. There was such sadness in her voice when she talked about Edna in that damp place—a prison, apparently." I shuddered, keenly aware of the balmy tropical air on my bare arms.

Jack shrugged. "But it's clear she wants to separate the Caulfields from some of their money."

"That's right. She's rather a desperate creature."

"Sprague called her a hophead. I guess he's been watching her and knows she dopes."

"Oh!" I said. "There was some stark white face powder on her dresser in that cottage on Waikiki. At least I thought it was face powder."

Jack narrowed his eyes. "Cocaine, I guess. It can be pretty bad."

Suddenly the little shady garden behind the house seemed oppressive. "Let's get out of here," I said. "Help me decide what to do. What to tell Antoinette, and how. And for God's sake, Jack, I hope you won't print a word of this."

Jack looked at me with a seriousness I couldn't remember

seeing very often in his face. "Don't worry, Iris. I know there are limits. And a dying mother's words—well, that's my limit."

I smiled a big smile of relief that Antoinette would be spared a public scandal, and relief too that Jack had some sense of propriety—rarely brought to the surface perhaps, but existing nevertheless.

My smile seemed to annoy him a little. He raised an admonishing finger. "But there's always a chance that the Montesquieu woman isn't on the level about Edna. And if this is connected with that coconut killing in any way," he said sternly, "it'll have to come out." We began to walk out into the street and down to our car.

"Well, naturally," I said, my face serious now. "But I can't see how it could be."

We drove back to the Royal Hawaiian, where I went up to our room and telephoned Antoinette immediately. I had thrashed things over in my mind and talked about them with Jack. It seemed to me that rather than my deciding for myself what part of Mrs. Montesquieu's story was factual, I should let Antoinette decide that. I had no doubt that these revelations might disturb her, but I felt very strongly that she was all grown up—well, very nearly, anyway—and had a right to know about her own people. Aunt Hermione had always said that a great deal of harm came from family secrets, and that those left in the dark could develop all sorts of morbid thoughts about the unknown, when the truth would be easier for them to face.

"Antoinette," I said firmly, "I do not believe that Mrs. Montesquieu is your mother, but I do believe she knew her." I outlined the conversation Jack and I had overheard. "She seemed to want to talk to you about your mother," I said, and I explained as gently as I could that according to Mrs.

Montesquieu, Antoinette's mother's last thoughts had been of her infant daughter, far away in Hawaii.

"Oh, I wish I could meet her," said Antoinette with a kind of desperate eagerness. "I do want to learn about Mother."

"Of course," I said, "the woman is not entirely reliable. She apparently dopes, and she wanted to get money from your family through blackmail or the nearest thing to it. She also did a very wicked thing, writing you and pretending she was your mother." I tactfully omitted the fact that she'd apparently been in prison, as Antoinette's mother had, too.

"But who else is there who'll tell me about Mama?" said Antoinette simply. "Oh, Iris, will you arrange a meeting? Please? I'll manage to get away from my grandparents and Walter for a little while." She paused and added earnestly, "It would be easier for me to begin my married life knowing about my past."

"I understand," I said. "I'll see what I can do." I didn't tell her that Sprague had threatened Mrs. Montesquieu and had told her to stay away from Antoinette. I would reveal that later if I had to—if Mrs. Montesquieu refused to see my friend.

I hung up with ambivalence. Was I opening a Pandora's box? I took a deep breath and placed a call to the place on Hotel Street Mrs. Montesquieu had mentioned, the LaGrande. A surly desk clerk indicated that the lady was in, and I was connected.

"This is Iris Cooper. I am a friend of Antoinette Caulfield," I began in a firm voice, trying to sound older. "She believes you can tell her about her mother Edna's last days and wishes to speak to you."

It was easier than I thought. Mrs. Montesquieu, with the air of someone used to drama, took my call in stride. "Is that so?" she said warily. "This isn't a trap of some kind, is it? Did

202

a Mr. Sprague put you up to this?"

"No," I said. "I'm a friend of Antoinette. I go to college with her. She's asked me to arrange a meeting, knowing her family would object. That's why she wants a very discreet meeting," I added.

There was a long pause, and then she spoke with a softer voice. "Funny you should call just now," she said. "I just wrote Edna's baby a letter. I don't know who you are, but you sound like a sweet kid. If she promises to keep our meeting secret, I'd be glad to tell her about her mother. Edna was a fine lady," she added, "who deserved better."

"Antoinette knows nothing about her," I said.

"How did you find me?" she said sharply now, as if she were changing her mind. "Sprague put you up to this, didn't he?"

I didn't know how to begin explaining that Jack intercepted her mail at the newspaper and that we had followed Sprague and eavesdropped on her in the empty house.

"It's a rather involved story," I said. "I can only assure you that Antoinette is eager to meet with you, and I have reason to believe that you had some finer feeling for her mother. I would hope that you could tell her what you know. It would mean a lot to her."

"You sound on the level, all right," said Mrs. Montesquieu. "Maybe I'm crazy, but I've half a mind to believe you. And you're right, I do have finer feelings." She said this last with the air of someone who has just surprised herself with the discovery that she truly does want to do the right thing. "But how do you know that? You know a lot."

"I know that because you just told me you wrote Antoinette a letter," I said glibly.

"Listen, it's possible I'm being followed, but if she can come here—come in the side entrance, perhaps. That might be best."

"Very well," I said, and we settled on four o'clock the following afternoon at the LaGrande Hotel.

With a deep sigh, I called Antoinette back and told her about the arrangements. "Oh, Iris, I'm so grateful," she said. "Let me get a pencil. I want to write the address and room number down clearly, I am so nervous." She came back on the line a second later, rather breathless, and I gave her all the information.

"She is a queer woman, Antoinette," I said, "and not an honest one, but I truly believe your mother was kind to her and she would like to return the kindness by meeting with you." I hoped it was true, and that Mrs. Montesquieu wasn't simply hoping to extort more money by befriending Antoinette.

"Iris, you must come with me," said Antoinette suddenly. "First of all, it will help me get away. We can pretend we're shopping or something. And secondly, well, I'm rather frightened, to tell you the truth. This woman seems so demimonde."

"All right," I said, secretly thrilled.

I would probably never again in my life get to meet a woman who'd led such a wicked life. While she was no doubt a pathetic creature, she also fascinated me. There seemed to be something at once foolish and brave and a little mad about the woman. A strange mixture of greed, for drugs perhaps, and for money, as well as a dangerous life of prison and indebtedness, a haggard kind of beauty, a strange mixture of the cultivated and the toughened. She seemed like a woman balancing all the time on the very edge, the edge of respectability, perhaps even the edge of sanity.

At about half past three the next day, Antoinette fetched me in her roadster. She looked strained and apprehensive.

"What if I don't like what I learn about my mother," she

said to me after we had parked the car some blocks from our rendezvous.

I took her hand. "Antoinette," I said, "your character is your own, and your mother's mistakes cannot taint it in any way."

She blinked back a tear and squeezed my hand. "Iris, you are a wonderful friend," she said.

"Are you sure you still want me to come with you?"

She nodded, and I smiled at her. Antoinette had always seemed rather frivolous, but I couldn't help but admire the way she was facing her past and her origins in this way. Always rather helpless, she seemed to possess hidden resources all of a sudden.

We set off down the street and managed to approach the hotel from the side entrance Mrs. Montesquieu had told us about. As far as I could tell, we weren't observed, which was probably a good thing, as we were both wearing dark glasses. My red hair being rather noticeable, I had wrapped it in a turban of white silk, and Antoinette wore a navy blue hat with a diaphanous brim of organza. Rather than appearing inconspicuous, I realized as I glimpsed our reflection in the window of the hotel, we looked obviously disguised. Only the importance of the occasion for Antoinette kept me from giggling at the sight of us.

Once inside the small lobby, I took off the dark glasses, and we went up in a slow, creaky elevator to the third floor.

We knocked firmly on Mrs. Montesquieu's door, but there was no answer. Looking nervously at Antoinette, I turned the knob slowly. The door was open.

"Let's wait for her inside," I said.

The room was very untidy, much like the bungalow Jack and I had examined. Antoinette entered gingerly, shocked, I was sure, at the disarray—a silk kimono spread out over the back of a chair, newspapers strewn about, an overflowing ash-tray on the dressing table, more clothing draped over the open lid of a trunk.

The bed itself appeared unmade, and strangely lumpy. It took a second before I realized that it contained a body. The covers were pulled up over it, and the face was turned away from the door, but there was a spill of blond hair on the pillow and a limp arm hanging from beneath the bedclothes.

I gripped Antoinette's arm. "Don't scream," I said.

"I won't," she whispered. Her eyes wide, she just stared at the bed.

I tiptoed over to the other side of it. If there had been any doubt, it was gone now. Mrs. Montesquieu's tongue was thrust out and her eyes were open in a glassy stare, strangely pale against her purplish skin. Around her throat was a yellow chiffon scarf, drawn so tightly that it disappeared between ridges of the flesh of her neck, the ends flopping in front.

I turned to Antoinette. "We should get you out of here," I said. "There might be a scandal. I shall call the police."

She nodded slowly, swallowing, and looking very dizzy. She turned her head away and let it fall to her chest. I realized I would have to get her out of there myself. She could easily pass out on the stairs. I thought it best to avoid the elevator, as there was no need to have the operator get a look at us twice.

"There's just one thing," I said as an idea leapt into my head. "Perhaps—" I walked over to a small desk. There were a few papers there, and an envelope, facedown. I turned it over. Antoinette's name was written on it. I decided that this was personal correspondence and none of the police's business, so I swept it into my bag and led Antoinette from the room. I walked her to her car and she got behind the wheel.

"My God," she said, "I never imagined anything like this."

"The poor woman," I said as the reality of the situation began to sink in.

"I know I should think of her," she said bitterly. "But all I can think of is that I didn't learn anything about my mother."

I opened my bag and handed her the envelope. "Maybe you still can," I said.

She seized it and read her name. "You found this on that desk?"

I nodded. "She'd told me she had written you a letter," I said. "I thought it might still be there."

She opened the envelope and read a letter of several pages of close script. There was almost a hunger in the way she devoured the words. I sighed, watching her. I knew that by removing something from the scene and getting Antoinette away, I had behaved improperly, but right now, watching Antoinette, that didn't seem important.

# 15

*As soon* as she left, I planned to call the police. Before I had a chance, however, I began to panic. How would I ever explain what I'd been doing in the hotel room? If I told the truth, Antoinette would be involved, and the whole world would know about her mother's scandalous past. She was so determined to keep this knowledge from Walter. No matter how broad-minded he was, it was certainly possible he'd fault her for keeping the story from him. I was very confused.

I thought first of seeking Aunt Hermione's advice, but I knew she would worry. When I had discovered that first body —poor Miss Blodgett splayed out beneath the coconut palm —my aunt had found the whole thing fascinating, but to have discovered a second corpse so soon after, and in an untidy second-class hotel room—well, it might be too much for her. She was always worrying that she was a poor chaperone.

I called Jack. He had moved into the Royal Hawaiian, and they were able to page him. "Where are you?" he said sharply after I blurted out the fact that the woman in white had been strangled and that I hadn't called the police yet. I glanced up at the street signs and gave him the address.

"I'll be right there," he said.

By the time he arrived, I was in turmoil. I knew it would be wrong to keep the truth from the police. After all, hadn't Sprague threatened Mrs. Montesquieu? It would all have to come out eventually.

"Jack," I said, rushing up to him as he pulled up in his borrowed car. "I've been thinking about this and—"

His eyes were shining. "Take me to the body," he said. "Then we'll call the cops."

"No," I said. "We'll call them now. I'm just not sure what to do about Antoinette."

"Okay, we'll call them now and meet them there," he said, elbowing me aside and striding to the telephone booth. And so it was that Jack and I found ourselves presently in that stuffy little hotel room, staring down at the corpse of Mrs. Montesquieu.

"We can't keep your friend out of this," he said solemnly. "You know that, don't you?"

"I suppose I do," I said. "But Jack, she's rather fragile. I'm not sure she can take it."

"She won't have much choice." He gave me another solemn look. "Why don't you tell me what happened?"

"After you and I overheard Sprague and this woman talking, I told Antoinette about it. She wanted to meet Mrs. Montesquieu and learn what she could about her mother. She asked me to arrange it, and I did. When we arrived, well, this is what we found." I wondered whether I should confess that I'd taken Antoinette's letter from the room.

"Did you tell anyone what you had planned?"

"No one," I said. "And I doubt Antoinette did either. She's so worried Walter would be shocked at her mother's past. Walter is rather stuffy," I added.

Just then, Detective Dietrich and his retinue arrived with much clomping of heavy shoes down the hall. "Well, well, well," he said, pushing his straw hat back a little on his head. "We're not used to this much excitement on our sleepy little island. Two middle-aged mainland ladies in a week, and you two found the body again." He walked slowly around the bed and lowered his face until it hovered across from Mrs. Montesquieu's.

I turned away. "Suppose you kids tell me what you were doing here?"

"Well," I began, taking a deep breath. I was prepared to divulge the truth, but before I could, Jack interrupted with a complete story.

"You see, ever since Miss Blodgett was killed beneath that palm tree, we wondered if maybe there hadn't been some mistake. You see, Miss Blodgett led a rather blameless life, by all accounts, and there's reason to believe this lady didn't. They were both from Boston, they both arrived on the same boat, and they were staying in similar bungalows on Waikiki. We wondered if the killer hadn't made a mistake the first time around, so we set out to find this Mrs. Montesquieu. We traced her here," he explained, waving a hand airily and neglecting to explain how we had done so, "but we were too late." Jack allowed his face to take on a melancholy aspect.

"Is that so? Well, you two run on down to the lobby, while I take care of things here." Detective Dietrich shook his head sadly. "This kind of thing isn't good for the tourist trade." He looked up again sharply at us. "Don't leave the lobby until I speak with you," he said, narrowing his eyes. He shook his finger at Jack. "And no press."

We descended to the lobby in silence. Why, I wondered, had the detective made me feel guilty? It's true, I had discovered two bodies, but I hadn't killed them. Still, what was it that drew me to the center of brutal crimes? Was there something morbid in my own nature? I shuddered.

"What's the matter?" said Jack, who, with his usual perception, had caught my little moment of horror.

I crossed my arms and rubbed myself. I felt suddenly rather chilly. "Oh, Jack," I said with a sigh. "It's all so horrible. Murder. On this beautiful gentle island. Evil. I'm afraid of it contaminating me, sometimes." Our elevator creaked to a stop, and he took my arm in a rather protective gesture.

"I know what you mean, Iris," he said. "I feel the same way about newspapering sometimes. Evil is my beat—"

We were silent a moment.

"But evil festers when it's not exposed to daylight," he said in a more cheerful tone. "Which is why we'd better find out who's responsible for these killings."

"And I had better call Antoinette before the police do," I said.

It was an unpleasant duty, but I saw no way out of it. I called her from the lobby telephone, figuring she'd be home by now. She was.

"I'm glad you called, Iris," she said. "I've been thinking about a lot of things, and I've decided that I should come forward and tell the truth. Reading this woman's letter has opened my eyes. I've already talked to Walter about it, and I realize how silly I've been. He's been wonderful."

"That's grand," I said. "The police are here now, and I'll tell them to contact you."

I was immensely relieved. I hadn't even dared think about the strain of lying to the police. Unlike Jack, who seems to relish inventing falsehoods, I'm a terrible liar. I was glad, too, that she'd discussed her family secrets with Walter. It seemed like the wisest course of action.

"Iris, come when you can," she said. "I'd like to show you the letter. That poor woman. Who could possibly have killed her, and why? I want to talk to you about it. You're so clever."

Antoinette sounded quite calm and more grown up somehow.

I didn't feel particularly clever just now. Two women had died violent deaths, and I didn't know why. A few moments later Detective Dietrich came down to the lobby. We sat on squeaky rattan chairs among some dusty potted aspidistras.

"How about you two telling me what you've found out about this woman," he said.

Jack and I told him what we knew about Mrs. Montesquieu. She had been in financial difficulty. She had come from Boston. Very reluctantly, in spite of Antoinette's expressed desire to be candid, I told him we had reason to believe she had some connection with the Caulfields. The detective gave rather a start at this last information.

Dietrich's eyebrows rose. "You don't say," he said calmly, in strange counterpoint to the intense look I'd just observed at the mention of the Caulfield name.

"There's a private eye in town, name of Sprague. Ask him what he knows," said Jack. "The Caulfields were paying Mrs. Montesquieu to leave the islands, and this Sprague was handling the payoff. By the way, Sprague seems to think the lady used dope."

"Very interesting," said Dietrich.

When he'd first questioned us, he'd seemed rather suspicious of us, pointing out rather obviously that we had discovered two bodies lately and that this seemed like more than coincidence. Once he heard the Caulfields were involved, however, he lost interest in us completely.

I added the final revelation. "Actually," I said, "Antoinette Caulfield was supposed to meet with her this afternoon. I accompanied her. When we came, we discovered the body. I've just spoken to Antoinette, and she says she'll be glad to tell you what little she knows about the case."

Dietrich looked quite taken aback. "I see," he said. "Well, yes, I'll get on that right away." He paused for a moment, then said with a great deal of seriousness, "This could be a very complicated murder, or it could be very simple. In any case, there is no need for you two to go poking into it. That's what we have a police force for.

"And another thing," he added, scowling. "It's my intention to handle this matter discreetly. Get my meaning? There's no point embarrassing people by their association with this woman. I trust you'll do the same."

After we were dismissed, I telephoned Aunt Hermione, who was by now, no doubt, wondering what had become of me.

"Oh, Iris dear, I'm so glad to hear from you," she said. "I'm simply exhausted. I've been arranging Miss Blodgett's funeral. It was rather difficult choosing the flowers. Nothing too showy and tropical, I thought. Don't you agree?"

"Let's discuss it when I return," I said. "There's a lot to talk about."

I hoped I could tell her about finding Mrs. Montesquieu's body in a casual sort of way so that she wouldn't be too perturbed. If she thought I was in any sort of danger, she might forbid any further detecting, or at the very least she'd worry a great deal.

"Oh, how dreadful," she said after I had told her the whole story. She and Jack and I were dining together at our hotel, beginning with delicious alligator pears. "There is such a lot of wickedness in the world. I would be horrified to think that the Caulfields might be behind this in some way. I shouldn't even mention it, but—"

"It certainly comes to mind," said Jack. "She had information they wanted suppressed. Of course, the woman may have had other enemies, and if she were really mixed up in this coke business, there might be an angle there."

"So sordid," said Aunt Hermione. "To die, wretched and alone, far from home. An ending, no doubt, to a reckless life."

"Yes," I said. "Mrs. Montesquieu was rather a mysterious woman. I'm afraid she will not be mourned. But she was trying to do the right thing by Antoinette, I'm sure of it."

"While she was blackmailing the rest of the family," said Jack cynically.

"Speaking of mourners, I do hope you'll come to the services for Miss Blodgett tomorrow," said my aunt. "Naturally, it will be rather small, but I think it would cheer up Miss Pomfret if we managed to round up a few extra people."

"Of course," I replied.

"I'll be there," said Jack, with a gleam in his eye.

I knew he probably hoped he'd find some clue to Miss Blodgett's killer among the mourners.

"She'll be buried next to her great-great-uncle Josiah. There was a suitable spot right next to him, isn't that nice? Miss Pomfret was pleased." Aunt Hermione smiled happily.

"How is Miss Pomfret managing?" I asked.

"Very well, considering how devoted the ladies were to one another. Her new friend, Rose Carlmont, has been most helpful. They are dining together tonight. And a telegram arrived for Miss Pomfret today." Aunt Hermione waved her fork in the air, agitated, perhaps because she'd forgotten to tell me this interesting news. "Apparently, Miss Blodgett left a few small bequests to nieces and nephews, and Miss Pomfret shall receive the bulk of the estate."

Aunt Hermione leaned forward confidentially. "The fact that a woman like Miss Blodgett, with such a strong sense of family, left her money to an outsider confirms my view that the ladies were very good friends, indeed."

"So," said Jack thoughtfully, "Miss Pomfret benefited by her friend's death."

"And quite handsomely, I would guess," said Aunt Hermione, squeezing lemon on some lovely, delicate tropical

214

fish. "If Miss Blodgett's jewelry was any indication. It was very valuable, and very old. No doubt her fortune was, too."

"I wish we knew who ransacked that bungalow," I said.

Later, when we went upstairs, we had very good reason to wonder again. Our own rooms had been searched, our trunks turned out, our drawers pulled onto the floor.

The door connecting our room with Miss Pomfret's hung open. This room, too, bore signs of a search, and here the frenzy had evidently been more intense. Even the bedclothes had been stripped and the gaily printed cushions from the chairs flung about.

# 16

**Neither my** aunt nor I had brought black or gray to Honolulu. We both managed, however, to appear in a sort of half mourning—me in lavender, Aunt Hermione in beige—at Miss Blodgett's short service.

It took place some miles out of town in a whitewashed chapel. Sunlight streamed through the windows in a very nonfunereal way, and insects batted against the window screening. There were just a few of us: Jack, Aunt Hermione and I, Miss Pomfret, her friend Rose Carlmont, and the minister's wife wearing a black straw hat that had turned rather greenish with age. In the back pew, Detective Dietrich sat, watchful and respectful, with a man I didn't recognize—another policeman presumably.

It was a short, austere ceremony. We sang one or two of the grimmer hymns—favorites, apparently of Miss Blodgett—emphasizing the narrowness of the path to salvation. There were a few white roses on the coffin, fanned out on a palm frond. I couldn't help but think that it was the fruit of the same plant that had crushed Miss Blodgett's skull. I hoped Miss Pomfret wouldn't notice this irony.

Afterwards, several strong Hawaiian men, members of the congregation recruited for the task, lifted the coffin onto their shoulders and carried it out to the well-kept churchyard. I couldn't help but think how they carried the coffin the same way the natives bore their heavy surfboards into the waves.

A few more words were spoken as the coffin was lowered into the ground and vivid red volcanic earth tossed onto it. Miss Pomfret began to collapse. She was supported on one side by Aunt Hermione and on the other by Rose Carlmont, her own plain face blotched with sympathetic tears. The minister's wife produced a vial of smelling salts. I imagined her keeping them next to her rusty black hat on a particular shelf, especially for funerals.

A few moments after Miss Pomfret had been revived, Kimo Kawena admitted himself carefully through the white picket gate and joined us in the churchyard. He carried a spray of orchids, the waxy petals, pink and purplish, curving over bristling, velvety stamen that trembled in the slight breeze.

Miss Pomfret gasped and then closed her eyes in horror. Kimo Kawena shifted the brilliant flowers in his arms, such a contrast to the demure roses that lay on the coffin, and stood looking down at the grave as it was filled in, a large tear running down his handsome coppery cheek.

"At least he brought some expensive flowers," I whispered to Jack.

"Probably stole them out of somebody's yard." Jack sneered.

When the ceremony was over, Kawena nodded curtly at all of us, placed his floral tribute on the grave, turned on his heel, and left. Detective Dietrich, who'd been lingering in the background, stepped forward as if to follow him, then seemed to think better of it and stopped.

I looked down at the headstone next to Miss Blodgett's grave. It was plain white marble. "The Rev'd Josiah Samuel Blodgett," it read. "1810–1878. He Came To Bring The Word Of The Lord To A Savage Land And Save The Souls Of A Heathen Race."

After the funeral, and the two policemen's somewhat embarrassed departure, we had a cup of tea and sandwiches at the parsonage. As we sat silently on horsehair chairs I reflected that Miss Pomfret was no doubt relieved Kimo Kawena had left abruptly and not stayed to tea.

The minister, a thin, ascetic type, turned pinkish from the tropical sun, spoke up. "Such a comfort it would have been to her, I am sure, to know that she was buried next to one of her own family."

"Yes," murmured Aunt Hermione, tempering her enthusiasm for the arrangements she had made by the solemnity of the occasion.

"Of course, she never knew him," said Miss Pomfret. "Except through his diary, of course."

"I have often paused before his tombstone," said the minister, "and read his inscription, wishing I'd had the privilege of knowing him. This was his church for a time, you know; in fact, he built it. And you say there is a diary?"

"Yes," said Miss Carlmont. "He describes his activities here in Hawaii, as a missionary."

"How fascinating," said the minister.

"I would be glad to let you read it," said Miss Pomfret. "It is mine now, of course, but I think the Blodgetts would prefer that it remain with the family papers. Otherwise, I would give it to you." She put a handkerchief to her face and added, "Perhaps someone else will want to finish Viola's work on the Blodgetts of Massachusetts."

Miss Carlmont leaned over and patted her hand. "It's in my room," she explained to the minister. "I can have it sent around for you to examine, if you would like. I've made a transcript of it. Perhaps you'd like that for the church records."

"Splendid," said the minister. His wife fluttered enthusiastically. "We know less than we would like to of the history of our church. When we came, the records were in a sad state."

"Mildew," said his wife.

I turned to Jack and wondered if he was thinking what I was thinking. Viola Blodgett's bungalow and later Miss Pomfret's hotel room had been ransacked, and ransacked thoroughly. There was no sign that the search was ever stopped, that the item sought after was ever found.

Now it appeared that one thing the ladies possessed that wasn't in the bungalow, or later in Miss Pomfret's room, was Great-Great-Uncle Josiah's diary. It had been in Miss Carlmont's room at her women's residence downtown during both searches.

Jack was looking at me in a puzzled way. "The diary," I whispered, under the minister's remarks about Miss Blodgett being reunited with other Blodgetts in heaven. "They must have been searching for the diary."

Jack's eyes took on that gleam they got when he was hot on a new lead. He stood up.

"Seeing as I have a car," he said, "I'll be glad to run that book over here." He bowed to Miss Pomfret. "You mustn't worry about a lot of details at a time like this."

Hours later Jack and I found ourselves on the beach in our bathing suits, drinking tall glasses of lemonade. I was reading aloud to him from Uncle Josiah's diary.

It was a plain reddish book, quite thick, with each square of paper covered with the Reverend Josiah's close, crabbed hand in ink that had faded to brown.

The Reverend Blodgett had not been a faithful diarist. The earlier entries, from the 1830s, contained his first impressions of the islands. I tried to imagine the young man, about the age I was now, writing about the spot that must have seemed so strange and far away.

*The squalor and sinfulness are oppressive, and while I had been warned of the habits of the people, I had, until now, no idea of the depths of degradation to which these poor creatures had fallen. Lewdness such as cannot be imagined is everywhere, and corrupts even the youngest of the natives. To live among these poor creatures is to learn the harsh lesson that a life without submission to His will is to live a wretched life indeed.*

Jack yawned. "Go on," he said, lying on his back facing the sun with his eyes closed. I noticed that he was getting rather tan, and the sun had lightened his sandy hair a little, so there were glints of gold at the temples. "Get to the part where he's tempted by a native girl."

"I don't think he was," I said. "And if he was, he'd never write about it." I looked back down at the book and continued reading. There were some homesick entries:

*Oh, for the grayness of New England! How the colors of this place begin to sicken me. The birds and flowers are too bright, the sky and sea too blue. God, in His infinite wisdom, chose to decorate this part of His creation in colors to please the simple natives here, while in parts of the globe where the sensibilities are more delicate, the human soul more finely shaded, he chose a more refined palette.*

"Do you think someone ransacked that cottage and the hotel room to learn about the decorating schemes of the Almighty?" said Jack a little impatiently.

"Be patient," I said. "We've got forty years or so to cover." Jack groaned.

"Take heart, the entries seem to be dropping off now. There's nothing for several years."

"Aha!" said Jack. "He probably spent them in a little grass shack with some Hawaiian maiden, lounging in a hammock while she wove flowers in his hair and sang Hawaiian love songs." He sighed happily.

*Building the church has been an arduous, back breaking task.*

*It has ruined my health and taxed my constitution greatly. But now, by the grace of God, the work is completed. I pray now, that I might be the instrument of His will in bringing His light to the most wretched of His children.*

"Poor salesmanship," Jack mused. "Those natives must've known how wretched he thought they were. No wonder they weren't buying it."

"Oh, but they were," I said, leafing through more entries, most of which seemed to be head counts.

*Twenty-seven souls at Sunday services. The hymnals in the Hawaiian language have arrived, praise the Lord. Five more infants, baptized in Jesus' name. Thanks be to God. If my coming here means just one more soul is allowed into Paradise, then my efforts will not have been in vain.*

Later he wrote:

*A day which gives me so much satisfaction, that I fear my soul will burst from happiness.*

"There it is," interrupted Jack. "The native girl."

"Oh, be quiet," I said, continuing.

*Irregular relations between native girls and white men are the scourge of these islands and a disgrace to the white race. That these ignorant natives should live thus is one thing, but that the European and American men who prey upon these simple, compliant girls should embrace such a way of life and set such a revolting example is the height of wickedness.*

*Today, I regularized twelve such liaisons, in a long ceremony that I found both fatiguing and joyful indeed. Oh! to have washed away the stain of sin, to ennoble a sinful way of life with the sacred bonds of matrimony! To give innumerable*

*half-caste babies, born and unborn, a father as well as a*
*mother. What a joy it is!*

*In my sermon, for in spite of the length of such a ceremony,*
*I was still given the strength to speak at length from the pulpit,*
*I told these new husbands that I expected them to accompany*
*their wives to church in the future. I am full of hope on this*
*point, but I fear I caught a glimmer of rebellion in the eye of*
*that young reprobate, Abner Caulfield, who has at last made*
*an honest woman of Pualani Apaka—and just in time to give*
*his child whom she carries, and will deliver soon, a name.*

Jack sat bolt upright and brushed sand from his arms.
"Read that again," he said. "Young Abner Caulfield, eh?
What's the date?"

"March of 1876," I said.

"That's only fifty-some years ago," said Jack.

"And Antoinette's grandfather is in his seventies now," I
said. "It could well be he."

"Whatever happened to his wife and child, I wonder?"
said Jack.

"All I know is that Antoinette's grandmother was writing
to him when he came over here as a young man. They were
engaged for eight years or something."

"I doubt he bothered to mention his wife and child," said
Jack. He was scrambling to his feet now. "I better go down-
town and find out where they keep the records around here.
This could be one swell story."

"Do you think Mr. Caulfield could have been a bigamist?"
I said thoughtfully.

# 17

*I'm coming* with you," I said, scrambling to collect my things. "Why Jack, this gives Miss Blodgett a link to Mrs. Montesquieu. I couldn't help but think their deaths were related. They were both connected to the Caulfields."

"And to Caulfield family secrets," said Jack.

"If Miss Blodgett knew that Mr. Caulfield had married before—" I began.

"And had a child of mixed blood," added Jack, standing and watching impatiently as I folded a towel and thrust it into my beach bag, carefully placing the diary on top.

"I suppose it would cause a scandal," I said. "Although no one here in Hawaii seems to care about any of that. They all seem very proud that they're a melting pot. Old Mrs. Caulfield wouldn't like it, I can tell you that. But would it be worth killing Miss Blodgett over?" I frowned, concentrating. "Did Miss Blodgett even know? Did she connect the diary entry somehow with Antoinette's family?"

"Maybe she was blackmailing the Caulfields. Who knows?" said Jack.

"More in Mrs. Montesquieu's line, I'd say. Oh, there's so much we don't know," I said, feeling a little overwhelmed at the task before us.

"A previous marriage might cause a social scandal," said Jack. "But what happened to the first Mrs. Caulfield and the child? If old Caulfield's second family isn't legitimate, then you've got more than a scandal. You've got a question of inheritance."

"He doesn't have a will," I said.

"This gets more and more interesting," said Jack. "I'd sure like to meet Antoinette's grandparents," he added wistfully.

I'd been trying to keep Jack away from Antoinette's family until now, hoping to prevent him from writing scandalous articles about them. But, I thought, solving these crimes was more important than the amour propre of the Caulfields.

"I'll try to arrange it," I said. "In fact, Antoinette said yesterday she wanted me to come over as soon as I could, and I really should go this afternoon. You could drive me over."

"Iris," he said with a wide smile, "you're a real pal. 'Your reporter gains entrée to society family linked to murders.' " He bent over and kissed me on the forehead.

"Jack!" I said with a frown. "I want you to help me solve these murders. Not just spy on my friends."

"I can do both," he said. "I'm a very versatile fellow." He glanced at his wristwatch.

"What about your research?"

"We can stop at the *Star-Bulletin* on the way over. There's someone there who can give us a hand. Great reporter. We had a few drinks together with some of the boys when I first blew into this burg."

We went into the hotel, where I left Uncle Josiah's diary in the hotel safe and went upstairs to dress. Soon we were on our way to the *Star-Bulletin* offices in Jack's borrowed car.

"It's sort of like being an Odd Fellow or a Mason," he said as I followed him inside a door with frosted glass. "A newspaperman is among friends in any port of call."

A burly fellow in a wrinkled white suit was coming out as we went in, and practically ran us over.

"What are you hanging around here for, Clancy?" he said gruffly. "You're old news." He stopped and stared at us. "You aren't looking for a job, are you? You'd have island fever in a week. Go on back to 'Frisco."

"I'm looking for O'Herlihy," Jack said with dignity.

The man in the wrinkled suit gestured over his shoulder with his thumb. "Back there," and barreled past us.

"Is that one of your friends in any port of call?" I said sarcastically. "I didn't notice him slipping you the secret handshake."

"Oh, don't mind him," said Jack airily, plunging into the newsroom. "O'Herlihy!" he shouted over to a knot of reporters. They all turned and drew back, revealing a woman in her middle or late twenties sitting on a desk and wearing a peach-colored jersey ensemble trimmed with blue. She looked up at us and waved to Jack, then slid off her perch and came over to us.

"Well, it's Mr. Clancy," she said, and looked me over carefully. "And a friend."

"Iris Cooper," I said.

"That's right," said Jack. "Iris, this is June O'Herlihy. Listen, I'm working on a swell story. I just need a little help in the research department."

"Really?" Miss O'Herlihy had dark, nicely waved hair, blue eyes with dark lashes, and creamy Irish skin, which she had wisely managed to keep out of the sun. "Why should I do that? So you can take the fair Miss Cooper here to the beach?" She gave a sly little smile.

"This story is developing on all fronts," said Jack importantly. "I thought it'd be a swell scoop for you."

Miss O'Herlihy laughed. "I'm a society reporter," she said.

"Jack needs you to do some research about the Caulfield

family," I said simply. "There seems to be a scandal in their past, and it may have something to do with these tourist murders."

"Now you're talking," she said, leading us into a quiet corner of the newsroom. "Tell me all."

When we'd revealed what we wanted her to check, her blue eyes lit up. "A story like this and I'd be banned from every social function in the islands." She paused. "It's rather an intriguing idea."

"Well, keep it all under your hat until we're ready with the full story," said Jack. "Then I'll cut you in on it. You can scoop everyone in the South Pacific."

Miss O'Herlihy fairly wriggled with excitement at the prospect. We left to her the task of checking old birth, marriage, and death records and set out for Antoinette's house.

"So much has happened," I said to Jack on the way over. "Do you think we are any closer to discovering why Miss Blodgett was killed?"

"Maybe." At the wheel, Jack's face looked rather grim. "But let's face it, we've got plenty of suspects. Take Kimo Kawena for instance. Who knows what a fellow like that might do."

"Nothing violent, I am sure," I said. "He strikes me as a rather gentle soul. I know he's a gigolo, but—"

"Of course, Miss Pomfret came into a fortune," interrupted Jack. "And she was pretty cut up about Blodgett and the beach boy."

"I suppose," I said.

"And then, of course, there's the diary," he said with a satisfied air. "Miss Blodgett had proof that old Caulfield had married a Hawaiian girl and presumably had had a child. We'll decide how damaging that would be when O'Herlihy gets through with her research. That might open up a whole new batch of suspects."

I sighed. "I know. I'm afraid the Caulfields might be involved. That Mr. Sprague sounded so ruthless. Remember how he threatened Mrs. Montesquieu?"

"We'd better decide right now how much to tell your friend Antoinette," said Jack as we drove into the shadow of the sinister banyans on the Pali Road.

"What do you mean?"

"Someone's killed two people, Iris," he said. "We can't go blabbing everything we've found out, especially not to the Caulfields. Not until we know more, at least not until we hear from O'Herlihy."

"You're right, Jack," I said. "It could be dangerous."

I shuddered, remembering my ransacked hotel room. The thought that a killer could have been in the room I shared with dear Aunt Hermione was horrifying all of a sudden. Of course, the hotel had said they would post a man near our room, but I felt a sense of danger.

"Jack," I said, "I'm frightened. We could be very close to someone who kills."

"That's right," he said. He put his arm around my shoulder and pulled me across the car seat nearer to him. "I want you to be very careful, Iris. Stick close to me, kid."

"Oh, Jack," I said, trying to sound casual, "you just want to be close to me so you can get one of your scoops and spy on my friends." Still, I felt more secure with Jack's arm around me.

I thought he would laugh at what I'd just said, but he looked serious for a minute. "Let's just remember," he said, "that when we're visiting Antoinette, we'd better be on our guard. The Caulfield home might just be where all this trouble is coming from."

I shuddered once more, thinking of the bougainvillea-covered house, so festive and lovely, surrounded by its beautiful garden. Yet, despite the beauty, there was a heaviness there, an oppression that could be evil.

"The way I see it," continued Jack, "we're there to pump 'em, not to give away what we've learned."

"I'm there because I'm Antoinette's friend, too," I replied, but I knew that now my primary purpose was to solve the mystery of two horrible murders.

When we arrived, I was interested to note the old Ford belonging to the mysterious Mr. Yamagamuchi parked in front. At least he had stopped parking out of sight. "Jack," I said, "we should find out who this Mr. Yamagamuchi is. Mr. Caulfield seems to have some mysterious business with him. I know the family has been curious about it. That's his car."

"Should be easy enough to find out," said Jack. "But right now, tell me about the old man, Iris. What's he like?"

"Whimsical," I said. "He likes to talk to me."

"Good," said Jack. "I'm glad to hear that."

A maid led us out to the lanai, where Antoinette sat alone. She looked drawn and pale but full of nervous energy as she rose to greet us. "Oh, Iris, I'm so glad you're here." She embraced me. "Hello, Jack."

When we were sitting, she poured us some lemonade and said, "Does anyone know what happened to poor Mrs. Montesquieu? Is there any word?"

"I'm afraid not," said Jack.

Antoinette looked away from us and said in a strained voice, "If she died because she was meeting with me—it's horrible but I did think it—if my grandparents didn't want me to know—that horrible man Sprague, he's been up at the house."

"Sprague?" said Jack.

"Yes. I've always had the impression grandfather uses

him for unsavory sorts of things." She shuddered. "That's what Charlie Spaulding told me once." She turned back to look at both of us. "I know I shouldn't even intimate my family might be mixed up in something unsavory, but I'm to start my own family now, and I feel less and less loyalty."

She began to weep a little. "Walter has been a prince," she said. "He says we can go far away if I want, or he'll stay here. It's all up to me. He's been so patient and kind. I told him all about Mother. He says he doesn't mind a bit."

"There, you see," I said, trying not to sound condescending. "Honesty is the best policy. And isn't it comforting to know Walter loves you no matter what?"

Just as I said this last, Walter and Charlie Spaulding appeared on the lanai, carrying tennis rackets and looking flushed, hot, and cross.

Walter went to Antoinette's side and bent down and kissed her. Next to me I saw Charlie Spaulding's hands turn into fists as he glared at them.

"Have you met everyone, Jack?" I said, trying to smooth over an awkward moment. As I introduced them Charlie gave Jack a perfunctory nod and slumped into a rattan chair.

"Thank you, Walter, for playing with Charlie," Antoinette said pointedly. "Grandmother's been worried he's feeling left out."

"I can never be left out," Charlie said, with a rather cruel smile. "I'll be your partner someday, Antoinette. Someday, you'll be the only Caulfield and I'll be the only Spaulding."

"I won't be a Caulfield after I'm married," said Antoinette.

She looked as if she was just about fed up with Charlie Spaulding, and I didn't blame her. With all the other things on her mind, it was too much for her to have to put up with a boorish, unwanted suitor. I imagined her grandmother insisted, and Charlie Spaulding was too gauche to know or care that he was unwanted.

"Would you rather change the name to Spaulding and Spaulding?" said Charlie.

"Steady," said Walter in a firm tone. "She's marrying me, you know."

"Who won at tennis?" said Jack innocently. "Gee, I bet you fellows really must have had quite a game going there."

Walter permitted himself a small smile.

"I would have won if he hadn't cheated," said Charlie flippantly.

There was a shocked silence as Walter walked over toward him.

"Take it back," he said menacingly.

"It's true, and you know it," said Charlie.

Walter reached down and gave Charlie's shoulder a little push.

"Keep your hands off me." Charlie stood, pushing over his rattan chair in the process. I glanced at Jack, who was leaning forward eagerly, as if amused at the prospect of a fight.

"Take it back," said Walter. "I don't want to—" He stopped himself.

Charlie leaned into his face. "You don't want to hit me? Go ahead. Just try it."

"There are ladies here," said Walter stiffly. "And we are guests of the Caulfields."

"Well, then, I'll hit you," said Charlie, pulling back his arm and preparing to swing.

"Wait a minute, fellows," said Jack easily, interposing himself between the two men and putting a shoulder into Charlie and a hand against Walter's chest.

"Step aside," shouted Charlie, trying to reach around Jack.

"What's going on here," said an imperious voice.

We all turned to see Antoinette's grandmother, standing at the French doors glaring at the scene. With her was a man in his middle forties, with receding temples flecked with gray and the tanned look of someone who'd been in the islands for a while.

"Charlie," he said sharply.

"Hello, Father," said Charlie, standing up and smoothing down his hair. "Golly, Mrs. Caulfield, I'm sorry. This temper of mine sometimes gets the better of me."

Walter smoothed his hair, too, and glared at Charlie, but he offered him his hand. Charlie glanced down at it, scowled, strode over to the lemonade pitcher, and poured himself a glass.

"Maybe you'd better go home, son," said the elder Spaulding, looking embarrassed.

"Nonsense," said Mrs. Caulfield. "The boy's always welcome here. Our families are too inextricably intertwined for any bad feelings."

Antoinette jumped up. "Please meet my friends, Mr. Spaulding," she said, and introduced me and Jack. "And this is Walter Carlson, my fiancé." She said it defiantly, jutting her chin out a little.

"Ha!" shouted Charlie.

"You'll have to excuse my boy," said Mr. Spaulding to Walter with equanimity. "The truth of the matter is, he's always expected to marry Antoinette, and it's been a blow to him."

"So it seems," said Jack, sipping lemonade.

"Well, there are no hard feelings," said Walter. "At least not on my part."

"You young people will simply have to get along," said Mrs. Caulfield, as if we were naughty children.

"She's not going to marry you, you know," said Charlie Spaulding to Walter in a normal conversational tone. I wondered if he were quite right in his mind.

"Charlie Spaulding, I am too," shouted Antoinette, stamping her foot. "I love Walter and he loves me. I've even told him our hideous family secrets, and he still doesn't mind!" she shouted with a defiant look at her grandmother. "I told him my mother was in jail. So there."

"She was?" said Charlie Spaulding.

"Nonsense," said Mrs. Caulfield. "Who's been telling you such things? That hideous Montesquieu person, surely. When you come from a family such as ours, my dear, you must remember, there are all sorts of strange people attracted to it like a moth to a flame. I had hoped we were rid of that woman." Two bright spots of red had formed in her cheeks.

"Don't distress yourself, please," said Mr. Spaulding. "Let us go inside." He gave her his arm. "Charlie, I'm ashamed of you," he said. "You'll have to take Antoinette's decision like a man." He escorted the old lady back through the French doors.

"Family secret, eh?" said Charlie. "Well I've got a better one than that about your family, Antoinette. And mine, too, It's a real corker."

"Perhaps we should go," I murmured to Jack.

"Not on your life," he said, sotto voce. "They're all so riled up they forgot about us. Shut up and listen."

"A real corker, eh? Well, what is it?" Antoinette demanded.

"Never mind," said Charlie. "But I'll use it if I have to." He glanced contemptuously over at Walter.

"Just go," said Antoinette. "Please, Charlie. Just go away. Don't you see I want you to leave?"

"You didn't always feel that way," he said, and then, mercifully, he turned and left, swinging his tennis racket belligerently.

# 18

*I fully* expected Antoinette to break down and cry after the scene we had just witnessed. The Antoinette I knew back at school might have done just that, but she seemed stronger now. There was something very determined about the set of her chin and the gleam in her eye.

"I'm not going to apologize for Charlie," she said. "I don't even want him around."

"He doesn't seem to believe that," said Jack.

"It's all Grandmother's fault," replied Antoinette. "She wants me to marry him, and she thinks if she gives him free run of the place, he'll wear me down. It's comical really. She's always said the Spauldings were an inferior bunch. When Charlie's grandfather became a partner all those years ago, he was some kind of a government clerk. But now, to secure the family fortune she wants to marry me off to them."

"She didn't take me into account," said Walter with a certain satisfaction. "I'm not going to let that brute hound you." He was perched on the wide arm of the huge rattan chair where Antoinette sat, looking small and brave.

She patted his hand. "Oh, Walter, you're wonderful." She turned back to us and leaned forward with animation. "You know, thanks to you and Mrs. Montesquieu, I understand it all so much better. Grandmother forced my mother to marry my father, just as she would like to force me to marry Charlie. It's all in Mrs. Montesquieu's letter." She turned to Walter.

234

"Would you get it for me, darling?"

"Of course. It's still in your jewel box?"

"That's right."

He bounded off happily on this errand, and she watched his retreating back fondly. "Walter's family is so normal," she said. "But when I broke down and showed him the letter, he took it all in stride. Coming from such a normal family, these revelations must have been a shock, but bless him, he pulled himself quickly together and told me nothing matters but us. I'm glad I was honest with him."

"It's usually best," I said.

"Poor Mrs. Montesquieu," she said after a moment. "I hope she didn't suffer."

"Well, it can't have been pretty," said Jack.

"At least she did me a great kindness before she died," said Antoinette.

I was struck by the ego behind this remark. There was often more than a little of the princess about Antoinette.

Walter came back and handed an envelope to her. It appeared to be the one I'd discovered on the desk.

*Dear Antoinette,*

*I wrote you before, but I wasn't on the level then.*

*I don't know why I expect you to believe me now, but here it is, the truth as Edna would have wanted you to know it.*

*I met Edna in 1909, when you were just a little baby. I'd had some troubles that I won't go into here, and I ended up in the Massachusetts Women's Prison. Your mother was there, too. Poor Edna, she'd been tried for murder and a jury found her guilty of stabbing a man to death, but she only did what any woman would have done.*

*I don't know how much your family's told you about your mother. Not much, I'd bet. Edna and I had plenty of time to talk* about our old lives. She loved the islands where she came from, and thought of them often, and of you.

Edna's trouble started many years before. She was in love with a young man who managed to get your grandparents dead set against him. They ran him out of the islands, and he went back to the mainland where he'd come from.

Instead, they practically forced her to marry your father. He was older and more respectable. She obeyed them—life was a great deal different for girls then—but she couldn't bear it. To tell you the truth, I think it was living with her parents that made it harder, but her husband was perfectly content to do just that and let his in-laws run his life.

One day the boy she'd loved came back. They ran off. It was madness, of course, but Edna was at the point of breaking. To avoid suspicion, she went on her own to the boat, arranging for your baby nurse to bring you separately to the dock.

Well, my dear, things took a tragic turn. Her lover was insanely jealous of the child she'd had by her husband. He made sure your grandparents learned of the plot and that you stayed behind.

She learned that you were still ashore just as the boat lifted anchor. She was frantic, but her lover convinced her he'd get you with them. Of course, he had no intention of doing any such thing. And your grandparents, when they learned she'd run off, were horrified. After that, they never would have let you go. They put around the story that Edna had sailed to California after a nervous collapse.

Edna went on to Boston, struck by grief and still in love with the scoundrel who'd separated her from her baby. After months of promising to get the child, he admitted the whole thing. She tried to leave him, to return to the islands, but he wouldn't let her go.

She stood at the door and pleaded with him, her hat and coat on and her bag in her hand, but he barred the door and vowed he'd never let her pass. Edna took a great huge hat pin out of her hat

*—the kind we used to wear back then—and plunged it through that villain's heart.*

*She was tried under another name—the name of the man she'd run off with. The two of them had posed as a legally married couple. She was glad of that, because she didn't want the scandal to reach the islands. She imagined if that jury let her off, she could go back to you, and no one ever need know she'd run off.*

*Well, the men on that jury were a hard-hearted bunch, without any sympathy for a young woman who'd been ruled by her heart. Edna was only twenty.*

*It was damp in that prison, and Edna died there. She caught a cold that settled in her lungs, and nothing seemed to help. I nursed her, but it's my belief she lost the will to live. She asked me many times to tell you the story of what happened to her. She feared your father and your grandparents wouldn't, being a proud lot. "Tell her I loved her," she said many times. "She'll always have enough of the world's goods, but she won't have a mother's love."*

*I know I wrote a foolish letter to you. I thought maybe you'd take to me as your own mother. I looked a little like Edna back when we were both twenty. I thought your proud grandparents would never receive me and wouldn't find out I wasn't Edna. We could stay on the mainland together.*

*I never had a child of my own, just a little girl that was stillborn many years ago, and I thought, you being a motherless child, maybe we could have had some kind of a life together. It was a crazy scheme, and maybe I wasn't thinking straight just then. I guess I knew that sooner or later you'd tumble to the fact I wasn't Edna, but you'd forgive me somehow. I knew plenty about her old life. There's so much time to talk in prison.*

*Later I thought your family could help me with some of my financial problems. I've had lots of ups and downs, and I figured they could share some of what they had with an old pal of Edna's.*

*Be that as it may, I still want to do right by you. I promised*

*Edna I'd set you straight, and I have. I don't know how you'll take it, but I thought you should know your mother was a fine woman—a girl, really—and she loved you.*

The letter was signed "Maria Montesquieu."

"May I?" said Jack softly, and Antoinette nodded. I passed it over to him. An earlier conversation with Aunt Hermione came to mind. The story I had just read was rather like a Victorian melodrama.

I could see it all so vividly—the mustachioed lover, barring the door, the weeping woman, cornered, desperate, plucking the long, sharp pin from her hat, a hat which I saw in a heavy black-draped velvet, trimmed with egret feathers and a jet clip, and then the damp prison walls, and Edna coughing her last, while half a world away a little child played beneath a tropical sky.

The story seemed almost like something from an opera. I wiped away a tear and looked over at Antoinette with pity and curiosity. She was now in possession of tragic knowledge, yet it seemed to have given her peace. Jack set down the letter and, after a moment, said to Antoinette, "I'm sorry about your mother."

"Thank you. At least I know now," she replied. "It makes such a difference."

"I guess it must have been a pretty tough break for your grandmother, this coming out now," Jack continued.

Antoinette closed her eyes momentarily. "I haven't talked to her yet. The time never seems right." She opened them again, her blue eyes looking strangely innocent. "I talked to grandfather, though."

"What was his reaction?" I heard myself say.

"He started to cry. I've never seen him cry before. He said they hadn't known she was in prison until she died. They were sent a packet of her things. She had never told them where she was. Mrs. Montesquieu explains all that in her letter. My mother wanted to be acquitted and come home without a scandal."

"A pretty tough story all around," said Jack.

Antoinette continued. "Grandfather says the prison authorities sent a death certificate and a letter. He said it was Grandmother's idea not to tell me and that he'd agreed. They thought it would be easier for me."

She turned earnestly to me. "But it wasn't. It wasn't. I never knew she loved me." She paused for a moment. "Grandfather says he was sorry for keeping it a secret. He said secrets were wrong, and there wouldn't be any more."

"There is a possibility," I said solemnly, "that this information might have something to do with those two murders."

"But how?" said Antoinette.

"Maybe someone didn't want Mrs. Montesquieu to spill the beans about your family," said Jack.

It was rather a bold thing to say, as the implication was that one of the Caulfields was involved, but the time had come, I supposed, to begin to tackle the question of the two murders.

"But I can't imagine—" began Antoinette, looking flustered.

"You said two murders," said Walter. "What would poor old Miss Blodgett have to do with Mrs. Montesquieu?"

I opened my mouth to speak, but Jack touched my foot with his under the table, and I followed his gaze over to the French doors. Mr. Caulfield was being wheeled out onto the lanai. Doing the pushing was his mysterious visitor, Mr. Yamagamuchi.

"Oh," said Mr. Caulfield abruptly when he saw me. "It's that girl with red hair."

"Hello, Mr. Caulfield," I said. "Have you met my friend Jack Clancy?"

Jack came over to his chair and shook hands, then Caulfield gestured vaguely at the Japanese behind him. "Have you young people met Robert yet? Robert Yamagamuchi?"

We all nodded. Mr. Yamagamuchi looked slightly flustered while Jack shook his hand, too, and the rest of us nodded.

"I'm showing him the garden," said Mr. Caulfield, and half turned in his chair. "Say, Robert, what are you doing tomorrow evening?"

"I'm taking a class at the Y," he replied.

"Oh," said Jack, eyeing Mr. Yamagamuchi keenly. I knew he wanted to learn more about him, just as I did. "The YMCA, eh?"

"No," replied Mr. Yamagamuchi. "The YMBA."

"Young Men's Buddhist Association," supplied Antoinette.

"Well that's interesting," said Jack. "What are you taking?"

"I'm brushing up my Japanese," said Mr. Yamagamuchi. "I speak it well enough, but I never learned to write it."

"Good, good," said Caulfield with approval. "Should help in business."

"That's the idea." Mr. Yamagamuchi seemed to be relaxing just a little.

"What kind of business are you in?" said Jack affably.

"I'm a lawyer. Just starting out, actually."

"Well, the day after that then, why don't you come to dinner? Bring that secretary of yours." Mr. Caulfield gestured vaguely at the four of us sitting on the lanai. "You young people can come, too, and Charlie, of course. Young people. That's what this place needs. Bring your aunt too, Miss Cooper."

Antoinette looked a little startled at this impromptu invitation. The old man had been acting whimsical lately, she'd said. Inviting Charlie was certainly ill advised after this afternoon's outburst, although perhaps he didn't know of it, and why Mr. Caulfield should expansively include Mr. Yamagamuchi and his secretary, I didn't know, but I welcomed the opportunity to find out more about them. Before Antoinette had a chance to jettison these rather strange dinner plans, I spoke up. "That would be lovely," I said. "I'll look forward to it."

Mr. Caulfield beamed. "Good. Glad you and Mr. Clancy here can make it. Let's see, about seven? Is that when we have people to dinner, Antoinette?"

"I suppose so," she said, looking vaguely uncomfortable. "You'd better tell Grandmother so she can tell Cook."

"I'll tell Grandmother, all right," he said, and then burst out with a rather wild cackle. "Come on, Robert," he said cheerfully.

The two of them wheeled off down the path, and Antoinette turned to Walter. "What is going on around here?" she demanded. "Grandfather is behaving so strangely. Who is this Mr. Yamagamuchi? All our legal business is in the hands of an ancient old firm downtown."

Walter frowned. "I can't imagine," he said.

"Oh, Walter, I can't bear any more. Charlie invited to dinner! He's just boorish enough to accept and make a scene." She turned to him and her face lit up all at once. "Let's get married right away. Let's not wait any longer."

Walter looked somewhat taken aback. "Would that be proper?"

"Who cares if it's proper," Antoinette demanded, running a hand rather fiercely through her hair.

Jack rose and took my arm. "You kids figure it out. Iris and I will see ourselves out."

"How about a little stroll through the garden first," he whispered when we were barely out of earshot.

I glanced over my shoulder. Walter and Antoinette seemed to be gazing rapturously at each other and took no notice of us.

"So that's your mysterious Mr. Yamagamuchi," he said. "I'm not sure what he has to do with anything, but I've been wondering if that old robber baron was behind these murders. He couldn't do it himself, naturally, but we've met Sprague, a tough customer if I ever saw one.

"Maybe this Yamagamuchi is helping him with the kind of thing that respectable downtown firm wouldn't handle, payoffs to Sprague or something."

I shrugged. "Who knows what Mr. Caulfield is up to? He's acting very whimsical lately, everyone says. And his health is poor—heart disease. He may not last much longer."

"And he hasn't got a will. More and more interesting, when you know what we do about that first wife and baby. I hope O'Herlihy's come up with something."

We took the upper path toward the tennis courts, a different path than Mr. Caulfield and Robert Yamagamuchi had taken. What I didn't realize, however, was that the two paths ran very close to each other at one point. You couldn't see, though, because a small latticed structure heaped with trumpet vines blocked the view. You could, however, hear.

Caulfield was saying, "I think I've finally decided. I'll ask you to do one more draft."

Mr. Yamagamuchi spoke more softly, but distinctly, and we were able to hear him when we strained. There was a slight note of impatience in his voice.

"I would advise you, Mr. Caulfield," he said, "to be absolutely sure before you sign another one. If it comes to light that you've had seven different versions, there might be grounds for someone to contest the will."

"You mean they'd think I was out of my mind?"

"Something like that," said Yamagamuchi. "I'm in business, and I don't mind taking your money to draw these things up, but what we really want is for you to be happy with the results and get together a good sound will."

Jack and I looked at each other wide-eyed and stood stock-still. I hoped that they wouldn't walk out of earshot too rapidly.

"Well, let's see, in that last one I left everything to Queen's Hospital, right?"

"Right. Against my advice. I would hope you'd consider regular bequests to your heirs, too," said Yamagamuchi. "It is most likely they would contest the will."

"All right. Forget the hospital. Tell me again what happens if I die intestate."

"Your children would inherit, and as your daughter has died, her children, in this case Antoinette, would inherit. Your wife would receive her widow's mite. In this case, considerable, as it includes all the land."

I could tell that Yamagamuchi had been over all of this before. It was too much to hope, of course, that we would hear any more. The squeak of the wheels and the crunch of the gravel continued at a decorous pace while Mr. Caulfield apparently mulled over his will in silence.

Now at least I knew where Mr. Yamagamuchi fit in, although there seemed no reason the Caulfields' regular firm of lawyers couldn't do his will. But then, maybe they had, and it sat in a safe somewhere while Mr. Yamagamuchi and his secretary drew up a slew of alternatives. One thing seemed clear. Mr. Caulfield was indeed acting very fancifully. It seemed to concern Mr. Yamagamuchi, who was no doubt torn. As a young lawyer starting out, he probably needed Mr. Caulfield's business, but he couldn't keep writing up wills and charging him for them if he thought the old man had gone around the bend. Jack and I discussed all this in whispers as we went back to the house. "We can go in this way," I said as we reached the French doors that led from the study, that neglected room where I had stumbled across the family album.

As we entered, we encountered a strange sight—two people rummaging through a large leather briefcase. "Here's another one," said the first, exasperated, flapping some papers.

"What's the date on it?" asked his companion sharply. "This is too terrible."

The first speaker was Mr. Spaulding, Charlie's father and Mr. Caulfield's partner. The other was Mrs. Caulfield herself, looking less than dignified in her dark tea gown, bent over the papers with a nasty gleam in her eye. They both looked up at us, startled. A quick glance at the briefcase told me what I wanted to know. The gilt initials on its side read "R. Y."

# 19

*No,"* *said* Aunt Hermione. "Absolutely not. I know I've been a very liberal chaperone, Iris, and I trust your judgment in most things, but this time I'm putting my foot down. You may not accompany a young man to a leper colony. There are limits."

"Of course," I said. Secretly, perhaps, I was a little relieved. "Jack says it's not really very contagious, but I wouldn't want to distress you."

It was the following morning and my aunt was sitting under a large beach umbrella in front of the hotel fussing with some knitting. The wool yarn looked so itchy and hot in this climate. I was sitting in the beach chair next to her, and Jack stood before us with his Panama hat in his hands, a sea breeze lifting his tie and rumpling his white suit.

"Distress me! I should be absolutely horrified. What would your father and everyone else in Portland think? Gadding about in a leper colony!" She shuddered.

"Well, hardly gadding about," I said, rather breathlessly. "It's just that Miss O'Herlihy seems to think the trail may lead there."

"Your aunt has a point," said Jack solemnly. "I'll catch that interisland steamer by myself. In fact, I'd better check with the hotel and see when it leaves."

"Run along then," said Aunt Hermione rather severely. "Iris can tell me all about it. I don't mind you two off

245

detecting, but I do insist that I be kept up-to-date on your progress."

While we had been at the Caulfields, Miss O'Herlihy had managed to check through territorial public records and come up with some interesting facts.

One of them was that there was no record of a marriage between Mr. Caulfield and anyone on the date in March of 1876 mentioned in the Reverend Josiah Blodgett's diary. There were, however, records of other marriages officiated by him on that day, so, apparently, he had complied with territorial law and turned over the records of his mass wedding to the county clerk, but one seemed to be missing.

The only proof that he had presided at the wedding of Mr. Caulfield and a young Hawaiian woman had remained in a dusty old volume in Massachusetts for fifty years. And when it returned to the islands, its owner was killed and her bungalow ransacked, probably in a fruitless search for it.

I was glad that it now lay in the safe at the Royal Hawaiian Hotel. Jack and I had decided that until the mystery of Miss Blodgett's death was solved, it was too valuable a document to give to anyone, even the police.

A record of the marriage between Mr. Caulfield and the present Mrs. Caulfield, however, existed. They had been married in St. Andrews Cathedral on the twelfth of January, 1880. I remembered the wedding pictures from the family album. I explained all of this to my aunt.

"So what happened to the native girl," said Aunt Hermione, leaning forward, her knitting forgotten in her lap.

I shrugged. "There is no record of her death."

"Then might she be alive? And what of the child?"

"That's the fascinating thing," I said. "There is a record of the child's death. He lived three days. A little boy named Kimo Caulfield, and he died on Molokai."

"In a leper colony?" Aunt Hermione's eyes widened.

"Actually," I said, "most of Molokai isn't a leper colony, but the village of Kalawao was where this infant died. That's the leper colony."

"Which means—" began my aunt.

"—that its mother was a leper," I finished.

"So she undoubtedly died," said Aunt Hermione.

Jack joined us again. "That's what I aim to find out on Molokai," Jack said. "Apparently, the lepers generally lived for six or seven years at Molokai before they died. Today, however, they are having some success with a cure. In fact, I've arranged to go over there and interview some of the doctors.

"It should allow me to do a little sleuthing and give my editor a story at the same time. He's been sending me more of those mean wires, suggesting I'm not working over here. Wants some hot copy, and right away, so I thought this leper angle was just the ticket. Generally, the place is off limits, you know."

"And a good thing, too," said Aunt Hermione.

"Well," said Jack, "I guess I'd better take off. I'll let you know what I find out."

"Be careful, Jack," I said.

"For goodness sakes, don't touch anything," said my aunt.

After he had left, my aunt resumed her knitting. She was working on a fancy sock for my sister Charlotte and was just about to turn the heel.

"Well, if the child died, I can't think why anyone would care that Mr. Caulfield had been married before. There wouldn't be any surprise heirs."

"That's what puzzles us," I said.

"But was there a death certificate for the first Mrs. Caulfield?"

"No," I said, with a little smile of triumph. "Jack thinks perhaps some of the records may have been destroyed. Significant, don't you think?"

"Perhaps," said my aunt, frowning and resuming her knitting slowly. "It certainly gives one pause."

It was going to be so hard waiting for Jack to come back with answers, if indeed the leper colony held any answers. I put my legs tentatively out from beneath the umbrella into the sun for a mad moment, thinking about getting a suntan on them and then reminding myself all I would get were more freckles and pulling them quickly back into the shade. I realized that Aunt Hermione might be feeling left out. It was true I had spent a great deal of time away from her trying to solve the mysterious murders.

Of course, Aunt Hermione had, as usual, made a great number of friends at the hotel and had been tied up at the bridge table most afternoons. Still, I knew she was keenly interested in the murders, and I felt I might have been neglecting her a little.

I was about to figure some way to apologize to her, without making an issue of it, when she spoke up. "I'll bet you're dying to find out what Jack discovers on Molokai as soon as you can," she said.

"Yes," I replied. "I am impatient, it's true."

"Let's meet his boat tonight," she said eagerly, putting her knitting aside. "And get all the facts immediately on his arrival. I'll hire a car."

"Wonderful," I said, grasping her hands.

It was very late at night as we pulled up to the docks in the machine she had rented. Aunt Hermione, an excellent driver, who as a young girl had been one of Portland's first female motorists, was at the wheel.

We parked some distance away, as we were rather unsure

of where we were, and made our way along the heavy planking. The dock smelled agreeably of creosote. There were a few others waiting, and the boat had apparently just arrived. The engine of the small, powerful launch was still throbbing.

An instant later it cut out, and passengers made their way down the gangplank. Jack was one of the first to appear. Aunt Hermione and I waved to get his attention. I was thrilled to see him descend that gangplank. I imagine it was because I was so eager to hear what he had learned.

"Say!" he exclaimed. "You came to meet the boat. That's swell. Boy, have I got a story to tell you. And one for my editor, too. All about chaulmoogra oil injections and leprosy. It's a very promising new treatment."

"Very interesting, I'm sure," said Aunt Hermione with a shudder. "You didn't touch anything, did you?"

"Never mind about all that," I said. "Let's get back to the hotel. Jack, tell us what you found out about the Caulfields on the way."

We set out toward the car. "I had a terrific voyage," said Jack enthusiastically. "They set out mattresses on deck and we just lay there and looked up at the stars."

"What about the Caulfields?" I said, my voice rising a little.

Jack took my elbow and leaned over to whisper into my ear. "Quiet," he said sharply.

Instinctively, I looked over my shoulder. We had gone some distance, and there was just one man behind us. He had a Panama hat pulled down low over his face, which seemed coppery and Hawaiian, although it was hard to tell by star-light. His body, however, was of the Polynesian type, large and broad-shouldered.

"Don't look now, but I think I picked up a tail," Jack said

out of the side of his mouth to Aunt Hermione, who walked on the other side of him. I glanced over at her, and she seemed suitably thrilled.

When we finally got to our car, Jack helped us in, then turned to face the man who seemed to be lingering behind the car. I cranked down the window and looked out, curious.

"Hey there!" shouted Jack, striding up to the man.

The man made his hands into fists and came forward.

"Mind telling me why you're following me?" said Jack affably, pushing back his hat jauntily.

"Who says I've been following you," said the man. He had a slight touch of pidgin in his accent.

"Oh, come on," said Jack. "You've been with me all day. You even tried to get into that leper colony, but you didn't have press credentials. What's the story?"

The man scowled and loomed up against Jack. "What are you talking about?" he said belligerently.

"Just that you did a lousy job tailing me," said Jack. "And that I want to know who set you after me." The two men were right next to the passenger side of the car.

"Lousy job, eh?" said the man.

He seemed to be bristling with anger. I saw him make a fist, a huge fist, as big as a ham, and step toward Jack. He began to draw back his elbow, and I was certain this huge man was going to strike Jack. Without thinking much about it, I opened the car door quickly and shoved it into the big Hawaiian, separating him from Jack. It seemed to knock the breath out of him. I heard a big "Oof."

Now he turned toward me. "What did you do that for," he demanded, grabbing me by the shoulder and pulling me out of the car with one hand. A minute later Jack had charged him and the man held on to me with one arm while Jack gave him what I believe is called a quick uppercut to the jaw.

"Iris," screamed Aunt Hermione.

Jack's blow did serve to loosen the man's grip on me. I was wearing my navy blue T-strap shoes with a stacked high heel. I brought one of those heels down on the man's instep with all the force I could. He cried out and let go of me immediately.

"Get back in the car, Iris," shouted Jack, who had stepped back a pace, had his fists up, and was weaving back and forth keeping his eyes on his opponent.

I didn't pay any attention to what Jack said. I was very angry, and even as Aunt Hermione leaned over and plucked at my sleeve to encourage me to do as Jack had said, I found myself rushing at the big man and giving him a huge push.

It seemed I put all my strength into it, but he didn't budge. He just looked down at me, startled. Then Jack said, rather foolishly, as it was I who had flung myself at the man, "Don't touch her!"

"Iris!" said my aunt sharply, and the man pushed me down.

I sprawled rather inelegantly on the ground and was dimly aware, as I scrambled to my feet again, that Jack and this huge fellow were grappling.

"Stop it!" I shouted, and the man gazed over at me for a second, while Jack managed to get in another punch.

The man hit him back, very hard, in the chest. Jack reeled a few steps and looked glazed over, but he managed somehow to keep his footing, then seemed to gather all his strength and come rushing back forward at the man, who just stood his ground with a blank expression on his huge round face.

"Stop it," I repeated, rushing between them, which was a very foolish thing to do, for the man was just about to hit Jack again, and instead, quite accidentally, hit me.

He hit my cheekbone. At the moment the blow struck, I

heard a great noise in my head, like thunder. My eyes seemed to stay in the same place while my head snapped back, and I fell against Jack like a rag doll. As he wrapped his arms around my waist, I began to hear a horrible ringing.

"Now look what you've done," said Jack.

The big Hawaiian stood staring at me, and looking truly repentant. Jack shifted my weight in his arms. I thought I saw stars, but I slowly realized that I was looking at two headlights. Another car had pulled up behind us, and a man was jumping out just as Aunt Hermione scrambled from our own car.

My legs were buckling under me and I began to slip from Jack's grip. He put one arm at the back of my knees and lifted me up. I put my arms around him, twisting a little to see who was getting out of the second car.

"You big jerk," Jack was saying. "You slugged her."

The man in the second car walked quickly over to us and took in the scene. It was Hugo Sprague.

"What's going on here?" he demanded of the big Hawaiian.

"So!" said Jack with triumph. "You sicked this big palooka on us, huh?"

"Settle down," said Sprague.

"Settle down? The big ape just slugged a girl."

"Get in the car," said Sprague to the Hawaiian, who gazed at all of us rather helplessly.

"I didn't mean to hit a girl," he replied. "She barged right in there."

"The car," repeated Sprague, and the big man turned on his heel and left us.

"What the hell's going on?" he demanded.

"Well, I guess we know who put a tail on us," said Jack to Sprague. "And I guess you're working for Caulfield."

Sprague narrowed his eyes. "You folks go on back to your

hotel," he said. "Stop nosing around these islands. It's good advice. Take it." He turned to Aunt Hermione. "If you have any influence over these kids, ma'am," he said, "you'll tell them to get on back to the mainland."

Aunt Hermione drew herself up to her full height. "My good man," she said frostily, "if you are, as Mr. Clancy suggests, in the employ of the Caulfields, I will speak to them tomorrow. We are to dine there."

The usually unflappable Mr. Sprague looked wary.

"Although," she added with her characteristic dubiousness, "if they are in the habit of employing brutes to strike young ladies, perhaps they are not the sort of people with whom we should be associating."

## 20

*Let's get* Iris back to the hotel," said Jack. "The doctor should look at her. There's no point standing around here."

He set me gently in the front seat of the car. While I protested that I seemed to be fine and nothing was broken, Aunt Hermione fussed at me from the driver's side.

"I'll be all right," I said, but I felt very weak.

Jack got in beside me and shouted out the window at Sprague as Aunt Hermione got the engine started, "You haven't heard the last of this, Sprague, I can tell you that."

"This is simply terrible," said Aunt Hermione. "And you say that horrible man was following you?"

"Yes," said Jack, "but he didn't stop me from finding what I was looking for."

"What!" I exclaimed, sitting straight up and realizing how much my face hurt, before I slumped back down and rested against the leather seat.

He patted my hand. "Plenty. Wait until my editor hears this. 'Island Aristocrats Bred in Shame. Blue Bloods Born on Wrong Side of Blanket.' "

"Tell us, tell us!" said Aunt Hermione, driving, I noticed, faster than usual.

"Well, I found out that Caulfield's Hawaiian wife died of leprosy, all right. In fact, I saw her tombstone." He reached inside his jacket for his pigskin notebook and flipped it open. "Pualani Apaka Caulfield. Departed This Life March Sixth, 1880."

"But Jack," I exclaimed, "he married Mrs. Caulfield in January of 1880!"

"Very courteous of you to call her Mrs. Caulfield," said Jack. "Actually, she's no such thing."

"Their marriage was bigamous," said Aunt Hermione. "Which means that their issue—"

"So if Pualani's baby had lived," I interrupted, "he would be the true heir."

"Her son was stillborn, all right," said Jack. He paused dramatically. "But his sister wasn't. It's all in the leper-colony records."

"What?" said my aunt and I in unison, and the boxy shape of an oncoming car loomed toward us, Aunt Hermione swerving away from it at the last minute.

"Settle down, ladies," said Jack, obviously relishing the fact that he had startling news to share.

"Twins?" demanded Aunt Hermione.

"That's right. A little girl. Named Elikapeka. Means Elizabeth in Hawaiian," he added. "Born May 12, 1876."

"What happened to her?" I said.

"Well," said Jack, "no one seems to know. The lepers, as you know, weren't allowed to leave. Still aren't, for that matter. And their children are reared off the island in an orphanage in Honolulu or with relatives and so forth."

"She'd be fifty-two now," I said.

"We've got to find her," said Jack. "She's the heiress to the Caulfield fortune."

"Antoinette's mother was illegitimate," said Aunt Hermione. "My, my."

"Why couldn't your friend Miss O'Herlihy find a record of Pualani's death or the baby's birth?" I said.

Jack narrowed his eyes. "That's what I'd like to know. It's as if all the records were removed from the files, except the ones at the leper colony."

"That stands to reason," I said. "It would be more difficult to penetrate the leper colony and destroy records."

"Yes," mused Jack. "They wouldn't have let me in if it hadn't been that they wanted to tell the world about the new cure they're working on."

"And Mrs. Caulfield—I can't help but call her that—" said Aunt Hermione, "would be devastated, I am sure, to learn that she isn't legally married."

"What if baby Elika—Elizabeth inherited leprosy?" I said.

"It's not inherited," answered Jack. "I learned that today. A lot of people think so, though, and more thought so back in the eighties."

"Poor little—" I began.

"Elikapeka," supplied Jack. "Well, if she's alive, she won't be poor for long. Not after her father dies." He sighed happily. " 'The Million-Dollar Baby in the Little Grass Shack.' How does that sound?"

"It sounds dangerous," I said. "Jack. If Miss Blodgett died because she possessed the Caulfield secret, Elikapeka could be in danger, too, wherever she is."

"You're right," he said, frowning. "And we should warn Miss Pomfret, too. What if the killer thinks she has the diary?"

"But who *is* the killer?" said Aunt Hermione as we pulled up in front of the hotel.

"There are a lot of people it might be," I said. I touched

my cheekbone tentatively. It felt swollen. The lobby was deserted, except for the Chinese lobby boys in their blue silk pajamas, and Aunt Hermione and I prepared to go up to our room.

"I've got to write that leper-colony story so I can wire it in early in the morning," said Jack. "We'll have plenty to do tomorrow." He walked us to the elevator. "You'd better have the doctor look at that face of yours," he added, peering at me with concern.

"I'll send for some ice," I said briskly. I was far too interested in the new things we had learned to think much about my injury.

"The nerve of that big lug," began Jack, his indignation renewed. "Why, if I catch up with him again, he'd better watch it."

"Oh, Jack," I said, with a crooked little smile that hurt my face, "he didn't mean to. I just got in between you."

"I know, Iris," he said with his own little smile. "You took the punch that was meant for me. You're a real pal, kid."

"Come along, dear," said my aunt rather impatiently. "It is very late and you must rest."

Once up in my room, however, I found it impossible to rest. I took a few aspirin tablets, put on my pajamas, and Aunt Hermione rang for an ice bag. Then, I went over to the desk, and on hotel letter paper I drew a genealogical chart of the Caulfields.

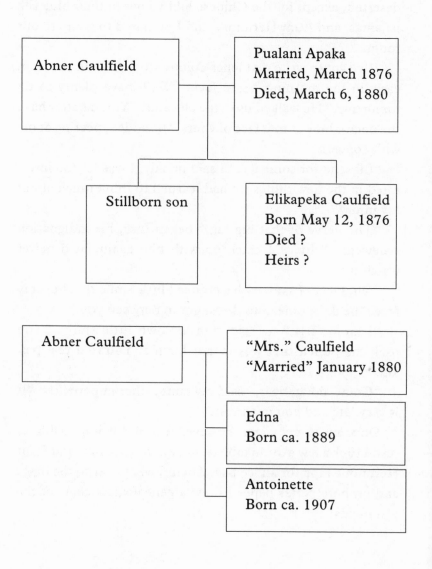

Aunt Hermione was still bustling around our hotel room, moving things from trunk to trunk, as I finished.

"Take a look," I said, and she came and sat beside me. We

were both too wound up to sleep. "I really should do the Spauldings next to it. I don't know much about them except that the original Spaulding, Charlie's grandfather, was some kind of a government clerk, and Charlie's father wanted to know pretty badly how the will stood." He and Mrs. Caulfield had looked like a couple of guilty schoolchildren going through that briefcase.

"I can see that a marriage between Antoinette and Charlie Spaulding would be very advantageous to all concerned," said my aunt.

"Too bad he's so impossible," I replied. "But, you know, he hinted at knowing some family secret as he left the other night. Could it be the secret Jack just uncovered on Molokai?"

"It's possible," said my aunt.

"He threatened to make the secret public. It almost sounded like blackmail—as if he would tell the secret if she didn't marry him."

"If Charlie Caulfield knew the secret," said my aunt, "well that's rather damaging, isn't it?"

"Yes. Who else would have known? Known enough to be able to take that entry in Miss Blodgett's diary and put two and two together?"

I closed my eyes and concentrated. "Someone who had seen the diary and made the connection. Maybe Miss Blodgett herself."

"Oh, she had made the connection, all right," said my aunt. "That was clear. She made some snide comments about half-castes and miscegenation, clearly designed to goad Mrs. Caulfield."

"But nothing about bigamy," I said. "She didn't know that the present Mrs. Caulfield married Abner while the first wife was still alive."

"No, she didn't seem to. You'd need the records, wouldn't you? The ones Jack found." She paused thoughtfully. "Let's take a look at the people who would suffer if the truth were known."

"Well," I said, "the heiress, Antoinette, chiefly, and Walter if he marries her, of course."

"And," said my aunt slowly, "Charlie, if he marries her. Which he, according to you, seems to think he will, against all odds. He would have more to lose than Walter, because he could combine his inheritance with hers and control all of Caulfield and Spaulding."

"In that case," I replied, "Charlie's father, Mr. Spaulding, might prefer the secret remain secret as well. He's of a different generation than Mr. Caulfield and has lots more years left. He might not want to share the firm with the unknown Elikapeka."

"And her heirs," said my aunt, shaking her head. "Oh, it's all so complicated."

"All money aside," I continued, "Mrs. Caulfield would of course be humiliated if the secret came out. I think respectability is more important to her than money. Mrs. Caulfield would die rather than admit she wasn't legally married. The inheritance wouldn't be as important to her as the respectability she might lose if the truth were to be made known."

"And we mustn't forget," said Aunt Hermione, raising an admonishing finger, "about Miss Pomfret. You realize, don't you, that she was very jealous of Miss Blodgett, and that she inherited a great deal of money from her. I believe the police actually suspect her."

"You do?" I said, startled. "Why?"

"Because," said my aunt, "she and Miss Carlmont have been asked not to leave Honolulu until the matter is settled."

"Rose Carlmont the typist?"

"Yes," said my aunt. "The two ladies have taken to each other." She raised her eyebrow and gave me a significant look.

"Interesting," I said. "Especially as they are offering each other an alibi."

We fell silent for a while, but I still wasn't sleepy.

"But what of Mrs. Montesquieu?" I said. "She had a Caulfield family secret—another one—about Antoinette's mother, the murderess."

"Quite a family, aren't they?" said my aunt, yawning. "A closet bristling with skeletons."

"And Mrs. Montesquieu was murdered, too," I persisted. "Jack and I actually heard Mr. Sprague threaten her."

Aunt Hermione frowned. "Well, I wonder if Mrs. Caulfield put him up to it?"

"She could be in it up to her neck, using that horrible man Sprague to carry out her orders," I said, shuddering. "She really is rather awful."

"Well, she was pretty decent about letting me photograph the garden," said my aunt, "but I know what you mean."

"And," I continued, "I did overhear her talking to her husband about hiring a private detective to handle a domestic matter."

My aunt tucked into bed and arranged her mosquito netting around her.

"Poor Mrs. Montesquieu," I said as I prepared to tuck myself in, arranging my ice bag on the pillow next to me.

"I know she was a pathetic creature," said my aunt in firm tones, "but she was an evil one as well. I'm afraid evil is often wrapped in foolishness, but it is evil, nevertheless. Toying with that poor girl Antoinette, suggesting she was her long-lost mother. It was very cruel. And it seems she was trying to blackmail the Caulfields."

"Blackmail," I said thoughtfully. "You know, perhaps we're looking at it from the wrong angle. Perhaps whoever wanted that diary intended to blackmail the Caulfields. Perhaps they didn't want to suppress it at all."

"That could be anyone greedy and ruthless," said my aunt. Her voice sounded sleepy, but I felt myself growing more and more agitated.

"Yes," I said. "Sprague, perhaps. Or even the Spauldings, who could get control over the firm. Or perhaps Kimo Kawena, although he seems too sweet. Or Mrs. Montesquieu herself."

I sat bolt upright. "Are you awake?" I said to my aunt.

She murmured a little and I didn't have the heart to wake her. Another theory suddenly seemed plausible. Mrs. Montesquieu had tried to find the diary and killed Miss Blodgett, perhaps because she was interrupted during the search. Then, when she tried to blackmail the Caulfields, she was killed. But by whom? This brought us back to the original motive—a desire to protect the Caulfield estate or name.

I began to drift off to sleep and became conscious once more of my cheek. It was throbbing. Right before I fell asleep, another thought occurred to me. Antoinette used her grand-parents' name—Caulfield. Had they actually adopted her? If so, wasn't she then a legal daughter? Only a lawyer would be able to sort it all out.

This made me think of Mr. Yamagamuchi and all those wills Antoinette's grandfather had been writing. Had the old man signed one yet? He was such a capricious old man. I tried to remember some of the odd remarks he'd made. Just one of them came back to me. "That's just the half of it." That's what he said when I'd been caught inspecting the family album. He'd cackled wildly as if it were some kind of private joke.

Now, I believed I understood the joke. That album was a chronicle of only half of his relatives. His other family, the legal one, had been hidden for almost fifty years.

What else had he said? I racked my brain. All I could remember was some vague remark about getting into heaven. About tying up loose ends. What had he said? I fell asleep.

## 21

*I was* shocked when, in the taxi on our way to Antoinette's and the dinner party her grandfather had arranged, Jack pulled out the Reverend Josiah Blodgett's diary.

"Jack! What are you doing with that?" I said.

Aunt Hermione glanced over. "Is that the diary? I thought it was in the hotel safe."

"Just a little hunch of mine," said Jack. "Thought maybe we could get to the bottom of this mystery tonight. Might come in handy."

"Well, for heaven's sake," I said, "be careful with it. There's valuable evidence there. Why on earth did you bring it along?"

Jack smiled. "I thought if I waved it around at the right moment, the guilty party would gasp or something."

"Oh no, Jack," I said.

I could imagine him holding forth in front of a startled group of people, dramatically producing the diary and glancing around to see who reacted. It sounded like something from a stage play.

"You never know." Jack flipped through the pages. "We've been rushing around so madly lately, we never finished reading this diary. We stopped when we found out about Pualani."

"You complained so much as I was reading it to you, it's a wonder we got as far as we did." I gave Jack a sharp look.

"Well, I trust, Jack," said my aunt, "that you don't plan to begin accusing our hosts and fellow guests of murder as soon as we arrive."

"I'll wait until after dinner at least," said Jack. "But you do understand my position. I've been foisting off these feature stories on cockfights and leper colonies on my editor while I've been pursuing the story of these murders. I've got to come up with the goods sooner or later. He's accused me of wasting *The Globe*'s time and money by staying here."

"Jack, there's no need to make a scene at the Caulfields," I said. "If we think we know something about these murders, we'd better go to the police," I added in a whisper so the driver wouldn't hear. "In fact," I continued guiltily, "we should have told them about the diary by now."

Jack dismissed this idea with a wave of his hand. "They'd have taken it away from us," he said. "And with the influence that family has, it might have disappeared forever."

"Oh dear," said my aunt in her own heavy whisper. "This is all beginning to sound so sordid. Perhaps we should not have come. I feel as if I am spying on the Caulfields."

"Remember how that thug struck Iris," said Jack indignantly. "We don't owe the Caulfields anything."

He returned to his perusal of the diary while I touched my cheekbone warily. I had looked rather peculiar in the mirror, with one cheek swollen and the eye a little squinty.

"Aha!" said Jack. "Just what I've been looking for. The old boy was human after all. Well, almost human." He read aloud.

*This strange restlessness is upon me once more. I gaze upon the smooth, naked limbs of these natives, and am overcome with deep feeling. I do not know whether these feelings come from God and represent a wholesome revulsion, or from Satan himself, who is dazzling me with the beauty of evil.*

*For if these islands harbor sin, it is also true that they possess a heartbreaking beauty as well. I no longer dream of the grayness of my childhood, but take delight in the jewel-like blossoms and birds, in the gleaming sea, in the azure canopy of sky.*

*But I digress. Apropos my disturbing thoughts: I have prayed for deliverance from the wild and savage notions that enter my mind unbidden. Perhaps if I had brought a wife with me to this place, she could have been put to good use sewing modest garments for the females of this place, and even, perhaps, consoling me in other ways.*

"He *certainly* should have brought a wife," said my aunt with a sniff. "I can't imagine them sending a young man out to this place without one all those years ago."

Jack turned the page. I supposed he was reading on to see if the Reverend Josiah ever gave in to his feelings. I sighed. I was glad the old boy had finally seen the beauty of the place. Even after having discovered so many evil secrets in the lives of the Caulfield family, not to mention two dead bodies, I had been struck by the way in which the sun beamed down, the waves lapped gently and persistently against the shore, the landscape persisted cheerfully. It was as if the land lived separately from the human dramas that acted themselves out upon it.

"Aha!" said Jack again, and I hoped he wouldn't embarrass me by reading any more about Josiah Blodgett's struggle with his baser self. Not in front of my aunt, anyway, who is reasonably broad-minded, I know, but there is no call to test her limits.

"Never mind," I said sharply as the taxi negotiated the broad, curving driveway in front of the Caulfields' house. "Anyway, we are here."

Jack had rather a wicked gleam in his eye as he slipped the

book back into his pocket and paid the driver. We went up the broad steps and Antoinette herself answered the door. She was wearing a dress of some festive native pattern, and around her neck and in her hair were leis of beautiful, fragrant blossoms. She looked relaxed and lovely—almost radiant. It was hard to imagine the pinched, troubled girl who'd been burdened for so long with family secrets.

"Come in, come in," she said. "I'm so happy to see you. We're having a special luau. Wonderful Hawaiian food." She embraced me.

As we were about to enter, Robert Yamagamuchi's little Ford pulled up. "Oh, there are those odd people Grandfather insisted on inviting," said Antoinette in a good-natured way.

She waved gaily at them, and we all stood on the porch waiting for them. Mr. Yamagamuchi was dressed in his usual somber suit. His secretary wore a simple, severely cut dinner dress of creamy white silk, setting off her smooth dark skin.

"Have you met my sister Betty?" said Mr. Yamagamuchi as we all gathered in the front hall.

"How do you do," we said as introductions were made all around.

"But Grandfather said you were Mr. Yamagamuchi's secretary," said Antoinette, looking confused.

"Betty is my sister and my secretary," he explained. "She's a pretty good one, too. She put me through law school at it."

Miss Yamagamuchi smiled benevolently at her brother. I recalled again the gesture that had seemed so motherly when I'd first seen these two in the Caulfields' hall. She had brushed off his jacket. Now, I realized it was the gesture of a big sister.

"Well, do come in," said Antoinette, leading us through the house. "And then out again," she continued as she led us out the French doors onto the lanai. "We are all outdoors.

We're having a luau tonight."

She seemed fairly bristling with energy. It occurred to me that Antoinette was a high-strung girl—as her mother, perhaps, had been before her.

"What fun," said my aunt. "Shall we be sitting on the ground and eat with our fingers?"

"Yes," said Antoinette. "But Grandmother always has finger bowls brought around. And we have cocktails in chairs on the lanai first."

Just a few feet away, on the lawn, stood a long, low table decorated with fruits and flowers and covered with bright green leaves.

The other guests were there, and they certainly made a rather peculiar group. Antoinette's grandmother sat glumly in a throne-like rattan chair, wearing a purplish beaded dress that looked hot and uncomfortable. Her husband sat beside her in his wheelchair, with a vaguely mischievous and rebellious expression on his craggy features.

The Spauldings, *pere et fils*, stood off to one side. The elder Spaulding had his eye on Charlie, as if he were ready to throttle him in case it might be made necessary by another jealous outburst. Charlie, in turn, had his eye on Walter, who was, no doubt because the man of the house was in a wheelchair, behaving like a genial, pleasant host, browsing over a tray of bottles and glasses, preparing cocktails.

I was sure that the ease with which Walter had assumed this role was driving Charlie into a jealous frenzy. He was clenching his fists, and his handsome face wore a scowl.

"Antoinette has taught me to make a special island cocktail," said Walter, carefully arranging glasses on a tray, pouring a fruity-looking concoction over shaved ice then slipping a wedge of lime and a sprig of white hibiscus in each glass and standing back proudly to admire his handiwork.

I had never seen Walter so domestic, and I smiled, thinking of how happy he and Antoinette would be and wondering if I would ever find anyone with whom to set up housekeeping. I glanced over at Jack and sighed.

"I've got some wonderful news for all of you," began Antoinette, clasping her hands together girlishly.

Walter made his way among us with his tray of cocktails and beamed at her. Charlie Spaulding fairly bristled, and I intercepted a warning look from his father.

"Wait!" said her grandfather. "There's something I want to tell all of you first."

He cleared his throat as we all turned, rather startled, for his manner seemed slightly agitated. In fact, he was gripping the arms of his wheelchair and attempting to rise. Beside him, his wife tugged at his sleeve.

"Abner!" she said. "Sit down. You mustn't strain yourself."

"Nonsense, my dear," he said brusquely, but not without affection. He smiled down at her. "I've been able to get around on my own for a long time. The only reason I'm in this chair is to conserve my strength. Well, I need it now, and I'm going to use it. After that—well, who knows, my dear, how long I can cling to life."

"Grandfather," said Antoinette gently.

"There's no point clinging," he said. "Not when all your work is done. I know enough to recognize when it's time just to say *pau*."

"Finished," murmured Jack at my side.

"Please, dear," said his wife, obviously embarrassed by the morbid turn his conversation was taking.

Walter respectfully handed Mr. Caulfield a cocktail and stepped back. We all stood in the hush for just a moment. Then Mr. Caulfield began to speak in firmer, younger tones than I had heard from him before, holding up his glass as if he were proposing a toast.

"Perhaps you've wondered why I've called you all here tonight," he said. We all turned to him expectantly. Was this another of his whimsical, enigmatic pronouncements? "This is," he said, "a moment of reckoning—one I've put off for many years."

With apparent effort, he walked over to Robert and Betty Yamagamuchi. "I've asked this young man to prepare a will for me," he said. "He's a plenty smart young lawyer, I can tell you that!"

Robert Yamagamuchi lowered his eyes modestly, and his sister smiled at him.

"In fact," continued Mr. Caulfield, "he's prepared a whole slew of wills for me." He began to laugh, and I saw Mrs. Caulfield exchange a worried glance with Mr. Spaulding.

"In case anyone's interested," he went on, "I've torn up all those wills."

Mr. Yamagamuchi looked decidedly nervous now. It seemed possible that his client was not of sound mind and wasn't fit to write a will. Mr. Caulfield cackled rather maniacally, further adding to possible questions about his mental state. He turned to the young Japanese and tilted his head in a rather birdlike fashion.

"You've been awfully patient with me, Robert," he said. "And I've learned a lot about you and your sister, too, while we were working together."

Betty looked frankly curious and gave her brother a sidelong glance from her beautiful almond-shaped eyes.

"But I never learned much about your family."

Now, brother and sister stared at each other, and I was struck by the fact that although I had assumed they were full-blooded Japanese, and Robert certainly looked it, his sister looked more Polynesian. Could it be that . . . ?

"What's Betty short for?" said Mr. Caulfield.

Startled, she looked down at his gnarled, blue-veined hand as it seized her slim brown one. "Elizabeth, of course," she said. "I was named after my mother."

"How charming," interjected Mrs. Caulfield. "Now Abner, let's not bother the guests with all sorts of personal questions. Come on, dear, and sit down in your chair. You know you shouldn't drink that cocktail, either. Doctor's orders." She was speaking exceedingly quickly.

He glanced down at the cocktail in his hand, and Betty Yamagamuchi continued. "Actually, her name was Elikapeka," she said.

"Dad raised us after she died," said Robert easily. "He's Japanese, and Mother was a *hapa-haole.*"

"Half-white," said Jack, who loved to show off his knowledge of Hawaiian terms. He had a gleam in his eye. "This is terrific stuff," he whispered to me, and on the other side of me, Aunt Hermione squeezed my hand in excitement.

"Real interesting," said Jack. "So you two are half Japanese, a quarter Hawaiian, and a quarter Caucasian?"

"That's right," said Robert Yamagamuchi. "People from the mainland are always surprised by the mixture of races here in Hawaii, but we just take it for granted."

Mr. Caulfield seemed annoyed that Jack had entered the conversation. He cleared his throat with annoyance. "Do you two know anything about your maternal grandparents?" he demanded.

He seemed determined to savor the moment of revelation, and I was almost tempted to burst in with the truth.

The Yamagamuchis looked nervously at each other. "Not really," they said.

"Well, I do," he said. "In fact, I'm your grandfather!"

Everyone looked absolutely flabbergasted, the Yama-gamuchis perhaps the most.

"But we never knew—" said Betty. "Mother never knew much about her own mother. She was raised by her grand-mother, a very traditional old Hawaiian lady, who called her by the Hawaiian name—Apaka."

"Really!" said Mrs. Caulfield, clearly horrified. "Well, I suppose we know the reason for that." She glared at her husband. "You've gone too far, Abner."

"I guess Mrs. Caulfield is intimating your mother wasn't legitimate," said Mr. Caulfield. "But she was. I married your grandmother, Pualani Apaka. And if the family never talked about her much, it was probably because she was a leper, poor child. She died on Molokai."

"Abner!" shrieked Mrs. Caulfield.

She put her hand to her forehead, went dead white, and began to slump. I ran to her side, careening into Walter, who was dashing to support her. I got to her side just in time to catch her under the arms. Walter stumbled backward and collided with Mr. Caulfield, knocking his cocktail out of his hand.

"There's more, isn't there?" said Charlie, sipping his own drink coolly. "A little matter of bigamy."

"Charlie!" said his father sharply.

"Come on, Dad. You know it as well as I do." He looked out over all of us. "Grandfather was a government clerk. He destroyed that marriage certificate years ago, didn't he? That's why Mr. Caulfield took him on as a partner. Let's face it, we're all frauds."

"Charlie, why didn't you ever tell me?" said Antoinette. "We never used to have secrets."

"I didn't want to jeopardize your inheritance," said

Charlie. "I knew your grandfather didn't have a will. I warned you the other day that I'd tell an old family secret if I had to." He glanced over at Walter, who was very gingerly picking up the broken glass. "I was going to use the fact that you might not inherit to scare off old Walter."

Walter stood up, scowling. "I've had about enough from you," he said.

"Oh, I can't bear it," said Mrs. Caulfield.

I had been rubbing her wrists, and now she shook off my hands. Her color was back, and I assumed she wasn't going to faint.

"You mean you knew about that marriage?" said Jack to Charlie. "You knew that the Caulfield line wasn't legitimate?"

"That's right. Grandfather told us before he died."

Robert Yamagamuchi cleared his throat. "Actually," he began, "it's a little-known point of Hawaiian law, but under certain circumstances, illegitimate heirs can inherit."

"They can?" said Jack.

"That's right. If the second, er, bigamous marriage was entered into without the woman's knowledge of its bigamous nature, she and her heirs can share the inheritance."

"I'm not dead yet," snarled Mr. Caulfield. "And I intend to put together a will that's fair to everyone. I just wanted to acknowledge all of my grandchildren before I died."

"You're my cousins," said Antoinette to the Yamagamuchis, sounding astonished.

"Half cousins," said Mr. Caulfield. "And they're fine young people. I wanted to make sure they were before I decided to bring them into the fold."

"So all those wills you had Robert draw up," began Betty.

He waved his hand airily. "Just a ruse to get to know you," he said.

273

"Abner," said Mrs. Caulfield, summoning all her strength, "why on earth did you marry me when you were already married?"

"Well, I never had the nerve to tell you about Pualani," he said. "After you'd kept writing me all those years. Then you rushed over and demanded we go ahead and marry. I didn't know what to do. I knew she wouldn't last long in any case." He turned away. "Poor little thing. I wasn't a good husband to her."

"This must be grounds for divorce," said Mrs. Caulfield to Robert Yamagamuchi.

"The question is moot," he said, "as you are not married. But there are very few grounds for divorce in Hawaii. Leprosy, however, is one of them."

"He says we are not married," said Mrs. Caulfield. "I refuse to believe it."

"Don't worry, dear, I'll be glad to make an honest woman of you. We can do it tomorrow," Mr. Caulfield said lightly.

"This is preposterous," she replied through clenched teeth.

"What do you say, Antoinette?" said Charlie. "Let's go along and make it a double wedding."

"You're too late," she said, smiling sweetly. "Walter and I were married this afternoon."

Walter went to her side, slipped an arm around her waist, and kissed her. They made a lovely couple. Aunt Hermione beamed at them.

"What!" said Mrs. Caulfield.

I really was beginning to feel sorry for the poor woman. She had just discovered that she was not married when she thought she was, and that her granddaughter was married when she had thought she wasn't. Just then a group of servants came around the corner of the hedge of yellow oleander, struggling under the weight of a huge cooked pig. Mrs. Caulfield glanced at it and fell back in her chair.

"I couldn't possibly eat a thing," she said.

"You're lying," said Charlie to Antoinette. "Tell me you're lying."

"Of course I'm not lying," she said.

"Come on," said Walter affably. "You'll drink a toast to us, won't you? I'll make some cocktails. But first, here's a replacement for Mr. Caulfield." He handed him a new glass, and it was then that I noticed the rash on Walter's hand.

"Why did you want to bring all this up," demanded Mrs. Caulfield of her husband, returning to her first shock. "You must be mad."

"Because," he said. "I am going to die very soon." As he raised his glass to his lips, I screamed, "Stop! Don't drink it!"

# 22

*What!" he* said.

I wasn't sure I was right. I didn't have any proof, but I believed it was possible that Walter was trying to kill Mr. Caulfield. Instantly, Walter hurried toward him.

"Stop him, Jack," I said, "before he knocks that one over, too."

Jack sprang into action, and in a second he had wrestled Walter away from Mr. Caulfield, who stood there looking slightly confused.

Charlie went over to the old man and took the glass gently from his hand, then led him back to his wheelchair.

"What the hell are you doing?" demanded Walter.

Jack looked at me for a reply.

"Let him go," I said, and to Charlie I added, "Just keep an eye on that glass."

"Iris!" shrieked Antoinette, running to Walter's side as Jack unhanded him. "What are you saying?"

"I think Walter wanted to kill your grandfather," I said. "He looked so clumsy when he knocked that glass out of his hand the first time. Remember when that was? It was right after he'd learned that the true, legitimate heirs to your grandfather's fortune were the Yamagamuchis. Then, when Robert explained that you would still inherit a portion of it, because of that quirk in Hawaiian law, he mixed up another cocktail for him."

"But poison? It's absurd."

"Perhaps," I said. "But the rash on his hand reminded me of the rash behind Miss Blodgett's ear. Yellow oleander. Highly toxic. Walter knew all about it. Jack and I told him when we were all at Shipwreck Harry's after we discovered Miss Blodgett's body. It works like foxglove. The victim would appear to have died of a heart attack—not so unusual in a man with heart disease like your grandfather—and there's a hedge of it over there." I pointed to the corner of the house.

"A rash on my hand!" said Walter. "It's absurd."

"It's simple," said Jack. "We'll pour half that cocktail into another glass and then you can drink it, Walter. Are you willing to do that?"

"This is ridiculous," said Walter coldly.

"Go ahead, Walter, drink it," said Antoinette.

"I'll get another glass," said Charlie.

"He had to wait until he was married to Antoinette, you see." I continued, "And that happened this afternoon. Then, because Mr. Caulfield was in poor health and seemed to be writing a lot of peculiar wills, he decided to strike immediately. When he thought that the Yamagamuchis would get everything, he tried to undo his plot and knocked over the drink. Then, a few minutes later, when he learned that you would still get a share, Antoinette, he decided he'd settle for that. It wasn't likely that even after a will was written, he'd get any more, and a will might make things more complicated. You might get it in trust or something. He wanted your grandfather to die intestate."

"Drink it," said Charlie, handing him a tumbler half-full of liquid. Walter tried to bat at the glass, then Jack seized him from behind and pinned back his arms. Charlie held the glass close to Walter's face and repeated, "Drink it!"

"This is horrible," said Antoinette. "Stop it, all of you. Oh, Walter, drink it and we can be done with this."

Instead Walter turned his head away from the glass and shrank back.

"Better save that and have it analyzed," I said. "And someone should call the police."

Betty Yamagamuchi said, "I'll do that. There's a phone in the hall, isn't there?"

"That's right," said a bemused Mr. Caulfield.

"It can't be true," said Antoinette. "It can't."

"We'll find out," I said.

I wanted to go to her side and take her hand, but I didn't dare. She might be furious with me. She had idolized Walter. He would have had no trouble getting complete control of her fortune.

Robert Yamagamuchi stood next to the table where Charlie had set the glass down next to the cocktail glass with the other half of the liquid.

"Let's make sure we keep an eye on this," he said. "If it is evidence, we must have witnesses that it is not tampered with."

Charlie stood next to him. Jack let Walter go once again and joined the other two men separating him from the cock-tail glass.

"Do you think Walter was behind Miss Blodgett's murder?" said Aunt Hermione.

"What?" said Antoinette. "But that's absurd."

"Not really," said Jack, pulling out the diary from his pocket. "Remember Great-Great-Uncle Josiah's diary? He's the reverend gentleman who married Mr. C. here and Pualani Apaka. He wrote about it in his book."

"Well how would Walter know that?" demanded Antoinette. "And what of it, anyway?"

"Don't you remember?" I said. "On board the *Malolo?* Walter told Miss Blodgett he'd read the diary. I remember thinking how he was so polite to old ladies. You see, when he read about that marriage, he worried that the girl he was marrying might not be a true heiress."

"Just because Grandfather had been married before? What would that prove?"

I stopped. She was right. Who would conclude that the second marriage was necessarily bigamous, simply from reading about his first marriage? I began to doubt my theory.

"Funny you should mention that," said Jack. He waved the diary around some more. "The date of that marriage was in here, and so was the date of Pualani's death. Iris, I started to read that entry to you in the car, but you cut me off. Listen." He read aloud. *"Today I said prayers for the soul of poor Pualani Caulfield. I received the news of her death at Molokai this week. Her little child is, praise the Lord, healthy and happy, although I fear she is not getting a Christian upbringing from her pagan relatives.* The date is on there. *March, 1880."*

I sighed with relief and gave Jack a grateful smile. He'd found the last missing piece of the puzzle. "There, you see?" I said. "All Walter had to do after that was find the date of your grandparents' marriage in that family album and perhaps check for any divorce records."

"He did go to town a few times. He said he was doing research on the history of Hawaii," said Antoinette, with just the first note of doubt creeping in.

I gazed at Walter and found I had to struggle to maintain that gaze, so horrifying were the accusations I was making.

"I rather imagine," I said, "that he went to retrieve the diary and was surprised by Miss Blodgett. She may even have made some remark about the family he was about to marry into. Aunt Hermione says Miss Blodgett seemed to be making allusions to that first marriage when she was here for bridge."

"She did go on about half-castes and so forth, didn't she?" said Mrs. Caulfield, astonished. "I had no idea she was referring to my family. What an odious person."

"But Iris," interrupted Antoinette with a note of triumph, "Walter was with me the evening Miss Blodgett died. Remember? We were all out dancing at the Moana. We ran into you afterward at Shipwreck Harry's."

"Yes," I replied. "But he wasn't with you the whole time, was he? You said he stormed off after catching you and Charlie together on the lanai."

Charlie looked a little smug at the memory. "We were there quite awhile," he said.

"Perhaps he just pretended to be in a huff, then set out on his errand," I mused. "Perhaps he was surprised in his search, or perhaps he actually decided that he must kill the owner of the diary to protect his position. We may never know."

"What about Mrs. Montesquieu?" said Jack.

"That's a little more difficult, but I have an idea," I said. "Do you remember that Mrs. Montesquieu pretended she was Antoinette's mother? Antoinette kept that letter in her jewel box, and Walter knew that's where she kept important papers. Remember when he went to fetch her other letter? If he killed Miss Blodgett to get that inheritance, he'd be annoyed to discover Antoinette's mother was still alive. After all, she would inherit. Isn't that right, Mr. Yamagamuchi?"

He nodded. "Yes, if Mr. Caulfield died intestate."

"So he killed her in cold blood. Absolutely not necessary, as she wasn't Antoinette's mother at all. But that's what he thought." I turned to Antoinette. "Remember when I gave you Mrs. Montesquieu's address over the phone? You wrote it down. Where did you put that address?"

"In my jewel box," said Antoinette slowly.

"That's how he found out where she was," I said.

"Great stuff, great stuff," said Jack, with unbecoming zeal. "All I want to know now is where Sprague fit into all of this."

"Sprague?" said Mr. Caulfield. "That detective we use once in a while? Well, I used him to find Robert and Betty here."

"And I used him to try and buy off that horrible Mrs. Montesquieu person," said Mrs. Caulfield. "She was trying to blackmail us."

"I guess he had that thug following me because he knew I took an interest in Mrs. Montesquieu."

Charlie's father spoke up. "He's always been very protective of the Caulfield interests," he said.

"Some detective," said Jack. "Going around having his goons trying to deck Iris here while he was supposed to be trailing me. And threatening the Montesquieu woman. But it took Iris to figure out that Walter was a cold-blooded killer."

I gave him a grateful smile, and he smiled back. Usually, Jack tried to take credit for all my detecting.

"Of course," said Robert Yamagamuchi with a lawyerly little cough, "these are just theories and not necessarily allegations. The police will arrive shortly, and they can question Mr. Carlson."

"Oh, this is terrible," said Antoinette. "Walter, please drink that cocktail. I have to know."

"All right," he said.

Charlie handed him the portion that had been poured out into a tumbler, but Mr. Yamagamuchi stepped between them.

"Please," he said, "let's leave this to the proper authorities. There are orderly ways of handling these matters."

Walter shrugged and reached into his pocket. It happened

so quickly, I had barely time to notice, but he unscrewed a little twist of paper and poured something into his mouth.

The Chinese doctor who had described the action of yellow oleander to me had been absolutely correct. Death was instantaneous. Walter clutched his chest, his face turned ashen and then became distorted in one last grimace, and he died.

Antoinette, instead of running to the body and bending over it as I had somehow expected her to do, simply stood there, frozen in horror. Charlie Spaulding went to her side and touched her shoulder tentatively. She turned to him, then fell against his chest and began to sob.

Two days later Aunt Hermione, Jack, and I tossed our leis into the water as our ship pulled away from the pier. "I do want to come back sometime, but not for a while," I said, peering over the rail to see if mine would lap back up on shore.

"I know what you mean," my aunt said. "This place is lovely, but entirely too hot this time of year. Besides, the family history of the Caulfields, not to mention all those murders and attempted murder and one suicide, right in front of our eyes—well, it is so tiring. Our next trip, Iris, must be somewhere cool and crisp and civilized. The Canadian Rockies, perhaps."

"I hope the Mounties would have handled those murders better than Dietrich and his crew," said Jack. "It was clear to me the whole thing is going to be hushed up. Mrs. Caulfield can thank her lucky stars that Walter did away with himself, saving the family a scandal."

"These things have a way of getting out nevertheless," said my aunt.

"Yes," said Jack with satisfaction. "Especially when

Clancy of *The Globe* is on the case."

"I knew that Walter Carlson was too perfect," said my aunt.

"I've never met such a cold-blooded killer in my life," said Jack.

"I think he just kept getting in deeper and deeper," I said. "He started out trying to protect his inheritance with that diary. After he'd killed once, it must have been easier for him the second time. He probably figured he might as well eliminate the woman he thought was his mother-in-law and get his hands on the money right away. He'd already killed for it. He began worrying what kind of a will the old man might draw up, and by then he'd been making a habit of murder."

"He may not have been completely sane," said my aunt. "What were you able to find out about him, Jack?"

We knew Jack had wired *The Globe* for background on both Walter and Mrs. Montesquieu.

"His dad runs a filling station in Lodi, California," said Jack. "A nice little business, but Walter had grander ideas. As for Mrs. Montesquieu, well she was in that prison for strangling her own baby. They never quite knew why."

"Oh, how perfectly awful," said my aunt. "There is so much wickedness in the world. So distressing, not for my sake, but for the sake of you young people. You are so fresh and young, and optimistic. I hate to see you learn that the world has its dark corners."

"If it wasn't for those dark corners, the bright spots wouldn't seem so bright," said Jack. "And besides, the readers of *The Globe* would be pretty bored."

"Yes, you're probably right," said my aunt, smiling but sounding nevertheless unconvinced. "I think I'll go down to our cabin, dear, and unpack the trunks. You know how I like to get organized as soon as we get into our cabin. And then I'll

283

order a nice sherry before dinner."

When she had left, Jack put his arm on my shoulder and gazed into my eyes. "I haven't had a chance to really thank you for taking that punch for me," he said. "You're a real pal."

"Oh, well," I said shrugging. It had been a silly thing to do.

"Still hurt?" he asked.

"Kind of," I said softly, feeling gauche.

He leaned over and kissed me very gently on the cheek-bone, and then whispered in my ear, " 'Comely Coed Kayoed by Hawaiian Hoodlum.' Great stuff."

Additional copyright information:

All stories reprinted by permission of the author.

"The Tell-Tale Tattoo," copyright © 2001 by K. K. Beck

"Hollywood Homicide," copyright © 1999 by Kathrine Beck

"Rule of Law," copyright © 1995 by K. K. Beck

"A Romance in the Rockies," copyright © 1992 by K. K. Beck

"Peril Under the Palms," copyright © 1989 by Kathrine Marris

The employees of Five Star hope you have enjoyed this book. All our books are made to last. Other Five Star books are available at your library, through selected bookstores, or directly from us.

For more information about titles, please call:

(800) 223-1244

or visit our Web site at:

www.gale.com/fivestar

To share your comments, please write:

Publisher
Five Star
295 Kennedy Memorial Drive
Waterville, ME 04901